THE RED COMMISSAR

THE RED COMMISSAR

Including Further Adventures of
the Good Soldier Švejk
and Other Stories

JAROSLAV HAŠEK

Translated by Cecil Parrott

Original illustrations
by Josef Lada

faber and faber

This edition first published in 2010
by Faber and Faber Ltd
Bloomsbury House, 74–77 Great Russell Street
London WC1B 3DA

Printed by Books on Demand GmbH, Norderstedt

A CIP record for this book is available from the British Library

ISBN 978-0-571-26049-2

Contents

OTHER STORIES

FROM AN OLD PHARMACY: A SERIES OF SKETCHES

STORIES FROM THE WATER BAILIFF'S WATCH-TOWER AT RAŽICE

A HOUSE SEARCH by JARMILA HAŠKOVÁ

THE GOOD SOLDIER ŠVEJK

THE PARTY OF MODERATE PROGRESS WITHIN THE BOUNDS OF THE LAW

PREFACE

Truant, rebel, vagabond, anarchist, play-actor, practical joker, bohemian (and Bohemian), alcoholic, traitor to the Czech Legion, Bolshevik, and bigamist, Jaroslav Hašek was born in Prague in 1883 and died at Lipnice, in Bohemia, in 1923 within a few months of his fortieth birthday.

Unlucky in love, work, and play, and always on his beam ends, he was fated after a promising beginning to achieve literary success and modest affluence only in the last months of his life, when he published the first instalment of his only novel *The Good Soldier Švejk*. Although recognition for the novel came slowly and only after his death, the book finally marked him as one of the great humorists of the age and a formidable satirist as well.

All the world has heard of Švejk, but few are familiar with the countless other characters Hašek created in his stories and sketches, which together with his feuilletons and articles are thought to number some twelve hundred. The best of these deserve to be made accessible to the western public and are included in this volume.

Although Hašek has a firm niche in the Communist pantheon in his own country and in Russia, thanks partly to his grotesque satires on the Austro-Hungarian monarchy, its nobility, church, and *haute bourgeoisie*, and partly to the practical services he rendered the Bolshevik cause in Russia, he was at heart a contradictory character. In Russia he felt himself a Slavophile and at the time of the Revolution found it initially difficult to shift his loyalties away from the Romanovs — or later from T. G. Masaryk. In his tastes he was a typical *bourgeois* product — anti-intellectual, philistine in questions of art and culture, and mildly xenophobic. He had no firm principles and drifted or allowed himself to be led where his intemperate emotions and self-indulgence drove him. It was never recorded of him that he was exactly chummy with workers. One cannot see him as a member of a trade union, although he was once sacked for trying to foment a strike. He is alleged to have worked in a mine for a period, but that period was exceedingly brief. He was most at home when drinking with his "court" of mainly second-class literary bohemians, whose company he enjoyed, and indeed needed, so long as they did not bore him with theoretical questions of literature and art. And he liked the company of ordinary men and it was his genius to be able to bring them to life in *The Good Soldier Švejk* and his countless stories. If his inability to bear the restraints of *bourgeois* conventions sorely tried his loving wife, broke up his marriage, and ruined his personal happiness, in fairness it must be said that any kind of compulsion — *bourgeois* or not — would have been too much for him to bear. Although his wife prided herself on being an emancipated woman, she remained at heart something of a stickler for convention.

By the time the war broke out Hašek had compromised himself so universally and so inescapably that it must really have come as a relief to him to bury himself in the anonymity of military life. It also afforded him the chance of making a new start. He made good use of such an opportunity during the two years he spent in Russia as a Bolshevik Commissar, where he at last found some purpose in life and gave the appearance of having become a changed man. His "finest hour" began in October 1918, when he was sent as "organizer" of the then townlet of Bugulma, hidden away in Eastern Russia among Bashkirs and Tartars and only recently liberated from the Whites.

The unusual note of mellowness which pervades the delightful "Bugulma Stories" speaks eloquently of Hašek's nostalgia for the days he spent in provincial Russia. We seem to be hearing the voice of a much more tolerant Hašek. While he makes fun of Comrade Yerokhymov and other Soviet officials, it is a gentle satire – far different from the sharp lash with which he flayed Austrian bureaucrats and some of his own countrymen. Even the Orthodox Church comes off a good deal better than the Catholic Church in Austria. The explanation for this is not far to seek: Hašek was a Slavophile at heart and he loved and understood these Russian characters and could be indulgent to them. It is for this reason that in his Russian stories he shows his best and most lovable sides as a writer. Another reason, perhaps, is that, while writing them, he was still under the tranquillizing influence of the milk of human kindness and had not yet become again addicted to stronger spirits and excited and stimulated by them. In Bolshevik Russia drunkenness could mean the firing squad.

Yerokhymov, the leading character in these stories, never existed, but he is a very vivid and faithfully drawn Russian character — especially a Russian at a time of anarchy. There was a certain Yerokhym who was sentenced to death for filching property when conducting house searches. His case came before the Revolutionary Tribunal of which Hašek was a member, and perhaps the name and the case suggested the stories.

But, while we read and smile, we should not forget that we are seeing Russian life through Hašek's distorting mirror. Yerokhymov threatens to shoot all and sundry, but Hašek presents it all as a joke — an idiosyncracy of the over-enthusiastic Russian red heroes which may be light-heartedly forgiven. Quite a different picture is shown in Babel's *Red Cavalry*. The Cossack Kudrya executes an old Jew for espionage. The Jew screams. Kudrya takes his head firmly under his arm. The Jew grows quiet and stretches out his legs. Kudrya takes a dagger in his right hand and "carefully cuts the Jew's throat so as not to stain his hands". Babel's account of the Civil War abounds with such episodes, where it is as simple to garrotte a human being as to wring a goose's neck. In *The Good Soldier Švejk* there are passages which tell of the stink of human corpses, of battlefields dunged with the excrement of troops driven to the slaughter by their capitalist masters. But in his vignettes from the Russian civil war Hašek shuts his eyes to all this and his presentation of life under Bolshevik rule is as one-sided as are the propaganda articles which he wrote day after day during his "finest hour". It is true that in his sketch *Before the Revolutionary Tribunal of the Eastern Front* Hašek comes close to applying the sharp edge of his satire to Soviet conceptions of justice and Soviet legal procedure as ruthlessly as he did to Austrian military court procedure. It is for that reason that, when these tales were first published in a Russian version, some of the former members of the Fifth Army protested, accusing Hašek of having disparaged the spirit of idealism in the struggle for the liberation of Siberia. But all that is now changed. Bugulma is not the only Soviet town to have a street named after him: it boasts a "Gashek" museum as well. None the less, it was perhaps lucky that the "hero" left Russia when he did. Had he stayed there longer he might not have been so well remembered, because it was characteristic of him that he could never work under any authority for long. And he certainly would not have been able to control his exuberant pen with so much good material for his satirical shafts.

If we look upon Hašek's life as the picaresque novel it was and if we shut our eyes to reality and accept the image his mirror throws back at us, we can be grateful for these stories, which are masterpieces in their genre and recall the gentler and more human sides of their author's great epic novel *The Good Soldier Švejk*. They have long deserved translation into English.

ACKNOWLEDGEMENTS

I owe a great debt to the late Dr. Dana Kňourková who, despite grave illness, spared no pains in reading through hundreds of Hašek's stories to help reach a final choice. She rendered me invaluable assistance too by reading through my manuscripts and helping me to solve problems connected with the translation.

I should also like to thank Mrs. Betty Graham for her cheerful readiness to type and retype many of my indecipherable scripts, a task which she accomplished with great skill in spite of the many difficult Czech names.

C.P.

THE BUGULMA STORIES

The commandant of the town of Bugulma

⟩⁻⟩

WHEN AT THE BEGINNING OF OCTOBER 1918 I WAS INFORMED BY the Revolutionary Army Soviet of the "Left-Bank Group in Simbirsk" that I had been appointed Commandant of the Town of Bugulma, I asked the chairman, Kayurov, "And do you know for sure that Bugulma has already been taken?"

"We haven't any detailed information" was the answer. "I doubt very much whether it's already in our hands at this moment, but by the time you get there I hope it'll have fallen."

"And shall I have any escort?" I asked quietly. "And one more thing — how do I get to this Bugulma? Where exactly is it?"

"You shall have an escort. You'll get twelve soldiers. And, as for your second question, look at the map. Do you think I've got nothing more to do than worry about where some idiotic Bugulma is?"

"I've got one more question, Comrade Kayurov. When shall I get the money for my fare and subsistence?"

He held up his hands in despair at such a question. "You've gone quite mad. On the journey there you'll of course have to go through some villages, where they'll give you food and drink, and at Bugulma you'll raise a levy. . . ."

My escort was waiting for me at the guardhouse below — twelve fine Chuvash lads who knew next to no Russian and so were quite incapable of explaining to me whether they were conscripts or volunteers. From their cheerful and terrifying appearance one could safely conclude that they were very likely volunteers who would stick at nothing.

When I had been given my papers and a pile of credentials where it was emphatically stated that from Simbirsk to Bugulma every citizen must provide me with every possible help, I left for the steamer with my expedition and we sailed on the Volga and the Kama to Chistopol.

On the journey I did not meet with any special incidents, except that one of my Chuvash escorts got drunk, fell overboard, and was drowned. There were now only eleven left. When we got off the steamer at Chistopol one Chuvash volunteered to go and collect some carts but never returned. Then there were only ten and we came to the conclusion that the Chuvash who disappeared was about forty versts from his home, Montazmo, and must have gone to see what his parents were doing.

When finally, after a lengthy interrogation of the local population, I had written down everything, where that town of Bugulma was and how we would get to it, the rest of the Chuvashes found some carts and we went along that region's awful, muddy paths towards Krachalga, Yelanovo, Moskovo, Gulukovo, Aibashevo. All of these villages were inhabited exclusively by Tartars, except for Gulukovo where Cheremisses and Tartars lived together.

Because there was frightful hostility between the Chuvashes, who had already adopted Christianity some fifty years earlier, and the Cheremisses, who were still pagan, a small misadventure occurred in Gulukovo. When my Chuvashes, who were armed to the teeth, searched a village, they brought its mayor before me — a certain Davledbai Shakir, who was holding in his hand a cage with three white squirrels in it. One of the Chuvashes, who spoke Russian best, turned to me with the following explanation:

"Chuvashes Orthodox — one, ten, thirty, fifty years. Cheremisses heathens, swine." Tearing the cage with the white squirrels from Davledbai Shakir's hands he went on: "The white squirrel is their god — one, two, three gods. This man priest, he jump with squirrels, he jump, he pray to them. You must baptize him. . . ."

The Chuvashes looked so menacing that I ordered some water to be brought and sprinkled it over Davledbai Shakir, mumbling some incomprehensible words, after which I released him.

My lads then skinned the Cheremisses' gods and I can assure everyone that the Lord God of the Cheremisses makes a very fine soup.

After that the local Mohammedan mullah Abdulhalei came to visit me and expressed his pleasure that we had eaten those squirrels. "Everyone has to believe in something," he said. "But to believe in squirrels — that's sheer beastliness. They jump from tree to tree and when they are in a cage they make a filthy mess. Fine gods indeed!" He brought us lavish helpings of roast mutton, and three geese, assuring us that if the Cheremisses were to revolt in the night all the Tartars would be on our side.

Nothing happened because, as Davledbai Shakir said when he came to see us off in the morning, there are lots of squirrels in the forest. Finally, we went through Aibashevo and, in the evening, without any incidents reached Little Pisetsnitse, a Russian village twelve versts from Bugulma. The local inhabitants were very well informed about what was happening in Bugulma. Three days earlier the Whites had abandoned the town without a fight. The Soviet army stood on the other side of the town and were afraid to go in for fear of a trap.

There was anarchy in the town, and the mayor and all his council had been waiting for two days with bread and salt to greet whomsoever entered the town.

I sent ahead the Chuvash who could speak Russian best and in the morning we moved on to Bugulma. On the outskirts of the town an endless crowd of people came to meet us. The mayor held a loaf of bread on a salver and some salt in a saucer.

In his speech he expressed the hope that I would have mercy on the town. I could imagine that I was Žižka at the gates of Prague, especially when I saw schoolchildren in the procession.

I thanked him in a long speech, cutting a slice of bread and sprinkling salt over it. I emphasized that I had not come to mouth slogans but that my aim would be peace, quiet, and order. Finally I kissed the mayor, shook hands with the representative of the Orthodox clergy, and went to the town hall, where offices for the Commandant of the Town had been assigned to me.

After that I had Order No. 1 posted up with the following contents:

Citizens!

I thank you for your warm and sincere welcome and your hospitality with bread and salt. Always cherish these old Slav customs, to which I have no objection, but at the same time please do not forget that I have been appointed Commandant of the Town and that I have my duties too.

I therefore ask you, dear friends, to hand in all your weapons at the town hall at the headquarters of the Commandant tomorrow at about noon. I don't wish to threaten anyone, but you are aware that the town is in a state of siege.

I should like to add also that I was to have imposed a levy upon the town, but I now declare that the town will not have to pay any dues.

Signed: Gashek

The next day, at about twelve o'clock, the square was full of armed men. Well over a thousand came with rifles. Someone had even brought a machine gun.

The eleven of us might easily have disappeared in this flood of armed men, but they came to hand in their weapons. They went on with it until late in the evening, while I shook everyone by the hand and said a friendly word or two.

In the morning I had printed and posted up Order No. 2:

Citizens!

I should like to thank all the inhabitants of Bugulma for the punctilious fulfilment of Order No. 1.

Signed: Gashek

That day I went happily to bed, unconscious that a sword of Damocles was hanging over my head in the shape of the Tver Revolutionary Regiment.

As I have said, the Soviet army stood on the other side of Bugulma about fifty versts to the south and, fearing a trap, did not dare enter it, until finally they received the order from the Revolutionary Army Soviet at Simbirsk to occupy it at all costs and secure it as a base for the Soviet armies operating east of it.

And so Comrade Yerokhimov, the Commander of the Tver Revolutionary Regiment, came that night to occupy and conquer Bugulma, when I had already been, for three days in the fear of God, the Commandant of the Town and was officiating to the general satisfaction of all classes of the populace.

When the Tver Regiment "penetrated" the town, they fired salvos into the air as they passed through the streets, and the only resistance they encountered came from my bodyguard of two Chuvashes, who were woken up while on guard at the door of the Commandant of the Town and would not let Comrade Yerokhimov into the town hall when, with a revolver in his hand, he was coming to take possession of it at the head of his regiment.

My Chuvashes were taken prisoner and Yerokhimov broke into my office and bedroom.

"Hands up," he said, drunk with victory and pointing a revolver at me. I calmly put up my hands.

"And who are you?" the Commander of the Tver Regiment asked.

"I am the Commandant of the Town."

"Of the Whites or the Soviet army?"

"The Soviet. May I put my hands down?"

"You can, but I beg you, according to the rules of war, at once to hand over to me the command of the town, because I have conquered Bugulma."

"But I was appointed Commandant," I objected.

"To hell with your being appointed. You've got to conquer it first."

"D'you know what?" he said, magnanimously after a short while. "I appoint you my adjutant. If you don't agree I'll have you shot in five minutes."

"I've nothing against being your adjutant," I answered, and called my orderly. "Vasily, prepare the samovar. We'll have some tea with the new Commandant of the Town, who has just conquered Bugulma. . . ."

All flesh is as grass, and all the glory of man as the flower of grass.

The adjutant of the commandant of the town of Bugulma

MY FIRST JOB WAS TO FREE MY TWO CAPTURED CHUVASHES AND go and make up for the sleep I had lost through the coup in the town. Towards noon I woke up and found, first, that all my Chuvashes had mysteriously disappeared, leaving behind a letter for me with fairly incomprehensible contents stuck in one of my boots: "Comrade Gashek, go look plenty help round about here and there. Comrade Yerokhimov *bashka-khawa* [head off]." Next, I found that Comrade Yerokhimov had been sweating from the early morning trying to compose his first order to the inhabitants of Bugulma.

"Comrade Adjutant," he said to me, "do you think it will be all right like this?" From a pile of draft orders covered with writing he took a sheet of paper with lines crossed out and words inserted and read:

> To the whole population of Bugulma.
>
> Today, with the fall of Bugulma, I have taken over command of the town. I am dismissing the former Commandant from his post on grounds of incompetence and cowardice and am appointing him my adjutant.
>
> Commandant of the Town: Yerokhimov

"That covers everything," I said approvingly. "And what do you intend to do next?"

"First of all," he answered gravely and solemnly, "I shall order a mobilization of horses. Then I shall have the mayor shot. Then I shall take ten hostages from the bourgeoisie and send them to prison until the end of the civil war. After that I shall carry out a general house-search in the town and prohibit free trading. That'll do for the first day, and tomorrow I'll think up something else."

"Permit me to point out," I said, "that I have nothing at all against a mobilization of horses, but I definitely protest against the shooting of the mayor who welcomed me with bread and salt."

Yerokhimov jumped up "He welcomed you, and hasn't come to see me yet? . . ."

"That can be put right," I said. "We'll send for him." And I sat down at the table and wrote:

The Office of the Commandant
of the Town of Bugulma
No. 2891
Operational Army
To the Mayor of the Town of Bugulma!

I order you to come immediately to the new Commandant of the Town with bread and salt according to the old Slav custom.

Commandant of the Town: Yerokhimov
Adjutant: Gashek

When Yerokhimov signed it he added, "If not, you will be shot and your house burned down."

"You can't add anything like that to official documents," I told him. "It would invalidate them."

I copied it out again in its original wording and formulation, had it signed, and sent it off by an orderly officer.

"Further," I said to Yerokhimov, "I am definitely opposed to ten people from the bourgeoisie being sent to prison until the end of the civil war, because that can only be decided by the Revolutionary Tribunal."

9

"The Revolutionary Tribunal," said Yerokhimov gravely. "But that's what we are. The town is in our hands."

"There you're mistaken, Comrade Yerokhimov. What are we? Just a damned rotten couple of ordinary people. The Commandant of the Town and his adjutant. The Revolutionary Tribunal is appointed by the Revolutionary Army Soviet of the Eastern Front. Do you want them to put you up against the wall?"

"Very well then," Yerokhimov replied with a sigh. "But surely no one can stop us from carrying out a general house-search?"

"According to the decree of the 18th June of this year," I answered, "a general house-search can only be carried out with the consent of the local Revolutionary Committee or Soviet. Since nothing like that exists yet, let's leave the house-search until later."

"You're an angel," said Yerokhimov tenderly. "Without you I would have been sunk. But surely we must stop the free trading?"

"Most of those who carry on trade and go to the bazaars are from the country," I tried to explain. "They are muzhiks who can't read or write. First of all they'll have to learn to be literate, and then they will be able to read our orders and understand what they're about. First we must teach the illiterate population to read and write, see that they understand what we want of them, and then we can issue orders — perhaps even for a mobilization of horses. Tell me, Comrade Yerokhimov, why are you so insistent on carrying out a mobilization of horses? Perhaps you want to change the Revolutionary Tver Regiment into a cavalry division? You know that for that there is 'The Inspector for Forming the Armies of the Left-Bank Group', don't you?"

"You're right again, Comrade Gashek," said Yerokhimov with a sigh. "What am I to do?"

"Teach the people of the Bugulma region to read and write," I answered. "And as for me, I'll go and see whether your chaps aren't up to some mischief and how they're billeted."

I went away and walked about the town. The Tver Revolutionary Regiment were behaving respectably. They were not oppressing anyone, they had made friends with the population, they were drinking tea, they had *pele-mele*, *shchi*, and *borshch* cooked for them, shared their shag and sugar with their hosts — in short everything was in order. I also went to have a look at Little Bugulma, where the first battalion of the regiment had been quartered. There too I found the same idyll. The men were drinking tea, eating *borshch*, and behaving respectably.

I returned late in the evening and at the corner of the square I saw a freshly posted placard which read:

> To the whole population of Bugulma and its Region!
>
> I order everyone in the whole town and region who cannot read and write to learn to do so within three days. Anyone found to be illiterate after this time will be shot.
>
> Commandant of the Town: Yerokhimov

When I came to Yerokhimov, he was sitting with the mayor who had brought with him not only bread and salt, which was carefully laid out on the table, but a few bottles of old Lithuanian vodka as well. Yerokhimov, who was in a good mood and was embracing the mayor, shouted at me as I came in, "Have you read how I've followed your advice? I went myself into the printing works and drew my revolver on the director: 'Print this at once, my little love-bird, or I'll shoot you on the spot, you son of a bitch.' He started to tremble, the vermin. He read it, and trembled still more. And then — I went *bang*! *bang*! at the ceiling. . . . And he printed it. He printed it beautifully. To know how to read and write, that's the main thing! Then you issue the order, they all can read, it's understood, and they are happy. That's right, isn't it, Mayor? Have a drink, Comrade Gashek!"

I declined.

"Will you have a drink or not?" he shouted.

I drew my revolver and shot at the bottles of Lithuanian vodka. Then aiming at my superior, I said with some vehemence, "Go and lie down at once, or. . . ."

"I'm going, my little love-bird, soul of mine. I didn't mean it seriously, just having a little fun and celebration."

I took Yerokhimov off, put him to bed, and returning to the

mayor, said to him, "It's the first time it's happened, so I forgive you. Run home and be glad that you've got out of it so easily."

Yerokhimov slept till two o'clock in the afternoon the next day. When he woke up he sent for me and, looking at me in some uncertainty, said, "I have the impression that you wanted to shoot me yesterday."

"Yes, I did," I answered. "I wanted to forestall what the Revolutionary Tribunal would have done to you when they learned that as the Commandant of the Town you had got drunk."

"But, my little love-bird, you won't tell anybody about it, will you? I won't do it again. I'll teach people to read and write. . . ."

In the evening the first deputation of muzhiks arrived from the region of Karlagin. There were six old grandmas between sixty and eighty years old and five old grandpas of the same age.

They threw themselves at my feet. "Don't destroy our souls, little father, *batyushka*. We can't learn to read and write in three days. Our heads can't manage it. Saviour of ours, have mercy on the district."

"The order is invalid," I said. "It was all the fault of that idiot, the Commandant of the Town, Yerokhimov."

In the night a few more deputations arrived, but by the morning new placards had already been posted up everywhere and sent to the villages around. The text was as follows:

> To the whole population of Bugulma and its Region!
> I proclaim that I have dismissed the Commandant of the Town, Comrade Yerokhimov, and have resumed office. Herewith his order No. 1, and his order No. 2 concerning the liquidation of illiteracy within three days are invalidated.
> Commandant of the Town: Gashek

I could afford to do this because during the night the Petrograd Cavalry Regiment had arrived in the town. My Chuvashes had brought them to deal with Yerokhimov.

The procession of the cross

THE COMMANDANT OF THE TOWN, YEROKHIMOV, WHOM I HAD dismissed from his post, issued an order to the whole Revolutionary Tver Regiment to evacuate the town in battle formation and encamp beyond it. He then came to take leave of me. I assured him that if he and his regiment ever tried to cause further unpleasantness I would have them disarmed and send him to the Revolutionary Army Tribunal of the Front. After all, we were putting our cards on the table.

Comrade Yerokhimov for his part assured me with great frankness that as soon as the Petrograd Cavalry Regiment left the town he would have me hanged on the hill over Little Bugulma so that I could be seen from all directions.

We shook hands and parted the best of friends.

After his departure with the regiment I had to find comfortable accommodation for the Petrograd Cavalry, which consisted mostly of volunteers, and get the barracks cleaned for them. Indeed I made up my mind to do everything possible to see that these splendid chaps were happy in Bugulma and would not rebel against me one fine day.

But whom was I to send to clean the barracks, scrub the floors, and make everything tidy? Definitely people who had nothing to do.

Among the local population everyone was doing something and working. I thought it over for a long time until I remembered that near the town there was a big convent, the Convent of the Most Holy Virgin, where the nuns did nothing else but pray and slander one another. And so I wrote the following official letter to the igumen [abbess]:

> The Army Command of the Town of Bugulma,
> No. 3896,
> Operational Army.
> To the Citizen Igumen of the Convent of the Most Holy Virgin:
> Send at once fifty maidens from your convent to be at the disposal of the Petrograd Cavalry Regiment. Send them straight to the barracks.
> Supreme Commandant of the Town: Gashek

The letter was despatched, and about half an hour later an extraordinarily beautiful and powerful peal of bells could be heard from the convent. All the bells of the Convent of the Most Holy Virgin groaned and wailed and were answered by those of the town church.

The orderly officer reported to me that the head priest of the main church, accompanied by the local clergy, was asking if I would receive him. I nodded amiably and a number of bearded priests poured into my office. Their spokesman said, "Mr. Comrade Commandant, I am coming to you in the name not only of the local clergy but of the whole Orthodox Church. Do not ruin the innocent convent maidens. We have just had news from the convent that you want fifty nuns for the Petrograd Cavalry Regiment. Remember that the Lord is above us!"

"At the moment only the ceiling is above us," I answered cynically. "And as for the nuns it must be as I said. I need fifty of them for the barracks. If it should prove that thirty will be enough for the job, I shall send the remaining twenty back. If fifty are not enough, I shall take a hundred, two hundred, or three hundred of them from the convent. It doesn't matter a rap to me. And as for you, gentlemen, I must warn you that you are interfering in official matters and so I am constrained to fine you. Each of you will bring me three pounds of wax candles, a dozen eggs, and a pound of butter. I authorize you, Citizen Head Priest, to arrange with the Abbess the time when she will send me those fifty nuns of hers. Tell her that I need them really urgently and that I shall return them again. Not a single one of them will get lost."

The Orthodox clergy left my office very downcast indeed.

In the doorway the most senior of them, with the longest beard and hair, turned round to me and said, "Remember that the Lord is above us."

"I beg your pardon," I said. "You will bring not three but five pounds of candles."

It was a glorious October afternoon. There had been a severe frost and the cursed mud of Bugulma had become crusted. Crowds hurrying to the church began to fill the streets. The bells rang gravely and solemnly in the town and in the convent. This time they were not sounding the alarm but calling all Orthodox Bugulma to a "Procession of the Cross".

It was only at the worst times in Bugulma's history that a Procession of the Cross took place — when the Tartars besieged the town, when pestilence and smallpox raged, when war broke out, when they shot the Tsar, and now. The bells rang meltingly, as though they were about to burst into tears.

The gates of the convent opened and out they came with icons and banners. Four of the eldest nuns with the Abbess at the head were carrying a large icon, a heavy one.

The image of the Most Holy Virgin stared aghast from the icon. And following it walked a number of nuns, old and young, all dressed in black, singing psalms: "And they led Him away to crucify Him. They crucified Him and two others with Him, one on the right hand and the other on the left."

And at the same time the Orthodox priesthood came out from the town church in gold-embroidered chasubles, followed by the Orthodox community in a long procession, carrying icons.

Both processions met and cried, "Christ liveth! Christ is King! Christ is victorious!"

And the whole crowd began to sing: "I know that my Redeemer liveth and that He shall stand at the latter day upon the earth."

The procession moved round the church and then turned towards the office of the Commandant of the Town where I had already made worthy preparations.

Before the building stood a table covered with a white cloth, on which there was a loaf of bread and salt in a salt cellar. In the right-hand corner stood an icon and around it there were lighted candles. When the procession came in front of the office of the Commandant I came out with dignity and asked the Abbess to accept bread and salt as proof that I did not harbour any hostile intentions. I also asked the Orthodox priesthood to cut off a slice of bread. They came, one by one, and kissed the icon.

"Orthodox men and women," I said solemnly. "I thank you for your beautiful and extremely attractive Procession of the Cross. I have seen it for the first time in my life and it has left on me an impression which I shall remember to my dying day. I see here a crowd of nuns singing and I am reminded of the processions of the early Christians in the days of Nero. It may be that some of you have read *Quo Vadis?* But I will not tax your patience any longer, Orthodox men and women. I asked for only fifty nuns, but now that the whole convent is here we shall be finished quicker, and so may I ask mesdemoiselles nuns to follow me to the barracks."

The crowds stood bare-headed before me and sang in answer, "The heavens declare the glory of God: and the firmament sheweth His handiwork. Day after day He exalts and night after night He reveals the wonder of His works."

The Abbess stepped forward before me. Her aged chin was trembling as she asked, "In the name of the Heavenly Father, what are we going to do there? Do not destroy your soul."

"Orthodox men and women," I shouted to the crowd. "The floors are to be scrubbed and the barracks cleaned so that the Petrograd Cavalry Regiment can be quartered there. Let's go."

The crowd followed me, and with such a quantity of industrious hands the barracks were put into perfect order by the evening.

The same evening a young and pretty nun brought me a small icon and a letter from the aged igumen containing the simple sentence: "I am praying for you."

Since that day I sleep in peace, because I know that up to this very day, in the old oak forests of Bugulma, there is the Convent of the Most Holy Virgin, where an aged igumen lives and prays for me, wretched good-for-nothing that I am.

In strategic difficulties

AT THE END OF OCTOBER 1918 THE FOLLOWING ORDER FROM THE Revolutionary Council of the Eastern Front reached me at my headquarters at Bugulma: "The 16th Division of the Light Artillery is on the march. Prepare sledges for its transport to the front."

I was at a loss what to make of the telegram. What sort of a division was it? How many thousand men did it have? Where would I get so many sledges? You see, in military matters I was a complete layman. Austria had not provided me with a professional military education and had resisted tooth and nail any attempt on my part to penetrate the mysteries of the art of warfare.

At the beginning of the war they threw me out of the officers' school of the 91st Infantry Regiment and tore off my one-year volunteer's stripes as well. While the others of my age-group received the titles of cadets and ensigns and fell like flies on all fronts, I sat locked up in the barracks gaol in Budějovice and in Bruck an der Leitha. When they finally let me out and wanted to draft me to the front with march companies, I hid in a haystack and in this way outlasted three of them. After that I pretended I had epilepsy, and they came very near to shooting me, but I volunteered for the front. From that moment on, fortune smiled on me, and when, on the march near Sambor, I managed to find Lieutenant Lukas an apartment with a very charming Polish lady and first-class cuisine, I was promoted to orderly officer.

When later, near Sokal, lice appeared in the billet of our battalion commander, I caught them all, anointed my superior with mercury ointment in the trenches, and received the Great Silver Medal for bravery.

But with all that, no one ever initiated me into the mysteries of the art of warfare. Today I still have no inkling of how many regiments make up a battalion and into how many companies a brigade is divided. And here in Bugulma I was required to know how many sledges were necessary for the transport of a division of light artillery. None of my Chuvashes knew either, and that was why I sentenced them conditionally to three days' imprisonment. If they found out the answer within a year, their punishment would be remitted.

I summoned the mayor and said to him sternly, "I have learned that you are concealing from me the number of men there are in a division of light artillery."

At first he could not utter a word. Then he threw himself on to the ground, started to hug my legs, and wailed, "Have mercy on

me. Do not destroy me. I never spread any such rumours."

I raised him up, treated him to tea and shag, and let him go with the assurance that in this case I was convinced of his innocence.

He went home and sent me a roast sucking-pig with a dish of pickled mushrooms. I ate the whole lot, but still didn't know how many men there were in a division and how many sledges were required for them.

I sent for the Commander of the Petrograd Cavalry Regiment and in the course of conversation casually referred to the matter.

"It's very peculiar," I said, "how the Centre is continually changing the number of men in the light artillery divisions. It's particularly awkward now, when the Red Army is being organized. You don't know by any chance, Comrade Commander, how many men there used to be in a division before?"

He spat and answered, "We're cavalry men and the artillery's no concern of ours. I myself don't know how many men I ought to have in my own regiment, because they never sent me any directives. I received an order to make up a regiment, so I collected the men. One man had a friend and another had one too, and that's how it gradually grew. When there are a lot of them, I'll perhaps call it a brigade. What are the Cossacks compared to us?"

When he went away, I knew just as much as I did before, and to crown my misfortune I received the following telegram from Simbirsk:

> Due precarious position on front you are appointed Commander of Front. In event of breakthrough of our positions on river Ik, withdraw regiments to position Kluchevo–Bugulma. Organize extraordinary commission for defence of town as soon as enemy comes within fifty versts. Mobilize inhabitants up to age of fifty-two and distribute weapons. At favourable moment blow up railway bridge over Ik and at Kluchevo. Send armoured train on reconnaissance and blow up railway track. . . .

The telegram fell out of my hand and, when I pulled myself together after my initial horror, I read on to the very end:

> Set fire to elevator. Destroy what you cannot take away with you. Await reinforcements and arrange billeting and regular provisioning of army. Organize supply train and regular dispatch of cartridges to front. Start publishing magazine in Tartar and Russian to satisfy inhabitants. Appoint revolutionary committee. Failure to execute these orders or any errors will be punished in accordance with wartime laws.
>
> Revolutionary Army Council of Eastern Front

It was towards evening and I had not lit the lamps. I sat in my chair and, when later the moon peeped through the window into my office, she saw a man sitting in the same chair, holding a telegram in his hand and staring idiotically into the grey gloom of the office.

And this is how the early morning sun found me. Towards morning the icon hanging in the corner could bear it no longer. It fell from the wall and broke in pieces.

The Chuvash on guard in front of my doors peered inside and reproachfully threatened the icon with his finger: "You bastard, you. You fall and fall and wake chap up."

Towards morning I took out of my pocket a picture of my late mother. Tears welled in my eyes and I whispered, "Dear Mama! When years ago I lived with you at No. 4 Milešovská in the Royal Vineyards in Prague, you never thought that fifteen years later your poor little son would have to withdraw regiments to positions at Kluchevo – Bugulma, blow up a railway bridge on the river Ik and at Kluchevo, blow up railway tracks, set an elevator on fire, and hold out to the last man in defence of the town — apart from other things. Why didn't I become a Benedictine instead, as you wanted me to, when for the first time I was ploughed in my examinations in the fourth class at school. I should have had peace. I should have served Holy Mass and drunk the monastery wine."

And, as though in answer, something began to rumble suspiciously in the south-eastern quarter of the town and after that it rumbled a second and a third time.

"That's some artillery fire!" said the orderly officer, who had just returned from the front. "Kapel's men have crossed the Ik and are advancing together against us on the right wing together with the Polish division. The Tver Regiment is retreating."

I sent the following order to the front:

> If General Kapel's group has crossed the Ik and is advancing with the Polish division against our right wing, cross the Ik on the other side and proceed against them on the left wing. I am sending the Petrograd Cavalry against enemy's rear.

I summoned the Commander of the Petrograd Cavalry. "They have broken through our positions," I told him. "It will now be all the easier for you to get to the enemy's rear and capture the whole Polish division."

"Very well," the Commander replied. He saluted and went off.

I went to the telegraph apparatus and wired to Simbirsk:

> Great victory. Positions on river Ik broken through. We are attacking from all directions. Cavalry in enemy's rear. Heaps of prisoners.

The glorious days of Bugulma

NAPOLEON WAS A PRIZE IDIOT. WHAT TROUBLE THE POOR fellow went to to probe the mysteries of strategy! What a lot he had to study before he hit upon the idea of his unbroken front! He was at military schools in Brienne and Paris and even had his own military tactics all worked out — and yet he took a beating at Waterloo.

Many others followed his example and always got a thrashing. Today, after the glorious days of Bugulma, the victories of Napoleon, from the occupation of Cape L'Aiquiletta, and on through Mantua and Castiglione, Aspern, etc., seem appalling nonsense. I am certain that if Napoleon had acted at Waterloo as I did, he would have decisively smashed Wellington.

In that battle Blücher fell on Napoleon's *right flank*, and Napoleon should have done what I did at Bugulma, when the volunteer corps of General Kapel and the Polish division were on our right wing.

Why did Napoleon not order his guard to fall on Blücher's *left flank*, just as I did in my order to the Petrograd Cavalry?

The Petrograd Cavalry worked sheer miracles, because the Russian land is indescribably vast and a few miles here or there do not matter. They rode as far as Menzelinsk, and came to the region of Chishma and God knows where else in the enemy's rear, and they drove him before them, so that his victory ended in a defeat.

Unfortunately the majority of our enemies used the opportunity to withdraw to Belebei and Buguruslan, and the minority driven from behind by the Petrograd Cavalry came to within fifteen versts of Bugulma.

In those glorious days of Bugulma the Tver Revolutionary Regiment with Comrade Yerokhimov at their head were constantly in retreat before the defeated enemy.

In the evening they always dispersed all over the Tartar villages and, when they had devoured all the geese and chickens, they retreated again nearer to Bugulma and dispersed all over other villages until finally they entered the town in full order.

From the printing works they came running to tell me that the Commander of the Tver Regiment, Yerokhimov, was threatening the manager with a revolver and insisting on having a certain order and proclamation printed.

I took with me my four Chuvashes, two Brownings, and a Colt revolver, and hurried to the printing works, where I found the manager seated in the office on one chair and Comrade Yerokhimov close to him on the other. The manager was in a rather

unpleasant predicament, because his neighbour was holding a revolver to his temple and repeating over and over again, "Are you going to print this or aren't you? Are you going to print this or aren't you?"

I heard the manager's manly answer: "I am not going to print it. I just can't, old man," whereupon his neighbour with the revolver implored him, "Print it, soul of mine, sweetheart, little love-bird, print it, I beg you."

When they saw me, Yerokhimov rushed forward to meet me in evident embarrassment, embraced me, and shook my hand cordially. Turning to the manager, he winked at him and said, "We've been chatting together now for half an hour. It's a long time since I've seen him."

I noticed that the manager spat and growled openly, "A fine chat, I must say!"

"I heard you wanted to get something printed again," I said to Yerokhimov, "a proclamation, an order, or something. Would you be good enough to let me read the text?"

"I was only joking, Comrade Gashek, only having a little joke," Yerokhimov answered in a very unhappy tone. "I didn't mean to make anything of it."

I took from the table the original of what was to be printed and what was never to be read by the citizens of Bugulma. They would certainly have been surprised at what Yerokhimov had prepared for them, because it ran:

> Proclamation No. 1.
> Returning at the head of the victorious Tver Revolutionary Regiment, I hereby proclaim that I am taking over the administration of the town and district. I am organizing an extraordinary revolutionary tribunal and I shall be president of it. Its first session will be tomorrow and the matter which is to be discussed is of great importance. The Commandant of the Town, Comrade Gashek, will appear before the Extraordinary Revolutionary Tribunal, because he is a counter-

revolutionary and a conspirator. If he is condemned to be shot, the sentence will be carried out within twelve hours. I warn the population that any revolt will be punished on the spot.

Yerokhimov,
Commandant of the Town and district

And my friend Yerokhimov intended to add to this the following order:

Order No. 3
The Extraordinary Revolutionary Tribunal of the Military District of Bugulma announces that by the decision of the Extraordinary Revolutionary Tribunal the former Commandant of the Town, Gashek, was shot for counter-revolution and conspiracy against the Soviet government.

Yerokhimov,
President of the Extraordinary Revolutionary Committee

"It's really nothing but a little joke, my little love-bird," Yerokhimov said in a soothing voice. "Do you want my revolver? Take it! Why would I want to shoot anybody?"

I was struck by his mild tone. Then I turned round and saw that my four Chuvashes were pointing their rifles at him and looking at the same time terrifyingly harsh and menacing.

I commanded them to order arms, took the revolver from Yerokhimov, who fixed his childlike blue eyes on me and said quietly, "Am I under arrest or at liberty?"

I smiled. "You're a fool, Comrade Yerokhimov. Nobody gets locked up for little jokes like that. You yourself said that it was really nothing but a little joke. But I ought to lock you up for something else — your disgraceful return. The Poles were crushed by our Petrograd Cavalry and yet you retreated before them all the way to the town. Do you know that I have a telegram from Simbirsk, ordering the Tver Revolutionary Regiment to win new laurels once more for its old revolutionary banner? I return you this revolver, which you handed over to me, but on one condition — that you immediately leave the town, encircle the Poles, and bring in prisoners. But you must not touch a single hair of their heads. I'm warning you that if you do, it will be all up with you. I'm sure you'll agree that we mustn't make fools of ourselves in the eyes of Simbirsk. I have already telegraphed that the Tver Regiment has brought in a lot of prisoners."

I struck the table with my fist. "And where have you got those prisoners? Where have you got them?"

And, brandishing my fist under his nose, I added in a terrifyingly angry voice, "Just wait! You'll pay for this! Have you anything to say to me before you go off with your regiment to get those prisoners? You realize I am the Commander of the Front, the highest authority here?"

Yerokhimov stood straight as a candle. Only his eyes twitched with agitation. Finally he saluted and declared, "This very evening I shall crush the Poles and bring in prisoners. Thank you."

I gave him back his revolver, shook his hand, and cordially took my leave of him.

Yerokhimov kept his word splendidly. By morning the Tver Regiment had begun to bring in prisoners. The barracks were soon full of them and we did not know where to put them. But when I went to have a look at them I nearly fainted with shock: instead of the Polish soldiers, Yerokhimov had collected peasants — the Tartar residents from all over the villages — because the Poles had not waited for the Tver Regiment's surprise attack but had fled like cowards.

New dangers

THERE WAS NO DOUBT ABOUT IT; COMRADE YEROKHIMOV COULD not understand that the peaceful Tartars, the local population, were not the Poles, and when I issued the order that all the supposed "prisoners", whom he was collecting in the villages, should be set at liberty, he felt insulted, went to the military telegraph office of the Petrograd Cavalry Regiment, and tried to send the following telegram to the Revolutionary Army Council of the Eastern Front at Simbirsk:

> Report that, after three days' fighting, I have destroyed enemy with my Tver Revolutionary Regiment. Enemy's losses enormous. Captured twelve hundred Whites, whom Town Commandant has set free. Request despatch special commission investigate whole affair. Town Commandant, Comrade Gashek, completely unreliable, counter-revolutionary, and has contacts with enemy. Request permission organize *Cheka*.
>
> Yerokhimov,
> Commander Tver Revolutionary Regiment

The head of the telegraph office accepted the telegram from Comrade Yerokhimov, assuring him that it would be sent as soon as the line was free. He then got into his sledge and came to see me.

"Well, here's a pretty mess, *batyushka*," he said to me with an expression of utter despair. "Read it." He handed me Comrade Yerokhimov's telegram.

I read it and put it calmly into my pocket. The head of the telegraph office began to scratch his head and blink nervously, saying, "You must admit that my position is a difficult one, a damned difficult one. According to the orders of the Peoples' Commissariat I have to accept telegrams from regimental commanders. And you seem not to want me to despatch this one. I didn't come here to put it into your hands, but just so that you should know about its contents and so that you could send another telegram against Comrade Yerokhimov."

I told the head of the telegraph office that I had a very high opinion of the Peoples' Commissariat for War, but we were not at the Base where they were. "This is the Front. I'm the Commander of the Front and I can do what I like. I order you to accept from Comrade Yerokhimov as many telegrams as he wants to write. But I forbid you to despatch them and I order you to bring them to me at once.

"For the time being," I concluded, "I leave you at liberty, but I warn you that the smallest deviation from our program will have consequences which you are quite incapable of imagining."

I drank tea with him while we talked about quite ordinary things and I took leave of him with the warning that he must tell Yerokhimov that the telegram had been sent.

After supper the Chuvash, who stood on guard, reported to me that the whole High Command building was surrounded by two companies of the Tver Revolutionary Regiment and that Comrade Yerokhimov was addressing them and announcing that the tyranny was over.

And sure enough, shortly afterwards Comrade Yerokhimov appeared in my office accompanied by ten soldiers with fixed bayonets who stationed themselves at the doors.

Without addressing a word to me, Comrade Yerokhimov began to post his men in various places around the office.

"You go here, you here, you stand here, you go there in the

corner. You place yourself by the table, you stand by that window, you by that one, and you will stay close to me."

I rolled a cigarette and, by the time I had lit it, I was surrounded by bayonets and could observe with interest what Comrade Yerokhimov would do next.

It was clear from his look of uncertainty that he did not know how to set about it. He approached the table with official documents, tore up two or three of them, and then walked up and down the office for a while, a soldier with a bayonet close at his heels.

The others, who stood around me in all corners, assumed solemn expressions, until one of them — a very young one — asked, "Comrade Yerokhimov, may we smoke?"

"Yes," answered Yerokhimov and sat down opposite me. I offered him tobacco and cigarette paper. He began to smoke and said in a hesitant tone, "Is that Simbirsk tobacco?"

"No, it's from the Don region," I answered briefly and began to leaf through the documents lying on the table as if he were not there.

There was a painful silence. At last Yerokhimov said quietly, "What would you say, Comrade Gashek, if I were President of the *Cheka*?"

"Then I could only congratulate you," I answered. "Wouldn't you care for another smoke?"

He lit a cigarette and continued rather sadly, "And now imagine that I really am that, Comrade Gashek, that I've been appointed President of the *Cheka* of the Revolutionary Army Council of the Eastern Front."

He stood up and added emphatically, "And imagine that you are in my hands."

"First," I answered calmly, "show me your authorization."

"Damn the authorization," said Yerokhimov. "I can arrest you even without authorization if I want to."

I gave a smile. "Comrade Yerokhimov, sit down quietly, where you sat before. They'll bring the samovar in a minute and we'll have a chat about how presidents of the *Cheka* are appointed."

"And you've got no business here," I said turning to

Yerokhimov's escort around me. "Clear off! Tell them to make themselves scarce, Comrade Yerokhimov."

Yerokhimov smiled in embarrassment. "All right, my dears, go and tell the men outside that they're to go home too."

When all of them had gone away and the samovar was brought in, I said to Yerokhimov, "You see, if you'd really had the authorization, you'd have been able to arrest me and shoot me, and do everything to me that you imagined you would—if you were President of the *Cheka*."

"I'll get that authorization," Yerokhimov replied quietly. "I'll certainly get it, my dear."

I took Yerokhimov's unfortunate telegram out of my pocket and showed it to him.

Yerokhimov was overwhelmed. "How did that get to you?" he said in a crushed tone. "They should have sent it off a long time ago."

"The position is, my dear friend," I answered affably, "that all army telegrams have to be signed by the Commander of the Front

and therefore they brought me your telegram for signature. If you wish to send it and insist on doing so, I shall willingly sign it, and you can take it to the telegraph office yourself, so you can see I'm not afraid of you."

Yerokhimov took his telegram and tore it up. He started to whine and sob. "My sweet soul, my little love-bird, I didn't really mean it. Please forgive me, my dear and only friend."

We drank tea until two o'clock in the morning. He stayed the night with me and we slept on one bed. In the morning we drank tea again and I gave him a quarter of a pound of good tobacco for the journey home.

Potemkin's villages[*]

EIGHT DAYS HAD ALREADY PASSED SINCE THE GLORIOUS DAYS of Bugulma and there was still no trace of the Petrograd Cavalry Regiment. Comrade Yerokhimov, who had been very zealous about visiting me since the last affair, expressed every day certain suspicions that the Petrograd Cavalry had gone over to the enemy. He proposed that I should, first, proclaim them traitors to the Republic; second, send a telegram to Trotsky in Moscow describing in detail their shameful desertion; third, organize a Revolutionary Tribunal of the Front and summon before it the Commandant of the Telegraph Office of the Petrograd Cavalry, because he must know what was happening — and if he did not, summon him all the same, because he was responsible for communications.

Comrade Yerokhimov was very punctual with his campaign of agitation against the Petrograd Cavalry. He arrived at eight o'clock in the morning and went on agitating against them until half-past nine. Then he departed only to reappear at two o'clock and start a new campaign of agitation which he continued until four. In the evening he came again and went on agitating over tea once more until ten or eleven o'clock in the evening.

All the time he walked about the office with his head down,

* When Catherine the Great was being shown around the Crimea, which Russia had just annexed, her lover, the Russian statesman Potemkin, constructed fake villages to make the region appear more populated. Hence, the expression "Potemkin's villages".

repeating gloomily, "What a frightful thing to do! What a disgrace for the Revolution! Let's telegraph. Let's get into direct contact with Moscow!"

"It'll turn out all right in the end," I consoled him. "A time will come, Comrade Yerokhimov, when you'll see the Petrograders return."

Meanwhile I received a telegram from the Army Revolutionary Council of the Eastern Front:

> Report number of prisoners. Your last telegram on great victory at Bugulma unclear. Despatch Petrograd Cavalry to Third Army at Buguruslan. Report whether all orders in our previous telegram carried out. Also report how many copies of propaganda magazine you have published in Tartar and Russian. State magazine's title. Send courier with detailed account of your activities. Send Tver Revolutionary Regiment to advantageous positions. Prepare leaflets appealing to soldiers of White Army to desert to our side and have them dropped from aircraft. Every error or failure to comply with individual points will be punished in accordance with laws of wartime.

In no time I received still another telegram:

> Do not send courier. Await arrival Inspector Eastern Front with Commander Political Department Revolutionary Army Soviet together with member of Soviet, Comrade Morozov. They have been invested with full powers.

Comrade Yerokhimov happened to be present at that moment. When I had read through the last telegram I passed it to him to see what effect an awe-inspiring inspection like this would have on him. After all it was just what he had wanted.

One could see that a difficult struggle was going on inside him. What an opportunity to avenge himself on me, to gloat over my misfortunes! But the happy smile which had lit up his face in the first moment soon disappeared and was transformed into a look of worry and mental torment.

"You're done for, my little love-bird," he said sadly. "You'll lose that wild and wanton head of yours."

He walked up and down the office, singing wistfully:

Oh, you bold head of mine!
How long will you stay on my shoulders?

Then he sat down and continued, "If I were in your place, I'd run away to Menzelinsk, and then to Osa and from Osa to Perm. And then I bet you wouldn't find me, my bright sparks! Now, hand over to me the command of the town and the front and I'll put everything right."

"I don't believe I've anything to be afraid of," I said.

Yerokhimov gave a meaningful whistle, "He's got nothing to be afraid of! Have you mobilized the horses? No, you have not. Have you got reservists from the local population? No, none at all. Have you levied a contribution on the town? No sign of it. Have you thrown counter-revolutionaries into gaol? Of course not. Have you found a single counter-revolutionary? Not one. And now tell me one last thing: have you had at least one priest or member of the merchant class shot? No, you certainly have not. Have you had the former district police officer shot? No you haven't done that either. And what about the former mayor of the town? Is he alive or dead? Alive. Well, there you are — and you go on telling me you have nothing to be afraid of! It's a bad look out for you, my friend."

He got up and walked about the office, whistling again:

Oh, you bold head of mine!
How long will you stay on my shoulders?

He put his hands to his head, and while I calmly watched the cockroaches swarming on the warm wall near the stove, he began to run from window to window and then back to the door, still with his hands on his head, moaning, "What's to be done, what's to be done? You're done for, my little love-bird. You'll lose that wild and wanton head of yours."

When he had been running about in this way for about five minutes, he sat down helplessly on a chair and said, "There's simply nothing to be done. If you could at least say that you have a full prison, that might be something. But who have you got there? No one. If you could at least show the inspectors that you'd set fire to some estate where the counter-revolutionaries had their hide-out, that might help. But you've nothing to show, nothing whatsoever. You haven't even made a house-search in the town. I tell you frankly, I'm fond of you but I've got a very low opinion of you."

He got up, strapped on his belt, thrust into it a revolver and a Caucasian sword half a metre long, shook my hand, and assured me that he wanted to help me — he didn't know how, but he would certainly hit on some way.

After his departure I telegraphed my reply to Simbirsk:

> Number of prisoners being ascertained. Mobility of front and lack of maps prevent detailed account of victory at Bugulma. Inspectors will verify on spot. Encountering difficulties over publication of magazine in Tartar and Russian. No Tartar printers available. Short of Russian type. Whites took away printing presses. If air squadron established at Bugulma, leaflets with appeals to White Army can be dropped by aircraft. Meanwhile am stuck here without aircraft. Tver Revolutionary Regiment in reserve in town.

I slept the sleep of the just, and in the morning Yerokhimov came to me and said that he had thought up a way of saving me, and that he and his men had been working on it the whole night.

He took me outside the town to a former brick kiln where I found a picket from the 5th Company of the Tver Revolutionary Regiment, who stood there with fixed bayonets and, whenever anyone passed, shouted, "Keep to the left. No entry here."

In the middle of this place a small surprise awaited me — three graves, newly dug and covered over, and on each of them a stake with a notice-board. The first grave carried the following inscription:

Here lies buried the former district police inspector. He was shot in October 1918 as a counter-revolutionary.

On the second was written:

Here lies buried the priest. He was shot in October 1918 for counter-revolutionary activity.

And on the third:

Here lies buried the mayor of the town. He was shot for counter-revolutionary activity in October 1918.

My legs shook under me and, supported by Comrade Yerokhimov, I started to make my way back to the town.

"We got it all done in a single night," said Yerokhimov. "I promised I'd help you, so that you'd have something to show the inspectors when they come. For a long time I couldn't hit on anything suitable and then I suddenly thought of this. Would you like to see them?"

"Whom?" I asked in alarm.

"Why, the priest, the mayor, and the district police inspector, of course," said Yerokhimov. "I have them all locked up in the pig sty and when the inspection is over I'll let them go home. Don't imagine that anyone'll be any the wiser. No one's allowed near the graves. My brave lads know how to keep mum and when the inspectors arrive you'll have something to show for yourself."

I looked at his profile. His features reminded me of Potemkin's. And I went to see whether he was telling the truth. I soon satisfied myself that he had not been lying. From the pig sty there rang out the bass tones of the priest, singing very doleful psalms with the refrain: "Lord have mercy, Lord have mercy!"

And then I thought of "Potemkin's villages".

Difficulties with the prisoners

THE PETROGRAD CAVALRY REGIMENT UTTERLY DASHED ALL Comrade Yerokhimov's hopes. They not only failed to desert to the enemy, but even brought in prisoners — two squadrons of Bashkirs who had mutinied against their captain, Bakhivaleyev, and gone over to the Red Army. They had mutinied because he would not let them burn a village on their retreat. And so now they had decided to try their luck on the other side.

In addition to the Bashkirs the Petrograders brought in other prisoners, youths in peasant sandals, aged seventeen to nineteen, who had been mobilized by the Whites and had been watching for the first opportunity to make a bolt.

There were about three hundred of them, emaciated young men in tattered homespuns. Among them were Tartars, Mordvins, and Cheremisses, who knew as much about the significance of the civil war as they did about the solution of equations to the power of x.

They arrived in full military order with rifles and cartridges, and brought with them one of their colonels whom they drove in front of them. The old Tsarist colonel fairly bristled with rage and rolled his eyes wildly. Even though now a prisoner he could not resist repeating to his former subordinates, who led him like a bear on a rope, that they were "scum" and that he would smash their "snouts".

I gave orders for the prisoners to be billeted in an empty distillery and for half of them to be fed with rations from the Petrograd Cavalry and the other half with rations from the Tver Revolutionary Regiment. Shortly after I had issued this order, Comrade Yerokhimov and the Commander of the Petrograd Cavalry both came running up to me and insisted categorically that, as Commander of the Front and Commandant of the Town, I should feed the prisoners myself.

In the course of the conversation Comrade Yerokhimov expressed the view that rather than feed the prisoners who were to be his responsibility he would have them shot. The Commander of the Petrograd Cavalry kicked Comrade Yerokhimov in the shins and told him to stop talking nonsense. He would not allow anyone to shoot his prisoners — he could have done that at the front without waiting till now, after his cavalry had been sharing their bread and tobacco with them all this time. If he were to have anybody shot, it would only be that Colonel Makarov of the 54th Sterlitamat Regiment.

I demurred and said that all officers of the old Tsarist army, even when taken prisoner, were to be regarded as mobilized by the decree of June 16, 1918. Colonel Makarov would be sent to the Staff of the Eastern Front, where there were already a number of former Tsarist officers serving in the Staff itself.

Comrade Yerokhimov remarked that this was how counter-revolution got spread all over the Staffs of the Red Army. I explained to him that these people were under the control of the political organs and were being used purely as specialists. But Yerokhimov in his radicalism nearly burst into tears. "My little love-bird, I'm not asking you for anything else, but please give me that colonel!" And then he started to threaten. "You know very well that one of these days the inspectors will be coming here. What are they going to say to you? A colonel has fallen into our hands and been allowed to go away safe and sound! To hell with these decrees! Perhaps they were drawn up by specialists too."

The Commander of the Petrograd Cavalry suddenly got up and thundered at Yerokhimov, "Is Lenin a specialist? Answer, you scoundrel! Are the Council of People's Commissars, who issue the decrees, specialists? My God, what a swine you are, you son of a bitch!"

He grabbed Yerokhimov by the collar, threw him out of the door, and went on raging: "Where was his regiment when we took Chishma and captured two squadrons of Bashkirs and a battalion of the 54th Sterlitamat Regiment with its colonel? Where was he hiding with his Tver Revolutionary Regiment? Where was he with his bandits, when Kapel's men and the Poles were only twenty-five versts from Bugulma? I'll take my cavalry and hound the whole of his glorious revolutionary regiment to the front. I'll have machine guns stationed behind them and force them to attack. Filthy scum!" He went on to swear horribly at Yerokhimov's mother and his regiment's mother, and only stopped when I pointed out that it was the Commander of the Front alone who had the right to station troops in that way, and then only on the authority of an order of the Supreme Staff.

So he reverted to what we had been talking about at the beginning, insisting that the maintenance of the prisoners in the town was the exclusive responsibility of the Commandant of the Town and the Commander of the Front. He was not going to pay a single kopek for them. He had in all only twelve thousand roubles in his regimental till and he had already sent to the field treasury three times for money without so far getting a single rouble.

I assured him that as Commandant of the Town and Commander of the Front I had only two roubles in my till, and if I reckoned up everything I owed that month to the various organizations which had furnished supplies to the units passing through the town, it would come to more than a million roubles. I was indeed sending the bills to the chief accountant in Simbirsk, as well as through the State Control Commission, but up to now none of them had been paid, so the balance of my month's stay here was: assets — two roubles, liabilities — more than a million. And, with such a magnificent turnover as this, for three days I had been drinking nothing but tea with milk and a small portion of white bread, morning, noon, and evening. I didn't have a single lump of sugar, I hadn't seen meat for over a week and I hadn't eaten *shchi* [cabbage soup] for over a fortnight. I could not even remember what butter or lard looked like.

At the description of such misery, tears came into the eyes of the Commander of the Petrograd Cavalry.

"Well, if it's as bad as that, I'll take over the feeding of all the prisoners. We have a great stock of provisions in our train. We managed to do a little looting in the enemy's rear," he said with obvious emotion. Then he asked me to give him the exact number of prisoners and went away. After his departure I got into direct communication with the Staff of the Eastern Front and exchanged a few telegrams with them, two on purely economic matters and one concerning the number of prisoners. I received the following answer:

Field Treasury has been instructed to advance you twelve million roubles. Enrol prisoners in army.

Bashkir squadrons should be incorporated in Petrograd Cavalry Regiment as independent unit, which you should complete with other Bashkir prisoners, to become first Soviet Bashkir Regiment. Captured battalion of 54th Sterlitamat Regiment should be incorporated in Tver Revolutionary Regiment. Distribute prisoners among companies of regiment. Send Colonel Makarov without delay to Staff of Eastern Front to be at their disposal. If he shows reluctance shoot him.

I sent for Comrade Yerokhimov and for the Commander of the Petrograd Cavalry.

Only the Commander of the Petrograd Cavalry came. Instead of Yerokhimov his regimental adjutant presented himself and informed me that Comrade Yerokhimov had just taken two armed soldiers with him and fetched Colonel Makarov out of the distillery where the prisoners were billeted. After that he had gone with him to the forest.

I rode after Yerokhimov and caught up with him, just as he was turning with his soldiers and the colonel into a low copse off the road to Little Bugulma.

"Where are you going?" I roared at him. Yerokhimov looked like a schoolboy, who has just been caught by the schoolmaster in his pear tree in the act of stuffing pears into his pocket.

For a moment he stared helplessly at the colonel, at the copse, at his soldiers, and at his boots, and then said diffidently, "I'm going for a stroll, just a little stroll into the forest with the colonel."

"Come on, now," I said. "I think you've been strolling long enough. You go on ahead and I'll go back with the colonel myself."

The infuriated colonel showed no sign of fear. I led my horse by the bridle and the colonel walked beside me.

"Colonel Makarov," I said, "I've just saved you from a disagreeable situation. Tomorrow I shall have you sent to Simbirsk, to the Staff. You are mobilized," I added affably.

Hardly had I finished speaking when the colonel struck me such a hefty blow across the temple with his enormous bear-like paw, that I dropped down without a sound in the snow by the path. I think that I should certainly have frozen to death if I had not been found a little later by two muzhiks, who were leaving Bugulma by sledge. They turned round and took me home.

The next day I crossed Colonel Makarov's name off the list of prisoners and the cavalry horse on which the colonel had escaped to get back to his Whites off the list of horses belonging to the Commandant of the Town. And it was just at that very moment that Comrade Yerokhimov, who had gone to Klyukven, was sending to the Revolutionary Army Council of the Eastern Front at Simbirsk the following telegram through the telegraph office of the railway station:

> Comrade Gashek has released prisoner Colonel Makarov of 54th Sterlitamat Regiment and given him his own horse to enable him go over to enemy.
>
> Yerokhimov

And this telegram actually reached Simbirsk. . . . .

Before the Revolutionary Tribunal of the Eastern Front

"...*böse Menschen haben keine Lieder*" — "BAD PEOPLE HAVE NO SONGS" — a German poet wrote, as he completed his couplet. That evening I sang some Tartar songs so late into the night that no one around me could sleep or go peacefully to bed, from which I concluded that the German poet was lying.

All the same, I think I was the first of the whole neighbourhood to go to sleep, because I got finally tired myself of those monotonous tunes, which all end with "Ek, el, bar, ale, ele, bar, bar, bar".

And then one of my Chuvashes woke me up to tell me that some sledges had arrived with three people who were showing their papers down at the guardhouse. His words, given in exact translation, were: "Three sledges, three people, down below heaps of papers, one, two, three papers."

"Talk to you," the Chuvash went on. "Bad people, swear!"

"Send them upstairs!"

Immediately afterwards the door flew open and the visitors pushed their way into my office-cum-bedroom.

The first was a fair-haired and bearded man, the second a woman wrapped in a fur coat, the third a man with a black moustache and an unusually penetrating look.

They introduced themselves one after the other. "I am Sorokin." "I am Kalibanova." "I am Agapov."

46

The last named added harshly and relentlessly, "We are the Board of the Revolutionary Tribunal of the Eastern Front."

I offered them cigarettes, upon which Agapov made the observation: "I can see, Comrade Gashek, that you're not too badly off here. People who honestly serve the revolution can't afford tobacco of this quality."

When the samovar was brought in, we conversed about quite different matters. Sorokin spoke about literature and declared that, when he had been a Left Social Revolutionary, he had published in Petrograd a collection of poems under the title *Resistance*, but it was confiscated by the Press Commissariat. Today he had no regrets about that, because what he wrote had been utter drivel. He had studied modern philology and was now President of the Revolutionary Tribunal of the Eastern Front. He was a really gentle, nice man with a soft, blond full beard, which I tugged gently when we drank the tea.

Comrade Kalibanova was a student of medicine and had also once been a Left Social Revolutionary. She was a lively, nice little person, who knew the whole of Marx by heart. Agapov, the third member of the Revolutionary Tribunal, held the most radical views of the three. He had served as a clerk in the office of a Moscow lawyer, where the White Guard General Kaledin had once been in hiding. According to his description the lawyer was the biggest scoundrel in the world, because he had paid him only fifteen roubles a month — while he gave the waiter in the Hermitage, who brought him a portion of salmon, three times as much as that as a tip and only demanded in return the privilege of spitting in his face.

From Agapov's whole appearance it was clear that everything which had preceded the fall of Tsarism had turned him into a cruel, relentless, harsh, and terrible man, who had long ago settled his accounts with those who had paid him those wretched fifteen roubles, and who continued to wage war on those shades of the past wherever he came, transferring his suspicions to his surroundings and always thinking of some unknown traitors.

He spoke briefly, in curt sentences full of irony. When I invited him to take a lump of sugar in his tea, he said, "Life is only sweet for some people, Comrade Gashek, but it will also get bitter too."

When in the course of the conversation the subject of my being a Czech came up, Agapov observed, "However much you feed a wolf, he always looks towards the forest."

Comrade Sorokin replied as follows to Agapov's observation: "Everything will be explained in the course of the investigation."

Comrade Kalibanova said, with a sneer, "I think we should show Comrade Gashek our full powers."

I told them that it would give me pleasure if I could see whom I had the honour of dealing with, because I would certainly not allow anyone to wake me up in the night without serious cause.

And then Agapov opened his briefcase and showed me these full powers.

The Revolutionary Army Soviet
of the Staff of the Eastern Front
No. 728-b.
Simbirsk
Full powers
Are hereby accorded to A. Sorokin, Kalibanova, and
Agapov who are appointed by the Revolutionary Soviet
of the Staff of the Eastern Front as members of the
Board of the Revolutionary Tribunal of the Eastern
Front and are authorized to carry out investigations on
the basis of their full powers with anybody anywhere:
We order all military units to place at their disposal the
number of men they require to carry out their sen-
tences.

> The Revolutionary Army Soviet
> of the Staff of the Eastern Front
> Signed:

"I think that's quite enough, Comrade Gashek," said
Kalibanova.

"Of course it is," I agreed. "But take off your fur coat,
because the samovar will be here in a moment, and besides it's
warm here."

Agapov did not let slip the opportunity to ask, "And aren't
you feeling warm? I think you may even be feeling hot."

"I've got a thermometer here," I said. "If you like, look by the
window and you'll see that the temperature here is just normal."

Sorokin, the most solemn of them, took off his short fur coat
and placed it on my bed, announcing that immediately after tea
they would get down to business.

If I still remember Comrade Agapov today it is because I liked
him for his frankness and openness.

He was also the first to ask me to have the samovar cleared
away, as now the main proceedings against me would start. He said

that there was no need to call witnesses. The charge which had been worked out in Simbirsk on the basis of a telegram from Comrade Yerokhimov was quite sufficient. He had stated that I had set Colonel Makarov at liberty and given him my horse to enable him to go over to the enemy.

He proposed that this should be the end of the trial proceedings and demanded for me the sentence death by shooting, to be carried out within twelve hours.

I asked Comrade Sorokin, who actually was the President in charge of the trial proceedings. I received the reply that everything was in perfect order, because Agapov represented the prosecution.

Then I requested that Yerokhimov should be called, because any man might send a telegram in the first flush of anger. He should be heard orally as a witness.

Agapov stated that that was quite right, because if Yerokhimov had sent the telegram he obviously knew a great deal more about my affairs.

We agreed that Yerokhimov should be immediately summoned to give evidence about me.

I sent for Yerokhimov. . . .

He was half-asleep and very surly when he arrived. When Agapov informed him that what he saw before him was the Revolutionary Tribunal of the Eastern Front, which had been sent to investigate the case of Comrade Gashek on the spot and give its verdict, Yerokhimov's face assumed an expression of boundless idiocy.

He looked at me, and to this day it is a psychological enigma what was going on inside him.

He looked from one member of the Revolutionary Tribunal to the other and finally at me.

I gave him a cigarette and said, "Have a smoke, Comrade Yerokhimov. It's the same good tobacco we smoked together that time."

Yerokhimov once again eyed the whole gathering stupidly and hopelessly and said, "My little love-birds, I sent that telegram when I was completely sozzled."

Comrade Sorokin then stood up and delivered a lecture on the green serpent of alcoholism.

Next, Kalibanova spoke in the same sense, and finally Agapov stood up and in an upsurge of indignation demanded severe punishment for Yerokhimov for drunkenness, because he had committed that crime while he was commander of the Tver Revolutionary Regiment.

Agapov, beautiful in his enthusiasm, proposed sentence of death by shooting.

I stood up and said that not a living soul could be found to shoot Yerokhimov. It would start a mutiny in the army.

Kalibanova proposed twenty years' forced labour, Sorokin that he should be reduced to the ranks.

They talked at length for and against every motion until the small hours, with the final result that Yerokhimov received a severe reprimand, coupled with the warning that if it was repeated the most severe penalty would be applied against him.

During the whole proceedings he was fast asleep.

In the morning, the Revolutionary Tribunal of the Eastern Front departed and, when Agapov took leave of me, he said once more, ironically, "However much you feed a wolf, he always looks towards the forest. Keep your eyes open, brother, otherwise it'll be 'off with your head!'" I shook hands with all of them. . . .

OTHER STORIES

INTRODUCTION

Hašek is supposed to have composed some twelve hundred stories and articles, of which more than a thousand have been published in Prague in a collected edition of his works. Most of these stories were written before the First World War and made fun of the Church and the "Establishment". As a boy at school Hašek used to make a little extra pocket money by acting as a server in neighbouring Catholic churches; since then all kinds of church ritual seem to have had a fascination for him — the mass, extreme unction, and the blessing of troops before battle. Another favourite target for his satire was the courts of law, where he always shows sympathy for the delinquent rather than the judge. Hašek also satirized vindictive schoolmasters, obstreperous children, and troublesome pets. He enjoyed depicting the misfortunes of quite innocent ordinary citizens like Mr. Tevlín (his humour always contained a liberal dose of Schadenfreude). When he was with the Bolsheviks in Russia, a lot of wild rumours spread through Prague about his activities. One was that he had been killed in a drunken brawl. In the last story in this section Hašek describes how he might have punished a journalist who had had the effrontery to publish a none-too-complimentary obituary about him.

Mr. Tevlín's thievish adventure

THERE ARE SOME PEOPLE WHO TAKE AN INTEREST IN EVERY SINGLE object, every single thing, every single happening which they notice in the street. One of these good people was Mr. Tevlín. For instance, if Mr. Tevlín saw a barrel of pickled herrings in front of a shop in the street he would stop, look, and wait until the servant rolled it away into the shop. Then he would nod his head in agreement and walk on.

If round the corner he saw a handcart standing in the street, he would look at it and again wait to see who would come and fetch it. It gave him pleasure that people were working. He liked to watch how they unloaded bricks and stones. He was interested in the work of paving and indeed in any work activity whatsoever.

He took an interest in anything which was part of life's daily round — horses which could not pull a load, and switchmen on the tram lines — and he was always agreeably excited when he saw someone doing a job. He also liked to speculate on what a passerby might be doing, and his eye would brighten if he succeeded in guessing that person's profession.

It was one of his pleasures to stroll along the streets — at least it was until this happened to him. He went out as usual into the street, and in a busy frequented thoroughfare noticed a bicycle standing by the pavement — an abandoned bicycle. He looked around, because he was interested to know who would be so careless as to leave a bicycle standing in the street like that. He did not see any shop. And so he thought that it could not belong to a delivery boy on a tradesman's bicycle, but that obviously something was being delivered here to a private individual at his home. He also noticed that there was no bar nearby. The bicycle stood by the pavement right in front of the entrance to an apartment block.

On the opposite pavement a policeman was standing, watching Mr. Tevlín with interest as he continued to stare about him and stand near the bicycle.

Mr. Tevlín considered that it was a great act of carelessness to leave a bicycle standing like that by the pavement, and he thought he would wait near it until its owner turned up. But then he wondered whether perhaps the bicycle might not have a padlock to prevent anyone riding off on it, and so he walked round the bicycle and inspected it on the other side.

Meanwhile the policeman was looking at Mr. Tevlín with ever increasing interest too, and even walked nearer towards him.

Mr. Tevlín ascertained that the bicycle had no padlock. "That really is careless," he sighed. "Anyone could jump on it and ride away."

He went on examining the bicycle. It was very well made. And what make was it? He took hold of the handlebars and leaned over it. The bicycle slipped out from under him, and as he got up he saw a face looking down on him. It was a severe, angry, and menacing face — the face of the policeman.

"What are you doing, messing about with someone else's bicycle?" the policeman asked sternly.

"I was looking to see what the make was."

"And why did you take it by the handlebars?"

Already a crowd of people had gathered around, the sort of people, like Mr. Tevlín, who take an interest in everything, just as Mr. Tevlín took an interest in that unfortunate bicycle.

"By the handlebars . . ." Mr. Tevlín stammered pitifully. "I'm waiting here for the owner."

"And what is the owner's name?"

"I have no idea."

"Then why are you waiting for him?"

"So that nobody steals it from him."

There was laughter among the crowd. "Perhaps so that no one *else* should steal it from him" said the policeman ironically. "Put it back where you took it from, and I arrest you in the name of the law."

That policeman was also just like Mr. Tevlín. He was interested in everything, every object, every little happening, and most of all in Mr. Tevlín.

Today one need no longer say, "He trembled like as aspen leaf." One might just as well say, "He trembled like Mr. Tevlín." Indeed Mr. Tevlín trembled so much that the policeman had sometimes to drag him along after him, like a puppy, from the place where the abandoned bicycle was still standing by the pavement in front of the apartment block, number 1912a.

He had still not stopped trembling when he was brought into the premises of police headquarters and heard the report: "Humbly report that this man was trying to steal a bicycle in front of apartment block number 1912a." And the policeman described how Mr. Tevlín had not succeeded, while Mr. Tevlín continually interrupted him, saying, "Me, why I'm not a thief. I can't even ride a bicycle."

He could not manage to find a better excuse. He went on repeating that he did not know how to ride a bicycle, that it would be pointless for him to steal one, and that, if he had wanted to have one, he could buy them by the dozen. Looking utterly miserable, he stood there repeating, "Honestly, believe me, I don't know how to ride a bicycle."

"And he immediately fell down with it when he was trying to jump on to it."

"How could I be jumping on to it," Mr. Tevlín moaned, "when I don't know how to ride anyhow." Then he added that he was just a well-intentioned idiot who wanted to help everybody.

At that moment the door opened and a young man rushed into the police station in a state of panic.

"My bicycle's gone," he cried. "It was standing in front of apartment block number 1912a and I've just heard that somebody has been trying to steal it!"

The policeman pointed his finger at Mr. Tevlín.

"Now, don't deny it," said the Police Commissioner to Mr. Tevlín, "and tell us the name of your accomplice."

"I can't," Mr. Tevlín said with a sigh.

"Then put him behind bars for the time being," said the Commissioner. Mr. Tevlín went down on his knees and shouted out, "In God's name, please don't do this, gentlemen."

The next day they took him off to the criminal court.

The examining magistrate, Counsellor Vincek, was a very nice man. He did not want to make things worse for any accused person and used all possible means to investigate most carefully the statements of the criminals who were under examination.

"Very well," he said to Mr. Tevlín. "You persist in maintaining that you cannot ride a bicycle. Tomorrow, then, a commission of this court will investigate the matter. We'll take you outside the gate and put you on a bicycle. Then we'll see whether you can ride or not."

The important day arrived and, in the presence of the Commission, the warder seated Mr. Tevlín on a bicycle on the main road near the Olšany Cemetery.

"I'll fall off!" Mr. Tevlín cried out in horror, never having sat on a bicycle before.

At a sign from the examining magistrate the warder gave the bicycle a shove, and Mr. Tevlín rode forward on the gentle incline of the road, calling out all the time, "I'm going to fall."

In a panic he stepped on the pedals for fear he would be killed. He stepped on them even harder, grasped the handlebars in a convulsive grip, and instinctively hurtled down the road to Strašnice like the most expert cyclist. He had done it. He called out, "I'm going to fall!" and rode off with great speed until he disappeared out of sight of the Commission.

Down at Strašnice he finally succeeded in falling into a ditch, after having run over a Jewess.

He got three months for having lied in saying that he could not ride a bicycle, when in fact he even tried to escape on it. And for that he had to suffer disciplinary punishment.

An idyll from the almshouse in Žižkov

WHEN GRANNY PINTOVÁ, FROM THE ALMSHOUSE AT ŽIŽKOV, looks back on it all, what she regrets most is that she has no teeth to gnash. But she raises her eyes to heaven and spits, and after that her bent, wizened figure shambles over to a corner of the room where she pulls a rosary out of the pocket of her grey skirt. And slowly but surely she prays for Chaplain Toman, that God may forgive him the treason he was guilty of at the Žižkov almshouse. When the other old women talk of that same event, Granny Pintová's grey eyes take on a brighter gleam and she observes that even in those days, when Chaplain Toman was still coming to visit them, she did not like the way he behaved — he was rather loutish, more like an ordinary servant, she said, than a servant of God.

Of course they often quarrel among themselves, because they do not like Granny Pintová's sharp tongue. But these quarrels are very entertaining and at least kill the tedium of those long hours in the almshouse.

The other day Granny Skuhrovská said that in fact Granny Pintová herself was at the bottom of it all. But in my opinion things developed of their own accord and the circumstances alone caused the catastrophe. It was, however, undoubtedly a catastrophe of very considerable consequences, which even affected the small flat flask which Granny Pintová kept in her suitcase. That flask is now empty, but when the stopper is removed an experienced nose can

— merely by sniffing it — at once detect the smell of sweet kümmel.

The flask will confirm that it used once to be full, and so, by a remarkable combination of circumstances, sweet kümmel, Chaplain Toman, and the almshouse mutually complement each other.

Of course an important factor in all this was Granny Pintová's dying, but that happened a long time ago. Now she curses the chaplain and she certainly does not lie in bed. But the chaplain's tender heart must bear the blame for the whole episode. He was called to the almshouse some time ago because Granny Pintová was on her death bed and was asking for extreme unction.

It was the first time that the new young chaplain had had to administer, and he set about the task with enthusiasm. The surroundings and the situation had such an effect on him that after the whole religious ceremony was over he put his hand into his pocket and placed a gold piece in dying Granny Pintová's hand. That was something that had never yet happened to the old women in the almshouse.

After the chaplain's departure Granny Mlíčková announced that he was very clever indeed at administering. And indeed the effect of the gold piece on Granny Pintová was such that that very same evening she actually ordered for herself some ham and kümmel.

When the doctor came next morning to give her an injection to relieve her death agony, he found her sitting at the table in a very cheerful mood and singing "I love my love dearest of all." A week later the kümmel ran out, because the money ran out. Then one day the sacristan came and knocked at the chaplain's door to say that Granny Pintová was dying again and wished him to come to her with the grace of the Lord.

When she saw the chaplain, she whispered happily, "O, my dear sweet Reverend Father, I don't know, I really don't, whether I shall have the strength today to hold that gold piece in my hand." She managed all the same, and Chaplain Toman said to the sacristan, as they were leaving the almshouse. "She's a tough one. She certainly hangs on to life." She certainly did. The next morning, when the doctor came, he heard her walking about the room and singing,

> She's my darling dear.
> I'm not the only one
> After her to run.
> There are thousands who
> Do the same too. *

"My dear Mrs. Pintová! What *is* the matter with you?" "But that chaplain's so very clever at administering extreme unction, doctor, sir."

That was on Wednesday. On Thursday the sacristan came running to Chaplain Toman, and while he was still in the doorway, called out, "Reverend Father, we must go to the almhouse again. This time we have to administer to that little old woman, Skuhrovská." But before they got there the dying woman had got

---

* This ribald song, "I love my love dearest of all", ends: "Do you know who she is? She's my Virgin Lady." (Translator's note.)

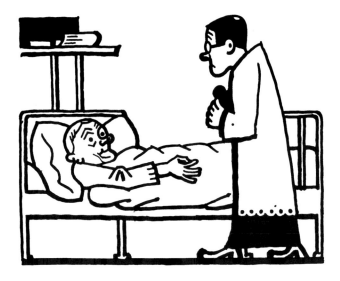

into a quarrel with Mrs. Mlíčková, who all of a sudden had insisted on lying down too so that the chaplain could administer to her at the same time. Mrs. Pintová had made the suggestion. The others had however persuaded Mrs. Mlíčková that her turn would come on Monday. Mrs. Mlíčková of course cried out that she wanted to die immediately that very day and she would not wait until Monday. What if something were to happen to her in the meantime? In the end she calmed down, but when she later saw the chaplain giving Mrs. Skuhrovská a gold piece after the spiritual consolation, she could not contain herself and said in a tearful voice, "Reverend Father, I feel it in my bones that it's going to come to me too very soon." When he remembers that day the young chaplain shakes his head and a cold shiver runs down his spine.

In the almshouse they still remember what a row and uproar there was when on Saturday old Mrs. Vaňková began to complain that she was unwell and was feeling faint. Mrs. Mlíčková said that it was a dirty trick on Mrs. Vaňková's part and that it was *her* turn first, and if that was the way things were going she would rather get her dying over and done with now on Saturday, and on Monday Mrs. Vaňková could send for the chaplain.

A lot of argument followed until finally Mrs. Vaňková, being the younger woman, gave way; she was after all only eighty-nine and Mrs. Mlíčková was eighty-nine and three months.

But when they came to fetch Chaplain Toman to the almshouse, he turned pale and said that the Senior Chaplain Richter could go today. Accordingly Chaplain Richter came and prayed fervently at Mrs. Mlíčková's bedside, blessed them all, and was about to go away without giving her a gold piece. Granny Pintová, who like all the others was keeping a careful watch, caught Chaplain Richter by the edge of his cassock.

"Reverend Father, forgive me, but I must stand up for Mrs. Mlíčková. We've always got a gold piece, when we have been given extreme unction. It's true, Reverend Father, that you prayed longer, but you forgot all about the gold piece."

And Granny Vaňková hissed, "And Mrs. Mlíčková was

obstinate enough to insist on dying today, just so that that good chaplain should come to her, although her turn was not until Monday."

Deeply crestfallen, Chaplain Richter gazed at the old women and then fumbled for his purse. . . .

The latest decision of the Žižkov town council is interesting. At the insistence of the chaplains it has decreed that the old women should be prohibited from dying on their own initiative. It has further laid down that extreme unction will in future always be administered in the almshouse once a month, and to all of them at one go. As a result the grandmothers' takings are now extremely meagre.

The flask smelling of sweet kümmel is empty and an air of great calamity hangs over the almshouse. Mrs. Vaňková hanged herself a fortnight ago, because the illustrious town council of Žižkov would not give her permission to die.

Justice and the lesser bodily needs

YESTERDAY I MET AN ACQUAINTANCE OF MINE WHO HAD A VERY strange expression on his face. He was muttering something under his breath, and finally it came out that he was swearing at the laws. It is the duty of every law-abiding citizen not to lose his head in such situations, but to say with complete loyalty, "Well, perhaps it won't be quite so bad."

This is in fact what I said, but the man swore even more and made one or two insulting remarks. First he started to swear at the cops, then he spoke about the Prague City Council and after that he began to abuse the police again. When talking of the district *hejtman's* * offices he spat contemptuously, and finally he cursed the whole judiciary. After pulling to pieces one by one all those institutions which were set up to protect humanity, cities, animals, and the State, he proceeded to hand me the following instructions on a half-sheet of yellowish paper.

Summons

You are required to report within three days for the purpose of commencing your sentence of six hours' imprisonment, passed by judgement of the City Council of the Royal Capital City of Prague on October 7,

---

* Officer in charge of a political district.

1904 (ref. no. P 23714/3), on grounds of an offence under para. 3 of the decree of the City Council of the Royal City of Prague of March 7, 1888, no. 165538. In case of failure to appear you will be forcibly collected.

Imperial and Royal District Court, Royal Vineyards, Prague, section VI, January 9, 1907.

[Signature indecipherable]

"Para. 3 of the decree of the Prague City Council of March 7, 1888, no. 165538! Who the hell would know that? What does it mean, my good friend?" I asked.

"Miserable rascal that I am," he said, "I broke this regulation three years ago. Blackguard that I am, I went so far as to perform my lesser bodily needs in the night. It's a shocking case in all its details. I'll tell you the whole story.

"Three years ago, at half past ten at night, when people were coming out of the theatre, I came out too. God knows what was playing that night. While I was in the theatre I'd already felt an urge to perform my lesser bodily needs, but I didn't want to go to the urinal there, because I can't bear the presence of other people when I'm doing it. I need quiet, and I always whistle to myself 'Feeyu, fee!' And so I went quickly along the Ferdinand Alley, and I didn't like to stand over the gutter — not with people coming out of the theatre and the glare of electric light there..... Listen carefully — it is an interesting story.

"At that time they were repairing the police headquarters in Karolína Světlá Street. It was nice and peaceful by those planks, nice and quiet, in short a very suitable place. I stood up against them and did what my health required of me. I also gave my usual whistle in the circumstances: 'Feeyu, feeyu, fee, feeyu.' Then suddenly the door of the police headquarters burst open, a policeman came out, seized me by the collar, and said, 'What are you doing here?'

"'Performing my lesser bodily needs,' I answered very readily.

"'Then come with me to the guard-room,' he said.

"'If you insist,' I said, 'I'll come at once, but first let me adjust my dress.'

"'No, you must not do that,' he declared. 'In this case unadjusted dress will be a *corpus delicti*.'

"As he led me away, I just had time to do up one or two buttons. At the police station he handed me over to an inspector, who wrote a report when he learned of my crime.

"'I can witness on oath,' the policeman said in a firm voice, 'that this man did not perform his lesser bodily needs over the gutter, but against the planks which were stacked in front of police headquarters.'

"'Tell me about the whole incident,' the inspector urged the policeman, who saluted and began to relate it. 'I was standing in the carriage-way and I saw a figure approaching the planks. I immediately had the impression that something illegal was going on there. Shortly afterwards I heard a trickle and some whistling. I ran out quickly and caught the perpetrator just as he was going to do up his trousers.'

"'Did you have the impression,' asked the inspector, 'that the accused was deliberately using a spot in the immediate proximity of police headquarters?'

"'I was struck by his remarkable calm,' the policeman replied.

The inspector then turned to me. 'Have you anything to say in your defence or do you admit to the offence?' I admitted it.

"'Your name?'

"'Josef Konvelský.'

"'Where do you live?'

"'1862, the Royal Vineyards.'

"'What place do you come from?'

"'Slaný.'

"'Have you ever been convicted?'

"'Certainly not.'

"'What was the name of your father?'

"'Antonín Konvelský.'

"'And your mother?'

"'Marie.'

"'Maiden name?'

"'Kautská.'

"'Have you a grandfather or grandmother still living?'

"'No.'

"'How old are you?'

"'Thirty.'

"The inspector then went to the telephone and called the police station at the Royal Vineyards. 'Hallo! Send a man to see whether at number 1862 there is living a certain Josef Konvelský, thirty years old, coming from Slaný, whose father was Antonín Konvelský and mother Marie, born Kautská.'

"Half an hour later the answer came through. 'The person in question does actually live in that house. The concierge there says that he is a disorderly man.'

"'You can go,' the inspector said to me, 'but next time remember that the street near police headquarters is not the place for performing bodily needs.'

"A fortnight later I received a summons from the office of the *hejtman* at the Royal Vineyards. I went there and was surprised to find in what low esteem a man is held who performs his bodily needs in the street at night.

" 'That was not very clever of you,' said the official there. 'You know perfectly well that if you were not doing it out of sheer luxury or frivolity, you could have done it over the gutter. The City of Prague has asked us to investigate the case. Did you do it with the intention of damaging the City, in its capacity as the authority responsible for upkeep of the pavement?'

" 'No, certainly not.'

" 'Good, then you performed your lesser bodily needs without any wilfully malicious intention?'

" 'Yes.'

" 'All right then. You can go home, but I warn you that the street near the police headquarters is not the place for performing lesser bodily needs.'

"Again three weeks elapsed, and I received a fresh summons to come to the office of the *hejtman*. Here I was told this much: 'The City of Prague issued a decree of the City Council on March 7, 1888, no. 165538. Are you aware of its contents?'

" 'Certainly not.'

" 'Nor of paragraph 3 of that decree?'

" 'Even less!'

" 'Ignorance of the law is no excuse,' said the official and sent me home.

"But third time lucky! I received yet another summons to the office of the *hejtman*.

" 'Now you're here for the third time,' the stern official said to me. 'The City of Prague firmly insists that after a thorough investigation of your case we should furnish them with an expert opinion on how far the Prague City Council has been injured by your action. Do you perhaps still remember how many square decimetres of the pavement were watered by you?'

" 'That could be investigated,' I said. 'Have me hanged and then conduct a post-mortem on my corpse. Cut out the bladder and measure its volume. I must warn you that you will also have to take into account whether the pavement slopes and how many holes there are in it. The climatic conditions are also important....'

" 'You can go home,' he said. So I did.

"A month later I received an official letter from the City Council of the Royal Capital City of Prague, in which it was stated that I was guilty of an offence under paragraph 3 of the decree of March 7, 1888, no. 165538, and for this offence they had considered it proper to sentence me to a fine of two crowns and, in the case of non-recoverability, to six hours' imprisonment. I was at liberty to appeal against this sentence to the office of the Governor within eight days.

"And so I appealed:

To the Most Honourable Office of the Governor,
    The City Council of the Royal Capital City of Prague have sentenced me to a fine of two crowns or six hours' imprisonment for an offence against paragraph 3 of the decree of the City Council of March 7, 1888. The undersigned begs that this sentence should be quashed on the following grounds:
    a) I performed my lesser bodily needs in the interests of safeguarding my health. The Honourable Office of the Governor will certainly be aware of cases where bladders have burst.
    b) I did not offend against public morals, because no one but the policeman saw me and it was at night.
    c) Finally I did not injure the City of Prague because I performed my lesser bodily needs on a heap of planks stacked near the police headquarters.

"A year later I received an order from the office of the Deputy-Governor, in which I was informed that my objections were not upheld and my act of performing my lesser bodily needs was consequently reinstated as an offence.

"After that they wanted to levy distraint on my property so as to collect that fine of two crowns. Three years later, because I had no money, I received a summons to start my six hours of imprisonment. Please, write a thesis on this case. I'm going to make them collect me forcibly."

I promised I would but, in the end, instead of writing a thesis, I wrote a story about the case of Mr. Josef Konvelský, who will never stop swearing at the laws. . . .

The judicial reform of Mr. Zákon, counsellor in the Ministry of Justice

"I'D LIKE TO KNOW WHAT THE OLD MAN IS THINKING UP FOR US this time," Mr. Vohnoutek, the usher of the regional court, said to himself, as he went home from the tavern at eleven o'clock at night and saw the light still burning in the office of the counsellor, Mr. Zákon. The expression "for us" applied not just to the ushers and messengers, but to the whole staff of the regional court, for Mr. Vohnoutek considered himself to be the representative of all the gentlemen who worked under Mr. Zákon, and for that reason he expected from the Old Man only such things as would give all the officials plenty to swear about.

It must be said, however, that in this particular case Mr. Vohnoutek was wrong. The counsellor had in front of him a sheet of paper covered with beautiful writing, but it was not a ukase for the regional court — it was a report, destined for His Excellency the Minister of Justice, which had almost the character of an academic treatise. The fact was that the Minister has issued a circular to all criminal courts, in which he had pointed out that the present state of justice in criminal cases was totally unsatisfactory. The courts, he wrote, continued to be guided by the outdated theory of retribution or, at best, the theory of the deterrent, whereas modern justice must aim principally at the criminal's reform. And it was just in this direction that the results up to now had proved unsatisfactory, because delinquency was not decreasing. And therefore the Minister asked the judges of all criminal courts to submit to him with the greatest possible haste their proposals for an appropriate reform of the criminal judiciary.

This circular from the Ministry came at such a particularly opportune moment for Mr. Zákon, who had been occupying himself with these questions for many years, that, after having assured himself that no one could hear him, he hissed between his teeth, "At last something sensible for once." Then he sat down and began to write out his proposals, and at the very moment when Mr. Vohnoutek was looking up at his windows he had just completed them. Then he lit another cigar and read through the most important bits of his expert opinion once more:

> It is true that criminals, who have been convicted, habitually promise the court that they will reform, but it is also no less true that this promise is very rarely kept. The criminal instinctively feels that the judge tries the case strictly according to the letter of the law, and so he promises to reform only in order to make out a case of alleviating circumstances for himself. But he does not keep his promise, because he regards the judge as merely the representative of a system of justice which is penal and therefore hostile to him. And so he thinks that a broken promise to reform is a permissable and useful stratagem.

> I regard it as quite out of the question that a simple assertion by the judge that he is not hostile to him could change a convicted man's opinion. One should therefore rather consider how it might be possible to make a promise of this kind binding in the eyes of the criminal. It would be appropriate to examine the question whether there exists any legal or moral bond which a criminal would consider as so particularly

venerable or sacrosanct that he would keep his promise in all circumstances.

The science of criminology, advancing with the spirit of the times, has paid special attention to the study of the psychology of the criminal, and has reached the conclusion, as the Most Honourable Imperial and Royal Ministry will be well aware, that a criminal in all circumstances keeps his word, when he has given it to another criminal. With the greatest respect the undersigned begs leave to see in this conclusion a possible basis for a judicial reform, which might lead to the noble results, which the Most Honourable Imperial and Royal Ministry wishes to achieve with its circular. The undersigned, again with the greatest respect, does not attempt to conceal that the reform which he proposes is a bold one. But he takes the liberty of mentioning that in his own modest opinion it is a simple one and, if carried out, will also be effective. The proposal involves the appointment as judges of criminals who would be the best-known ones in their circles. If it were to this kind of judge that a criminal were to make a promise that he would improve, then the feeling of solidarity among criminals would make that promise binding on the man who gave it and would bring about the reform of those unfortunates who have violated the law. . . .

With the deepest respect the undersigned does not attempt to conceal that three important objections may be raised against his project. The first might be that the exalted rank of judge should not be open to such doubtful elements. But this difficulty could be removed, if the names of these former criminals were changed and they were appointed exclusively to courts where they had never been convicted. The second objection might be that they would lack the necessary education. This could be alleviated by ensuring that when criminals, who have been specifically earmarked for duties as judges, have served their final sentence, special lectures could be arranged for them in the field of criminal law and the criminal code. Since these people obviously could not and would not be used in any other sector of the judiciary but the criminal branch, these two subjects will be quite sufficient. The third objection is finally the problem of finance. A young lawyer or a doctor of law, fortified in his knowledge of the laws, tolerates, if with some difficulty at least with a clean conscience, his long years of unremunerated practice. With these new officials one could not presuppose the same moral fibre and it is naturally to be feared that the poverty of such probationers and assistants might drive them back onto the path of crime. For this reason the undersigned, with the greatest respect, takes the liberty of proposing that such officials should be appointed judges forthwith, that is to say to the 9th-allowance grade of public servants. One cannot deny that as a result of this the expense incurred by the salaries of the officials of the criminal courts would involve an increased financial burden, but in compensation for this the expenses for the upkeep of prisons would be cut, since as a result of this reform the number of cases of conviction would be reduced to the smallest proportions.

The counsellor read through his work and an expression of deep satisfaction could be observed on his face. Then he wrote on the envelope the address, sealed the letter carefully, and the next day his expert judgement was on its way to Vienna.

Six months later the counsellor received a reply from the Ministry of Justice. He opened it with a trembling hand. For as long as he could remember the Ministry had never dealt with any question so quickly. What lay concealed in this envelope? Praise or a snub? The counsellor once more repeated under his breath the whole of his judgement. At first his proposal seemed to him to be nonsense, but then he began to defend it to himself. After a while he recalled that that was really unnecessary. An irrevocable decision on his proposed reform lay before him on the table. He began to count the buttons of his waistcoat — should he open the answer at once or only after lunch. His counting showed that it should be later. Then he remembered that it was really quite immaterial whether he spoiled his lunch or his dinner, so he sat down at the table and energetically cut the envelope. . . . His proposal had been accepted.

If it had been possible for the counsellor to abandon all ideas of the dignity of an official in the 5th class, he would have started dancing, but, as it was, he lit a cigar and looked into the distance. And he saw how, in a short time, he would move to Vienna, perhaps to the Supreme Court or to the Ministry of Justice. And then become President of the Senate or Head of Department. . . . People like that were sometimes given the title of Excellency. . . . The counsellor beamed with delight.

He selected one of the old criminals from Pankrác prison, who was serving a fifteen months' sentence for burglary with violence. He assured himself beforehand that this man understood German, since the authentic text of all laws was in German only, and then "Long Eda" was sent with the permission of the Ministry to the prison of the regional court, of which Mr. Zákon was the head. The latter spent more time in the prisoner's cell than he did in his office. Mr. Vohnoutek shook his head over it. The whole staff of the regional court wondered what it meant. The most famous town gossip affirmed that the mysterious prisoner was the counsellor's natural brother. But the greatest surprise came when the mysterious prisoner finished serving his sentence. Mr. Zákon became President of another regional court and "Long Eda" disappeared with him.

Fourteen days later Mr. Zákon appeared at one of the district courts in his new region for an inspection. Some tatterdemalion had come up before the judge, Mr. Eduard Pablásek, accused of theft and vagabondage. Mr. Zákon was delighted when he saw the dignity and energy with which the former "Long Eda" set about things. The ragamuffin had not got the nerve to contradict the judge; he only cast furtive glances of amazement at him and wiped his eyes. For a moment it looked as if he wanted to say something, but in the end he did not utter a word. And he accepted without demur the severe sentence of six months' imprisonment.

When they led the convicted man away the counsellor asked, "Did he recognize you?"

"Of course he did."

"You have made a really excellent start, but you forgot to get him to promise that he would never again embark on a career of crime. Moreover that sentence was too severe."

"Just let me carry on, sir. I'm his old comrade. We used to call him 'Smart Joe'. I'll go and see him now in his cell and everything will be all right."

In the afternoon the two old friends met again. "Smart Joe" embraced the man he supposed was only masquerading as a judge and assured him that, compared to him, the Captain of Köpernick was like lemonade to arsenic. Then he wanted to indulge with his old comrade in memories of a merry past. But the new judge interrupted him with the energetic question, "Joe, would you like to be judge or even counsellor?..."

In the course of the next two years there was an unheard of change in conditions in Bohemia. The courts occupied themselves at the most with cases of libel or tavern brawls. There were no longer any real criminals. Anyone who had once been one was now a secretary or a counsellor, and, because there was no school of crime, there were no longer any criminals. Mr. Zákon was already Head of Department in the Ministry of Justice, "Long Eda" and "Smart Joe" had already attained "out of turn" the ranks of senior counsellors. Mr. Zákon and his protégés had won. The Minister of Justice now applied his judicial reform over the whole empire and said to him that he had only one fear and that was that the criminal courts, which had up to now had such wonderful moral successes, would become totally redundant. But should this fear prove to be unfounded, then the Head of Department could look forward to the title of "Excellency".

After some years Mr. Zákon was indeed afraid that he might have gone a little too far in his attempts to wipe out criminality. But no. When he took up the evening paper he read that the police had caught an admirably organized band of young thieves and robbers. What was remarkable about this was that allegedly this whole honourable company was composed of probationary lawyers and those who had graduated in Law. This report should really have given pleasure to Mr. Zákon. It was a proof that in his humane effort he had not gone too far. But he was not pleased. He did not himself know exactly why. He had a kind of inkling that something terrible was going to happen. And this inkling proved to be right.

When the President of the Court of Justice asked the accused lawyers and probationers why they stole and burgled, he received this answer, unanimously, from all of them: "So that they'll make us counsellors too one day."

Mr. Zákon never received the title of "Excellency".

The criminals' strike

OF COURSE, IT WAS AGAIN THE SOCIAL DEMOCRATS WHO WERE to blame. Their papers continually carried reports on the class prejudices of the judiciary. Their speakers demanded that the equality of all citizens, which was theoretically enshrined in the laws, should actually be implemented in practice! These demands went so far that when a baroness in a jewellery shop by mistake secretly tucked into her pocket one or two precious diamonds, their newspapers insisted on her conviction as a common thief, in spite of the fact that in cases like that with baronesses it was always due to kleptomania. Similarly too these organs refused to stand up for a certain enlightened count when he went bankrupt, and as a result various creditors and officials lost a few paltry millions. No, they even had the effrontery to demand that His Serene Highness should sit in the accused box, and when this failed to occur they began to incite the people against the judiciary and the courts.

And so the inevitable happened. Criminals thought that the courts were not being just to them and that they were not being properly treated, and there came about a phenomenon unique in world history, which had — as readers will see — very serious consequences for the State. One day, or rather one night, without the knowledge and permission of the police, there appeared at street corners posters announcing a general strike of all criminals! That was the last illegal act to take place. From then on there were none. The strike was to last until the laws guaranteeing the equality of all citizens were implemented to their very last letter.

It must have been painful for the loyal citizen to see with his own eyes how from the very beginning the authorities underestimated the importance of this movement. Police and officials of the law courts went on holiday, rubbed their hands with satisfaction, and declared that they would take care to see that the requests of the strikers were met. Such glorious times as they had would never come again in their lifetime. The officials of the Public Prosecutor's Office sat the whole day in cafés and read newspapers out of sheer boredom. But then the first effects of the strike began to be apparent. The editors, those born criminals, were solid with the rest and took care not to offend against the smallest paragraph of the law. Even the Public Prosecutor himself, when he read copies of the Social Democrat publications *The People's Right*, *The Glow*, and *Stinging Nettles*, hoping in spite of everything to find something of interest to himself, was disappointed and threw them away in anger, saying, "They've become almost as boring as the *Prague Official Gazette*!"

From that moment he had been afflicted by a terrible bout of neurosis. Then quarter-day came and he had to fill in his returns. When he wrote in the column "Number of accused" "zero", in the column "Number of prosecutions" again "zero", and in the column "Number of convictions" a third "zero", he wrung his hands in despair and hanged himself.

But the neurosis spread by leaps and bounds. It was a neurosis resulting from boredom and idleness. The building of the Bohemian Provincial Criminal Court became quite derelict and its entrance was covered with cobwebs. Then suddenly there were frightful developments. All the Law Court reporters in the daily papers were given notice. And so they determined to resort to self-help. They founded the Society for Supporting the Families of Prisoners and began publicly to collect funds for it. According to its statutes the family of a prisoner would receive for the time of his imprisonment double his earnings. The readers of the column "From the Law Courts", as well as the publishers of the newspapers, flooded the new society with contributions so that it was able to announce that it would pay to the family of a prisoner not double but ten times his earnings. But even that did not help against the solid organization of the criminals.

But the worst misfortune of all befell *National Policy*. This paper, which as is well known never published anything except reports of crimes, appeared without any text at all — nothing but advertisements. When it transpired that the circulation fell, the paper decided on a great humanitarian action and announced that if a crime took place and its perpetrator was convicted it would pay his poor innocent family the sum of a hundred thousand crowns. But even that did not help.

Finally a certain Deputy Public Prosecutor hit on an idea which in his view was bound to help in this exigency. He asked the Archbishop's Office for a list of all monseigneurs and began to institute strict searches of all their houses, in alphabetical order, and merciless inspections of all books and holdings of factories and institutes. He then sat back and waited for the result. It was quite staggering; even the monseigneurs had given up stealing!

The defending counsel in all criminal cases had nothing to do. They had no clients. But at least they safeguarded their own futures. They were aware that the newspapers would pounce like vultures on any case, and that that would be excellent advertisement for them. And so the most illustrious and expensive barristers declared that in future they would defend any client *gratis*. Younger barristers who were only just starting to try to make themselves famous even went so far as to promise in the newspapers that they would pay anyone who would engage them for his defence. But these young barristers were not rich and the reward which they offered was consequently quite small, and, as the criminals' organization remained solid, the attempt failed completely.

At Police Headquarters they were in despair. All the police chiefs sat in their offices and twiddled their thumbs and by an ordinance of the Counsellor of the Imperial and Royal Court and the Chief of Police, policemen were ordered to go out and catch butterflies so as not to lose the knack of catching. But the

Counsellor tried other ways of improving conditions. The news-papers published a report that he had held an important conference with the leaders of the German Club the very day before the German students' processions were scheduled to start. The calcula-tion was that one or two members of the National Socialist Party would get themselves jailed, and the cause would be won. But when the processions took place, nobody took any notice of them. And so everything had failed. The police chiefs were desperate. If the truth is to be told, this despair had still another cause. Police Headquarters were prepared to hand over to the courts those policemen who had broken the law, maltreated the public with unnecessary inhumanity, or jostled people without due reason. And the Police Headquarters of that city of which we are writing here knew from experience that it was a dead certainty that even at only slightly disturbed times there would have been at least a hundred such cases. But all expectations were disappointed and the Counsellor began to have an unpleasant suspicion that his own staff belonged to the criminals' organization.

And then he had an idea to save the situation. He started to prosecute policemen for being in league with the criminals. But again he had no proof. The only complaint he had was that earlier on they had committed crimes but now did so no longer. He could not convict them on such slender grounds.

The importance of the counsellors and officials of the Crimi-nal Court began to dwindle rapidly. It was known that they drew their pay and did nothing. When someone went into an inn and said he was a Counsellor of the Criminal Court people began to edge away and the poor man could read on all the guests' faces the thought: "Again one of those parasites who eat up our rates and do nothing in return." The officials of the Public Prosecutor's Office no longer dared show their faces in the street.

In parliament, meanwhile, an urgent bill was introduced requiring the abolition of all relevant posts and offices in view of their inability to furnish proof of any activity.

Now things were really bad; this was the straw which broke the camel's back. The government took matters in hand. All convicts serving long terms of imprisonment received pardons and were released. They had heard nothing about the strike and there was a hope therefore that they would immediately allow themselves to be used to break the strike. But the strikers had their pickets at all the prisons and they explained at once to those who were released what it was all about and warned them against strike-breaking. The government failed totally with its action and the situation became much worse, because all authorities — officials as well as prison employees — became redundant.

For a time there was serious thought of awarding government grants to criminals. The Agrarian Party proposed that subventions should be given for committing a crime, but on mature consideration this bill was rejected.

Meanwhile the day was approaching when the bill for the Abolition of the Criminal Courts, the Public Prosecutor's Office, the police, prisons, and prison administrations was to come up before parliament. But on the day before, early in the morning, there suddenly assembled before the building of the Governor General's Office a crowd of many thousand people, as though they had been belched forth out of the earth. At its head there stood four men. There was the President of the Criminal Court, carrying a long pole at the end of which was fastened an enormous notice with the words: "Give Us Work!" Beside him, like a frowning god, walked the Public Prosecutor who carried an enormous banner: "Abolish Unemployment!" The interesting head of the Chief of Police was overshadowed by the letters of the slogan: "The Only Ennobling Thing is Work!" Finally came the President of the Chamber of Barristers, wiping his sweating brow as he trudged along under the heavy burden of the poster: "Give Us Back Our Criminals!" After these four gentlemen came a crowd of counsellors of the law courts, secretaries, investigating magistrates, assistant judges, probationary lawyers, assistant prosecutors, police officials, defence counsels — in fact, members of all classes who were suffering as a result of the criminals' strike.

The above-mentioned four gentlemen put down their banners and went into the palace of the Governor General. The policemen who had not taken part in the procession, because they found the present state of affairs quite agreeable to them, observed these peculiar demonstrations with unconcealed interest.

Then there appeared on the steps of the palace the four-member delegation. The President of the Supreme Court took hold of his pole and waved it as a sign that he wanted to inform the gathering of the result of the mission. There was a deathly silence. Then the President, with angry gestures and in a voice overcome with emotion, proclaimed, "He refused to receive us!"

"Refused to receive you! The bastard!" could be heard from the crowd, and thousands of clenched fists were raised towards the windows of the Governor General's Office. There was an uproar of shouts and oaths. Some stones flew straight at His Excellency's residence.

The police understood that if they did not intervene now it would be a crime. And because they were no longer committing any crimes, they started to intervene. Prague had never yet seen such a riot! The Public Prosecutor broke his pole and its slogan on the heads of policemen, the Chief of the Police tore the feathers off the hats of his own men just as though they had been members of the National Socialist Party. The scandal ended with the arrest of five hundred people, all of them high state officials or well-known barristers.

The next day the columns of *National Policy* were full and the law courts had their hands full of work again. The great majority of the rioters were discharged, because they had acted at a time when their minds were momentarily disturbed. Only a few less important people were sentenced to fines from five to ten crowns. But on that day the criminals' strike came to an end. They realized that they could quite easily be replaced. And the sentences passed on those who had replaced them convinced them that the equality of all citizens before the law could not be achieved. The strike had failed.

And so it happened that in the country where all this took place the equality of all citizens before the law continued to be valid only on paper.

Hašek's effort to improve the finances of the monarchy

TO HIS EXCELLENCY, HERR VON BILINSKY, MINISTER OF FINANCE, Vienna. Inspired by patriotic feelings, the undersigned respectfully takes the liberty of proposing to the Most Honourable Ministry of Finance a draft bill for the introduction of a tax on burials and deaths. The recent exceptional rise in the number of undertakers' establishments has inspired me with the idea of a means of improving the national finances by instituting a *State monopolization of death*. Since people continually die, the State would be thus assured of a permanent annual revenue, which in times of epidemics or war might register a gratifying increase according to circumstances. The proposed draft bill is as follows:

Para. 1

Every citizen of the Austro-Hungarian Empire, irrespective of sex, becomes *ipso facto* after death the property of the Ministry of Finance and pays on death a tax of 2 to 24 crowns according to the ascertained circumstances of his death and burial.

Para. 2

The tax is collected from the deceased concerned during his lifetime according to the circumstances cited in sub-para. c of para. 6. The deceased's next-of-kin have the right, if the deceased, due to circumstances beyond his control, has not paid during his lifetime the burial and death taxes, to submit to the Imperial and Royal Ministry of Finance a petition for the reduction of the prescribed tax. This written request must be furnished with a two-crown stamp.

Para. 3

Every citizen of the Austro-Hungarian Empire, irrespective of sex and age, is liable to the death tax. This includes those persons to whom the consequences of para. 4 of the law on the burial tax do not apply.

Para. 4

Every citizen of the Austro-Hungarian Empire, irrespective of sex and age, who has been properly buried is liable to a burial tax. If anyone has been buried alive, his next-of-kin have the right to petition for the concessions outlined in para. 2.

Para. 5

Every citizen of the Austro-Hungarian Empire is liable to a burial tax during his lifetime, according to para. 9, sub-paras. a to g. Persons who are minors, or of unsound mind, or having guardians, are exempt from paying the tax, but their next-of-kin must pay it for them, or if they have none, it must be defrayed by their native parish.

Para. 6

The collection of the tax takes place according to the circumstances, regulating the size of the tax:
- a) from healthy persons
- b) sick persons and
- c) persons afflicted with bodily defects.
- ad a) In the case of healthy persons, by the tax offices.
- ad b) In the case of sick persons, by appropriate doctors, bound by oath, wherever and whenever it may be.

ad c) In the case of persons afflicted by bodily defects, by
the police authorities.

Para. 7

The death tax must be distinguished from the burial tax, and in
cases where the tax-payer concerned has not been buried, his
corpse not found, or he has himself been declared unaccounted for,
and if he has not paid the tax while alive, the tax will not be exacted
from his next-of-kin or from his native parish respectively.

Para. 8

The death tax is obligatory even in cases where the missing person
has been officially declared unaccounted for.

Para. 9

In assessing the amount of death and burial tax, regard will be paid
to the following points:
a)   A healthy new-born infant up to 1 year of age will pay 2
crowns,
b)   from 1 to 5 years: 4 crowns,
c)   from 5 to 14 years: 6 crowns,
d)   from 14 to 20 years: 8 crowns,
e)   from 20 to 30 years: 16 crowns,
f)   from 30 to 40 years: 18 crowns,
g)   from 40 years till the end: 24 crowns.
These charges are to be regarded as doubled in the case of a
combined burial and death tax.

Para. 10

The collection of the tax will be carried out in all lands of the
Austro-Hungarian Monarchy in the following way: Charges under
para. 9 sub-paras. a to g must be paid by instalments, but never in
such a way that the total sum exceeds 24 crowns per burial and 24
crowns per death. The first payment will be collected within 8 days
of the child's birth. An unreported birth will be punished, accord-

ing to circumstances, by a fine of from 10 to 200 crowns or, if necessary, 3 weeks' imprisonment.

Para. 11

Whoever fails to report his death or his funeral will be fined double the amount of the highest tax, 96 crowns, or if necessary, will be sentenced to a punishment of 14 days' imprisonment with 4 days severe without food or drink.

I hope that the Most Honourable Minister of Finance will give sympathetic consideration to my most humble proposal and thus improve the finances of the Empire.

I am,

Your humble, obedient servant,

Jaroslav Hašek

A very involved story

THEY WERE TALKING ABOUT VARIOUS HORRIFYING STORIES AND it was the tale told by the innkeeper, Vidnava, which made the deepest impression on the company.

"It was early in the morning, on the day when I opened a new inn for the first time in one of the larger district towns. You can imagine how a chap looks forward to his first customer. At about seven a.m. he arrived—a respectably dressed young man, who ordered a glass of wine and a cigar. He seemed rather tired after his journey and mentioned that he was taking some money to the savings bank.

"I was in the midst of conversation with him when he suddenly fixed his eyes on a distant point, closed them, continued sitting for a while, and then all at once fell off his chair. I've never had such a shock in my life. I tried to revive him, but he'd ceased to breathe and his hands were as cold as ice.

"'My God, he's dead! That's a fine beginning! As soon as it gets about that the first customer in my new inn has died, not a living soul will dream of coming here!' But my wife was more energetic than I was and had more business sense. 'Let's carry him down to the cellar for the time being,' she said calmly, 'and in the evening we'll shove him into our neighbour's garden.' (You see, the restaurant of my main competitor was next door.) And so we put him in the cellar.

"It was not long before another customer appeared in the doorway. He was an elderly gentleman, of pleasant countenance, who ordered tripe soup and a glass of beer. Warming up, he told me that he had an appointment to meet his son here, who was taking some money to the savings bank. He described him in such detail that I soon realized that that son was that same unfortunate first customer who was at that very moment a stone-cold corpse lying in the cellar.

"The elderly gentleman began to show signs of nervousness. "'I'm afraid something may have happened to him,' he said. 'He may have been attacked and robbed. You can't trust a soul today. He had his money sewn into his overcoat.' You can imagine that I turned deadly pale.

"But my wife kept her presence of mind and went off somewhere. She came back looking even paler, and whispered to me that the lining in the dead man's overcoat which I had hidden in the parlour was ripped open and the money gone.

"The elderly gentleman grew more and more nervous and ordered a glass of wine after he had drunk up his beer. When he had finished his wine he suddenly announced that he was not feeling well. He stared at the corner of the room, lowered his eyes, and dropped his head on the table.

"Full of dire foreboding I pulled him by the coat, and the poor old man fell to the floor like a lump of lead. When we found we couldn't revive him, we carried him off to the cellar too.

"And so now we had both father and son down there. We locked the cellar and reflected on the awful calamity which had befallen us. Destiny certainly seemed to have played a terrible trick on us. It was a ghastly advertisement for the opening of our inn.

"Shortly after eight o'clock an elderly lady arrived and asked for her husband and son. She said a policeman had told her that they had come in here. She had been waiting for them in the market for half an hour already and was afraid that something might have happened to them, because both were taking money to the savings bank.

"With a trembling voice I told her that no gentlemen like that had come in yet. She said she would wait for them. . . . "

The innkeeper took a sip of wine, wiped his brow with his hand and slumped to the ground. . . .

He passed away in my arms without finishing his very involved story and telling us how it ended. Instinctively we were going to carry him down to the cellar like the others.

Man and woman in marriage

MR. HENDRYCH, THE GEOMETRY TEACHER IN THE GRAMMAR school, stood behind his desk like Caesar, like God, like the Supreme Being. Looking down at the class with an expression of sublime perfection, he announced the following to the gathering of boys on the school benches beneath him:

"A straight line can intersect a curve, in which case it is called a secant. Or it can touch a curve, and then it is called a tangent. A straight line which joins two points of a curve is called a chord." And with a vigorous gesture he pointed to the diagram he had drawn with a large pair of compasses on the smudgy school blackboard, exclaiming triumphantly, "These straight lines s, s_1 are, as you can see, secants. Straight lines t and t_1 are tangents, and straight lines AB and CD are chords."

He was beautiful in his grandeur, fearful and noble in his majesty, as, slowly lowering his hand from the blackboard to his pocket, he stared down the row of school benches.

Taking two quick steps back towards the blackboard, he was like a Bengal tiger about to spring at an unhappy Indian on a pilgrimage to the sources of the Ganges.

And then he said quietly, "Chaloupecký, can a tangent of a circle also intersect this curve?"

There was no reply. The teacher's voice took on a note of

urgency and he repeated the question more loudly, "Chaloupecký, can the tangent of a spiral do the same?"

There was a silence like the grave. The teacher sprang up. He made a wonderful leap from the blackboard to the first row of benches and shouted at the class, "Chaloupecký, what do you call a chord which goes through the centre of a circle?"

Again there was a deathly silence. All the boys in the front benches turned round and looked back at where Chaloupecký was sitting on the last bench but one. He was not actually sitting, because only his arched posterior could be seen jutting out between the desk and the back of his seat like Mount Říp rising out from the plains or the rump of an ostrich which, stupid thing, had stuck his head into the sand so as not to be seen.

With a majestic sweep of his hands, the teacher called out, "Pull him up!" When Chaloupecký's neighbours had done so, the schoolboy's face was revealed. He stood now face to face with his teacher, whose ears had caught the sound of a falling object, obviously a book, as they raised Chaloupecký up. Only a book can make that sound, the impact of a flat object on a flat surface.

Chaloupecký looked quite calm and resolute.

"What have you been doing under the bench, Chaloupecký?"

"I've been reading."

"What have you been reading?"

Chaloupecký looked round the class and announced with pride, "*Man and Woman in Marriage* by Debay."

"And what kind of book is that, Chaloupecký? A novel or something of that kind?"

And again Chaloupecký replied proudly, as he looked triumphantly over the whole class. "It's the biology and medical history of man and woman in the most specific details. It advances a new theory, sir, on the determination of sex during procreation, on impotency, and sterility. There's an annex too called 'Special Hygiene for Pregnant Women and New-Born Infants'. I've just finished the last page."

He stooped under the bench for the book, came out of the

row and, followed by the envious looks of the whole class, carried it to the teacher. After handing it to him he stepped up to the blackboard like an invincible hero on the steps of the gallows or the guillotine.

Calm was mirrored in his face. He knew that the teacher would now sit down at his desk, turn over the pages of the book, and rebuke him. Then he would enter it all into the class book like an examining magistrate and announce that he would hand him over to higher justice, to the extraordinary summary criminal court, the frightful inquisitorial tribunal, the Headmaster's Committee, which would be presided over by that old dotard, the headmaster himself.

He knew that he was lost and that the chaplain would declare him a reprobate and an outcast. But he had not had time to read the book anywhere in the park by himself. He had been lent it by a friend in the fourth class of the Second Grammar School for this morning only, and he had honestly tried to read it during the lessons of Czech, physics, and geometry. And he had managed it. Now the whole pattern of sexual life was clear as day to him, and that was worth much more to him than a straight line and a curve. *Après nous le déluge*. This evening he would explain everything to Máňa from the Girls' Commercial School. Anyhow, she had once given him fifteen crowns to buy *Sexual Hygiene* for her and he had lost the whole amount at billiards.

It turned out just as he had thought it would. The teacher sat down at his desk, opened the class book and Debay's *Man and Woman in Marriage* and, turning over the pages, started off, "Chaloupecký, you have always been an exceptionally immoral student. You smoked in the lavatory, and the year before last you rammed my boat with your canoe, yes, mine, your class master's. It's a miracle that you didn't capsize it. To this very day I am still convinced that you wanted to drown me. . . ."

"Like a puppy," a mysterious muffled voice could be heard calling out from somewhere in the class.

"Give me the pen," the professor ordered and solemnly announced, "It's a matter of indifference to me who it was who said that. I am not going to hold an investigation, but I shall enter the whole class in the class book. One for all and all for one."

"Hear, hear!" the muffled voice in the class repeated, followed by a burst of laughter from all the boys. When the laughter died down, the teacher went on, "You have behaved very badly, and today is no exception. Perhaps, indeed, it is the final *coup de grâce* for your immoral conduct. You were once the most capable student in the class. You did not know that the paths of diverging straight lines do not meet, but with the greatest relish you have been reading in this book ideas about marriage. In addition you have underlined the sentence, 'The existence and survival of living creatures is based on the reproductive instinct revealed in sexual intercourse.' Well, the Headmaster's Committee will certainly drive the reproductive instinct out of your head, and their decision to ask you to go elsewhere will be much too good for you. While I am explaining what are tangents and secants, you are reading under your bench that, from a physiological point of view, marriage is nothing more than the intercourse of both sexes for the achievement of the same aim, that is to say the lasting preservation of the species."

"Hear, hear!" the unknown voice repeated once more, but immediately afterwards some twenty voices shouted, "Shut your mug or you'll get beaten up." There was a death-like silence. If at that moment the strictest of all inspectors had come in, he would have had to say to the teacher, "I congratulate you. You have the most model class. Never have pupils shown such an interest."

"Chaloupecký," the teacher continued, "in the sixth school exercise you only know the right angle and the straight line, and you left out the acute, obtuse, and convex angles. That does not seem to worry you provided you can read that virginal chastity and abstinence are impossible, and passionate desires, if suppressed without hope of satisfaction, make a man and woman pensive and taciturn. Now, with the aid of a protractor, please draw for me an angle of $75°$. There you are, you see, Chaloupecký, you can't even do that, but reading in a geometry lesson all about erogenous zones, you consider that more important than knowing what a radius is, and immersing yourself in the description of the human body has far more point for you than trying to understand that an oval is a closed curve like an ellipse, made up of arcs of circles. Tell me, what is an ellipse? Can't you answer?"

The teacher paused, eagerly turned over the pages of the book, and exclaimed, "But if anyone were to ask you about an erotic malady I am sure, and I don't doubt it for a moment, that you would be able to explain it to him in great detail."

Looking at the book, he asked Chaloupecký, "Now tell me, for example, what is erotomania?"

One could hear the tick of Matoušek's pocket watch, who was sitting on the front bench.

And Chaloupecký answered promptly at the top of his voice, "Erotomania is erotic madness, which both sexes succumb to without distinction."

"Quite wrong, Chaloupecký," the teacher corrected him, looking at the text of the chapter, "not which both sexes succumb to, but which *attacks* both sexes."

"There's a great difference, boys," he observed to the class. "Erotomania attacks both sexes without distinction, but you cannot succumb to it. Go on, Chaloupecký, or don't you know any more?"

Chaloupecký continued with the same confidence of knowing his facts, "An erotomaniac is carried away by his passion for an object, whether it is real or ideal; he dreams only of love, happiness, sweet pleasures, and, being full of a fire which rages inside him, he constantly gives way to the object of his ardent desires. For all his passion the erotomaniac is chaste, as is explained by the following example."

"That's enough, Chaloupecký."

The teacher absorbed himself in the book, and after a long time turned to Chaloupecký in the tense deadly silence:

"Tell us, Chaloupecký, what are aphrodisiacs?"

"Under the term aphrodisiac," Chaloupecký answered without hesitation, "we understand various nutritive and healing substances, which we use to awaken in ourselves the dying fires of physical love and fan them into flame again, if they have completely gone out. In most cases the recipes for these products are made up from materials which are more or less unpalatable and unsavoury. Numerous facts recorded in ancient and modern history leave us in no doubt about that."

"Not altogether, Chaloupecký," the teacher said excitedly. "For instance, what is it that drove the Roman emperor Caligula mad? What were the ingredients of the love philtre which Kesonia gave him to drink?"

Chaloupecký, who had kept his nerve up to now, began to waver. Throughout his studies he had had a distaste for historical facts and so he had skipped those historical examples.

He gasped and looked appealingly at the front benches in the hope of getting some prompting from them, but none was forthcoming. Thirsting for knowledge, they were all of them waiting for the explanation too, as though it were the grace of God.

"Very well, then, I'll tell you, Chaloupecký. She made him drink a concoction of savory, peppermint, and garden nasturtiums. Note that down, boys. That is what made the emperor Caligula mad. It's quite clear, Chaloupecký, that you have not done your preparation."

The teacher turned over a few more pages, approached Chaloupecký with a notebook, and floored him with the following question:

"What is the average length in centimetres of a new-born baby? Quiet there!"

There was noise again.

Chaloupecký was lost. He had just the same aversion to figures as he had to historical facts. And he had only read quite cursorily about the hygiene of new-born babies.

"So, you don't know," the teacher roared, "and obviously you don't know either what their average weight is?"

The noise in the class grew louder. It was as though everything had livened up again.

Chaloupecký was silent.

"No marks, Chaloupecký. Go and sit down."

Before he had got to his bench, the usher rang the school bell, which brought the lesson to an end and helped to conclude this interesting case.

I am exceptionally obliged to that school usher.

A conversation with little Míla

I HAVE ALREADY BEEN HELD FOUR MONTHS IN CUSTODY WHILE under investigation and have still not confessed what I did with my little nephew — the four-year-old Míla Klogneru.

I am afraid that if I were once to say exactly where I left him, I would not be rid of him, after they had found him. I know that his first words would be "Why are you sitting here?" That unfortunate way of his of saying "Why?"

More than four months ago his parents promised him that his uncle, that is to say me, would take him for a walk. Like it or not, I had to take him, after having promised his unfortunate parents that I would bring that clever little boy back again safe and sound.

And so I said to him at once, as soon as we left the house, "Now hold my hand, so that nothing happens to you." And at once that clever child surprised me with the question, "Why mustn't anything happen to me?" "You know, my dear little Míla, they might run over you." "But why should they specially run over me? Why shouldn't they run over you?" "You're still small." "But why am I small?" "Because you're only four." "And why am I only four?" "Because you're not five." "And if I was five?" "Then you'd be a year older." "What's older?" "Look, that lady over there is older than you." "Why do you say that lady over there, Uncle?" "Because darling, I don't mean this one here who's just coming towards us." "What do you mean by this one here?" "Now, dear little Míla, be a good boy and keep quiet." "Why must I be a good boy and keep quiet?"

I gave him a box on the ears.

The boy burst into tears and so I said to him, "Now don't cry." He wiped his eyes with his sleeve and asked me innocently, "Why mustn't I cry?" "Because you're a man." "And why am I a man?" "Because you're not a little girl." "Why aren't I a little girl?" "Because, dear child, you wear trousers. As to the rest, you'll know about it when you're older." "But you wear trousers too, don't you, Uncle?" "Of course, you can see I do, dear little Míla!" "Then, Uncle, why aren't you a little boy like me too?" "Because I've grown up." "Shall I grow up too?" "You'll grow up too, and now shut your mug." "Why must I shut my mug?" "Because if you don't I'll chuck you in the river." "But that'd be fun, Uncle." Now it was my turn to ask him, "And why would you think it fun, dear little Míla?" "Because I'd be a little steamer." "And how would you be a steamer?" "I'd blow out steam, Uncle, and people would climb on to me and they'd ring. I'd be the steamer *Chuchle* and spit out fire."

Suddenly his attention was caught by a man who was watering the road. "Why is that man watering the street?" "He's washing off the dust." "And why doesn't he spray us?" "Because he mustn't." "Why mustn't he?" "Because he'd spoil our clothes." "How would he spoil our clothes?" "With the water, sonny." "And why with the water?" "Because he's watering the street with water and not with beer." "And why doesn't he water it with beer?" "Because he'd get drunk." "And why would he get drunk? You get drunk too, Uncle. That's what Mama says. Why are you a pig, Uncle?" "You don't understand these things, my dear little Míla. Now keep quite, or I'll spank you." "And why will you spank me?" "Because you're calling me names." "And why shouldn't I call you names? At home they call you names too." "But that's not nice of them." "It isn't very nice of you either, Uncle."

I gave him another box on the ears. He didn't blink and said, "You see, I mustn't cry. You don't cry either, when Auntie hits you. Why does she hit you?" I gave him a spank on the behind. He was quiet and then, for no apparent reason, he called out, "Why don't these houses here have a door at the back. Why do they have it just here?" "Because otherwise no one could get in." "And why should they have to get in?" "Because they live there." "And why do they live there?" "Because they have to." "And why do they have to?" "Because they don't want to sleep in the street." "And why don't they want to sleep in the street?" "Because they are orderly people."

He was silent and then said, "But you don't live here, Uncle." After that there followed a whole series of questions: Why is a tree called a tree? Why does that tree have branches on the top? Could bubbles be made out of the tree? Why does a bubble burst? Why do I look like a bubble when I burst (which he accompanied with the request that I should burst round the next corner)?

When we saw a dog, he asked why it wasn't a cat (another box on the ears). A long pause, during which new questions were taking shape inside his little head. "Why, Uncle, don't they make doughnuts out of a guardian angel?" "Why am I in a sweat?" "Why, when you're hot don't you hang out your tongue, Uncle, like a dog?" "Why aren't you a dog and why are you an elephant?" "Why do you have a trunk, Uncle?"

We walked past the station. I said to him in despair, "Wouldn't you like to go to Hungary?" "Why should I want to go to Hungary, Uncle?" "Because I'll buy you a ticket and we'll go there together. You know, on a puff-puff." He clapped his hands and called out, "I'll puff too." "Puff away, little boy." "I'll let off steam." "Do what you like, little Míla." And I bought two tickets for Puszta Magyarád, in the direction of Füzes-Gyarmat, the last station in the middle of the boundless *puszta*. Let me add that that clever child kept on asking all the time, "When shall we get there? When are you going to abandon me?"

Finally it happened. We walked out of the station of Puszta Magyarád into the middle of the *puszta* — it took us more than a day and a half— and there in the middle of it I told Míla to wait for me. "Why must I wait, Uncle?" "Because you're such a bright little boy." And I disappeared quickly. Behind me I heard his innocent little voice asking, "Why are you running away, Uncle?" And a moment later, "Why are the ants stinging me, Uncle?" ...

And that is my confession.

How I met the author of my obituary

IN THE COURSE OF THE FIVE OR SIX YEARS I SPENT IN RUSSIA I
was several times killed and liquidated by various organizations and
individuals. When I returned home to Czechoslovakia I found I had
been hanged three times, shot twice, and quartered once by wild
Kirghiz insurgents near Lake Kale-Yshel. Finally I was definitely
stabbed to death in a wild brawl with drunken sailors in one of the
Odessa taverns. I think myself that this was the most likely
possibility.

My good friend Kolman shared that sentiment. He found an
eye-witness to my ignominious and heroic death and wrote an
article for his paper about that whole affair which was so unpleasant for me. But he was not content merely with that tiny scrap of
news. His good nature drove him to write an obituary of me, which
I read shortly after my arrival in Prague. With great elegance he
vilified my posthumous memory, being convinced that the dead do
not rise from the grave.

I went to look for him to convince him that I was alive, and
that is how this story came about.

Not even that master of horror and dread, Edgar Allan Poe,
could think up a more grisly subject. . . .

I found the author of my obituary in one of the Prague wine taverns
exactly at midnight, the very hour when it closed according to an
Imperial and Royal decree of April 18, 1856.

He was staring at the ceiling. They were stripping off the stained tablecloths from the tables. I sat down at his table and said affably, "Excuse me, is this place free?"

He continued to observe some given spot on the ceiling, which appeared to interest him very much, and replied, logically, "Of course but they're just about to close. I'm afraid they won't serve you."

I took him by the arm and turned him round so that he faced me. For a while he stared at me in silence and said at last very quietly, "You haven't been in Russia by any chance?"

I smiled. "So you recognized me after all? I was killed in Russia in a low-down tavern in a brawl with rough drunken sailors."

He turned pale. "You are, you are. . . . "

"Yes," I said emphatically. "I was killed in a brawl with sailors in Odessa, and you wrote my obituary."

A faint gasp escaped his lips. "You've read what I wrote about you?"

"Of course I have. It was a very interesting obituary except for one or two small misunderstandings. And an unusually long one too. Not even His Imperial Majesty the Emperor himself, when he died, got as many lines. Your journal devoted 152 lines to him and 186 to me, at 35 hellers a line (that was the miserable rate they paid journalists then!), which made 55 crowns and 15 hellers altogether."

"What exactly do you want of me?" he asked in horror. "Do you want those 55 crowns and 15 hellers?"

"You can keep them," I answered. "The dead do not accept fees for their own obituaries."

He blanched.

"Do you know what?" I said nonchalantly. "We'll pay the bill and go somewhere else. I'd like to spend this night with you."

"Couldn't we put it off till tomorrow?" I stared at him. "The bill!" he called out.

At the corner I hailed a fiacre. I ordered him to get in and in a sepulchral voice told the driver, "Drive us to Olšany Cemetery!"

The author of my obituary made the sign of the cross. For a long time there was an embarrassing silence, broken only by the cracking of the whip and the snorting of the horses.

I leaned over to my companion. "Do you have the feeling that somewhere in the quiet of the streets of Žižkov the dogs have begun to howl?"

He trembled and drew himself up in the cab, stammering "You really were in Russia?"

"Slain in Odessa in a tavern in a brawl with drunken sailors," I answered drily.

"My god," my companion exclaimed, "this is worse than Erben's *The Spectre's Bride*."

Once more there was a painful silence. Somewhere dogs really did begin to howl.

When we got to the Strašnická Highway I ordered my companion to pay the driver. We stood together in the darkness of the Highway. "Isn't there a restaurant here by any chance?" He turned to me helplessly and pitifully.

"A restaurant?" I gave a smile. "Now we are going to climb over the cemetery wall, and on a gravestone somewhere we shall have a nice little chat about that obituary. You go first and then give me your hand.

Without a word he quietly gave me his hand and we jumped down into the cemetery. Beneath us the cypresses crackled. The wind moaned mournfully among the crosses.

"I am not going any further," my friend blurted out. "Where are you dragging me to?"

I held him up and said cheerfully, "Now we'll go and look at the tomb of the old Prague patrician family of Bonepiani. It's a completely abandoned tomb in the first section of row number six by the wall. It's been abandoned from the time they buried the last descendant there. They brought him in 1874 from Odessa, where he'd been killed by sailors in a brawl in a low-down tavern."

My companion crossed himself a second time.

When at last we reached the gravestone covering the dust of the last descendants of those Prague citizens, the Bonepiani, and sat down, I took him gently by the hand and talked with him quietly.

"Dear friend! In the secondary school our teachers taught us a beautiful and noble slogan: *De mortuis nil nisi bonum*. But the moment I was dead you tried to write as nastily as you could about me. If I'd written my own obituary, I'd have written that no death left such a tragic impression as that of Mr. So-and-So. I'd have said that the dead writer's finest virtues were his positive love for good and for everything which is sacred to pure souls. But of my death you wrote that I died a rogue and a buffoon. Don't cry! There are times when the heart burns with desire to write about the most beautiful moments of the lives of the dead — but you wrote that the deceased was an alcoholic."

He began to cry all the harder. His wails resounded mournfully in the silence of the cemetery and were lost somewhere far away in the distance near the Jewish Furnaces.*

"Dear friend," I said firmly, "don't cry. Now it's too late to put it right. . . ."

* A quarter in Prague.

On saying this I jumped over the cemetery wall, ran down to the gate-keeper, rang the bell, and reported to him that as I was returning from my overtime night-work, I had heard the sound of sobbing behind the cemetery wall in the first section.

"That's probably some drunken widower," the gate-keeper answered cynically. "We'll have him put behind bars."

I waited round the corner. In about ten minutes guards led the author of my obituary out of the cemetery in the direction of the guard-house.

He was resisting and shouting, "Is this a dream or reality? Gentlemen, do you know Erben's *The Spectre's Bride*?"

FROM AN OLD PHARMACY
A Series of Sketches

INTRODUCTION

When Hašek was thirteen, his father died. Until then he had done well at school, but he soon started neglecting his work and involving himself in street fights. Finally he failed his examinations and, following a series of complaints from the school and the police, he was expelled. In desperation his widowed mother tried to find him a job; thanks to her efforts, he spent the next three years working at two chemists' shops. These tales "From an Old Pharmacy" are based on his personal experiences as a chemist's apprentice.

It was not long before he was sacked from the first shop. There are two versions of how it happened. One was that Kokoška, the proprietor, fancied himself an artist and had covered the walls of his office with paintings of alpine landscapes. One day, when Kokoška was asleep, Hašek crept in and with a few strokes turned the face of one of the cows into a caricature of Kokoška complete with pince-nez and square beard. According to the other version, while up on the loft one day Hašek heard the sound of singing and the stamping of feet outside. Sticking his head out of the window he saw a procession of bakers on strike. Anxious to show his sympathy for them he tore down the red petticoat of Kokoška's maid, which was drying on the loft, and hung it out on the roof. The strikers broke into thunderous applause, shouting out the Czech patriotic greeting of "Nazdar" and singing "The Red Flag". The police came rushing up and cross-examined the proprietor. This was too much for the old man and he insisted that Hašek's guardian should remove the boy forthwith.

A job was then found for him with another chemist named Průša. He was a more easy-going man who had progressive ideas and could appreciate Hašek's gifts. After a year, he persuaded Hašek's mother that the boy had too much talent to be left to spend all his life at a shop counter. And so young Hašek was sent to the Czechoslavonic Commercial Academy for further education.

The first day at the pharmacy

ON THE VERY FIRST DAY OF MY NEW CAREER AS A CHEMIST'S apprentice, Mr. Kološka, my chief, called me into his counting-house, which was the name he gave to a corner of his shop shut off by a wooden partition.

Mr. Kološka — an elderly gentleman with a long beard, who was of such short stature that I, a fifteen-year-old boy, was taller than him by a short head — sat down on the chair before his writing desk, fixed his shrewd little eyes on me, and began, "Young man, from today on you are my new apprentice, and as such, you must listen seriously to one or two things I am going to tell you and see that you are guided by them throughout your life. You are probably familiar with the proverb 'Good advice is more precious than gold'. . . . Very well then, be all ears now and pay attention to what I am about to say.

"Your new profession, young man, is a very difficult one. Up to now you have been at school, and there you only had to worry about learning things by heart. None of it was of the slightest use for your future life, except Latin which, as a fourth-form boy, you probably have a smattering of and which you will need as a chemist. In the trade nobody will ever ask you when this or that king reigned or what a thing is called, what geometry is and so forth. Nobody wants to know how far away from us some star in the sky is or how 'pterodactyl' is spelled. When a customer comes into the shop he will not be interested in whether you speak correct Czech or not, and you certainly cannot ask him about his Czech either. It will be quite sufficient if you understand what he says and serve him to his satisfaction. In the shop all that is required of you is that you should be able to add up correctly and not lose out in the process. That's the right way to do things in business. You are a young man and you must learn from what you see, not from books as you did at school.

"When a customer comes into the shop, you must do exactly what he wants. If he wants sky-blue you must climb up to the sky and bring it down to him. Furthermore, you can think what you like about him, but you must not say it to him. A tradesman, remember, makes his living from the public. When anyone comes into the shop you must immediately call out, 'I wish you good day, your Honour', 'I kiss your hand, Madam', or 'Good morning, Miss'. And when the customer leaves, you must be just as polite, even if he has bought nothing. And when you are selling — and you will be doing that after a time — remember for the future to say, 'Please, sir, what can I offer you?' or something like that, and you must

bestir yourself, rush about, serve him promptly, and never lose money. If an item isn't in stock, don't allow the customer to go away, but offer him something else. Once he is in the shop you must make him buy something, whatever it may be. For example, if he comes in and wants a toothbrush, urge him at once to buy toothpowder. Or if he wants toothpowder, urge him to buy a toothbrush and tell him that it is a special bargain.

"And you must tell whatever lies come into your head; you will learn all that in the course of time. But it goes without saying that although you may deceive a customer by telling lies, you must never lie to me. To me you must always behave as though I were your father, and if at any time I should swear at you, I would not advise you to answer back, because I have a very quick temper. When I give an order, you must execute it at once. With me everything must be done as it is in the army.

"You must be scrupulously honest — I hope there is no need to tell you that. You must not scrounge food or break anything. What you do have to do is work. It's only for your own good. I am telling you all this, young man, as if I were your father.

"Every morning you must come to me in my flat to fetch the key-box. After that you must go and wait in front of the shop. When the clerk comes, you will both of you open the shop. You will then go and hang out the angel sign, come back again and dust the shop thoroughly so that it is clean everywhere. And when I arrive at eight o'clock I shall give you your instructions.

"At ten o'clock every morning you will come and see me in my counting-house. I shall give you money and you will buy me half a litre of beer, two rolls, and a portion of anchovies. At one o'clock you may go to lunch, but you must be back again by two. At four o'clock you will come and see me again in my counting-house. I shall give you money and you will go and buy me coffee from the café — be sure you ask for a lot of cream. At eight o'clock you will go with the messenger, take down the angel sign, and shut the shop. You will then put the keys into the key-box and the clerk will lock it. He will take the key and you will bring the key-box to my flat.

"Every other Sunday between ten and eleven o'clock I shall allow you to go to church somewhere. And there's another thing that I want to impress upon you. You must side with me and not with the staff. That is the most important thing. Today you will only clean the bottles. And while you are doing that, take a good look at the labels in Latin and Czech, so that you will know what is in them. That way you will gradually get to understand everything. So now, young man, remember all this very carefully. You may go."

When I left the counting-house I was deeply affected. All Mr. Kološka's instructions went round my head in a whirl. When I came back to the counter, the clerk, Mr. Tauben, said to me, "He bored you to death, I suppose, our Radix?"

"Whom do you mean?" I asked diffidently.

"Why, the old man, of course," the clerk answered. "We call him 'Radix'. We chemists like to use nicknames like that, you know. Our Radix is a bit weak in the upper storey, as the saying goes, but he's a good chap otherwise. You probably think that what he's just told you came out of his own head. Good Lord, no, my lad! He's had to learn that whole sermon by heart exactly as his wife taught it to him. We call her 'Acidum'. You mustn't look on our old man as though he were God Almighty. He's really nothing more than a cipher and it's his wife who is everything. As soon as she comes into the shop, you'll see at once who's the real boss. So, my boy, see that you stick with us.

"I expect the old man told you that you have to clean the bottles today. Well, clean them — but not at the double! D'you understand? Just take it easy. There mustn't be any 'at the double' about your work here. If there were, old Radix would soon twist you round his little finger. If today you clean fifteen bottles by the evening, you'll have done your stint. After all, you'll be cleaning bottles for the whole of the week, so take your time over it. Whatever you do don't go and bust yourself, otherwise he'll only shove more and more work on to you. And when his old woman comes here to see him, run straight up to her and kiss her hand. And if Radix sends you to a firm to fetch something or if you go anywhere to deliver anything, for heaven's sake don't run! Just amble along comfortably in your own time, as if you were going for a stroll. That's what I always used to do. And be sure you don't come back too soon. If you do, Radix'll only send you on more errands every day and get so used to your returning quickly that in the end he'll think you just can't help doing things at the double."

Mr. Tauben paused and then went on, "You know what, my lad? I see you're a good chap. Here's money for two litres of beer. Go to the storeroom at the back and in that barrel at the end — you can see it from here — you'll find a jug. Take it, go through the back exit from the storeroom and across the yard into the bar. Then buy two litres of beer. Bring the jug of beer back and put it in the barrel. You can drink as much as you like. You know, I was an apprentice myself once."

Mr. Tauben gave me the money and I did as he asked. When I had returned with the beer and hidden the jug in the barrel, I came back and cleaned the bottles — *very* leisurely, in fact as leisurely as anyone could imagine.

Half an hour later Mr. Kološka called me into his counting-house.

"By the way," he said, "there's one thing I forgot to tell you. If by any chance that Mr. Tauben sends you out to fetch beer for him, let me know at once. They say that he's rather too keen on sending the apprentices out for beer. . . ."

These were the events of the first day, but let me add that altogether I went five times to fetch that forbidden beer for Mr. Tauben, and when the servant asked, "Well, what about the young apprentice?" I heard Mr. Tauben answer, "He's already of our persuasion and calls the old man 'Radix'. . . ."

Mr. Tauben's instructions

FOR THE NEXT TWO DAYS I FOLLOWED MR. TAUBEN'S ADVICE AND cleaned the bottles very slowly.

"When Radix comes," Mr. Tauben said to me, "and asks you why you aren't ready with them, tell him you're carefully studying the instructions on the labels. But leave your work now and I'll show you round the whole establishment."

He took me over the building. Mr. Kološka's shop was in an old house which no longer exists today. In that blackened building you could always smell the characteristic aroma of dried drugs, which in the first days stupefied me and permeated my clothes so thoroughly that everyone could tell a mile off that I was apprenticed to a chemist.

The ancient building had a special charm of its own. It conjured up in my mind memories of alchemists' workshops and medieval pharmacies I had read about. These impressions were confirmed by the sight of two giant mortars which were in the storeroom, and some big retorts on stands which were black with dust and as dirty as the retorts themselves.

From the storeroom Mr. Tauben led me to the carriage entrance, where under the cross-vaulting there stood some troughs, buckets, rolling pins, and various objects belonging to the particular business carried on here by a lady who sat at a little table near the entrance to the street.

"That's Mrs. Kroupová, the cooper's wife," whispered the clerk. "Her husband is a real bad hat and everything she earns during the day he squanders in drink in the bar across the way. He sits there the whole day, and when he has no money left he comes to his wife and asks, 'Have you sold anything dear?' If, for example, she says, 'One washtub', he replies, 'But that'll only buy eight glasses of beer.' He reckons everything up by glasses. And, when you're a little older, my lad, you'll understand what it means when I tell you that she puts up with anything he does because she's living in sin with him!

"We don't need to go so quickly," Mr. Tauben continued. "If anyone should come into the shop, Radix will serve him. You already know the bar over there. When we get to around the twentieth of the month, I shan't give you money for the beer. You'll have to get it for me on tick. But the proprietor there is a cunning devil, my boy. Take care he doesn't book you for three litres instead of two as he's done sometimes. But his wife is nice. When later on you're despatching alcohol for brandy and she comes into the shop to buy it, give her the best we have — not mixed with water like we give the public. She uses it for making

cherry brandy and I sometimes nip over to get some, so let's keep it good and strong. The last apprentice once poured out that adulterated stuff for her, and don't ask what the cherry brandy tasted like after that! And later when you'll be selling across the counter, if the proprietor comes to buy some drops for his stomach, give it to him free, because he sometimes waits up to three months for me to pay him.

"There, where those two dirty windows are, is where the concierge, Mrs. Pazderková, lives. She always comes to us first thing in the morning for a glass of kümmel. We have to give it to her *gratis*, so Radix says, because she could upset the whole house. For the three days since you've been here she hasn't shown her face. She's ill. She's always like that when the teacher keeps her son in — ginger-haired Francek. He's eleven years old and a real hooligan. He doesn't give anyone any peace, gets up to all sorts of mischief, but you're not allowed to punish him, oh dear no! Once I caught him making a hole in the big metal drum where the oil is kept, and I slapped him. Well, after that old Mrs. Pazderková came into the shop and insisted that Radix give me notice at once. And you should have heard the row in the street in front of the shop! Lots of people collected outside; she was holding ginger-haired Francek by the hand, he was howling and blubbing, and she was shrieking out that there was a man in the shop who'd beaten unconscious this innocent and defenceless child. So we had to invite her to have a glass of kümmel and give Francek some sweets. That ginger-haired Francek has caused me a lot of trouble. In the summer you'll see a regular pantomime in the yard. Francek'll get undressed and climb into the washtub in the middle of the yard just as God made him. And he'll splash about in the water from morning till evening. There's an old maid living upstairs on the first floor and once, when she saw Francek bathing in his birthday suit, she fell into a faint. The concierge, Mrs. Pazderková, is allowed to buy all goods from us at half price.

"Next door, by those windows, lives the butcher, Mr. Kavánek, and whenever he makes galantine of pork, he always invites me to have some too and gives some to the messenger as well. The messenger and I both call this a *quid pro quo*. He doesn't cheat us and we don't cheat him either. You know, my boy, that's in the spirit of the German proverb: '*Leben und leben lassen*' — 'Live and let live.' It's true that we sell him spices at the normal price, but remember that when he comes in and wants a kilo of any spice, you must weigh out a kilo and a half, and bill him for only a kilo. Then he'll offer you some of his galantine of pork. But don't eat it in front of the boss. The last apprentice used to take it home with him. You'll learn all about that in the course of time. Now, come on, let's go down into the cellar."

When Mr. Tauben opened the door of the cellar and lit the lantern, my nostrils were assailed by the odour of acids and mustiness rising out of the darkness. At the same time a squealing sound could be heard.

"That's the rats," Mr. Tauben told me. "The last apprentice was bitten by one; you always get them, my boy, everywhere in old buildings. Ever since our Radix put down special poison for them they've multiplied quite considerably. In the summer months especially you'll see any moment a grey brute moving about somewhere in the cellar. And no cats have been able to survive here since a man who thinks he has consumption moved in next to the butcher. He catches all cats, skins them, and lays the skins on his chest. Be careful you don't slip on the steps. It's still damp from the time the messenger and I broke a drum of distilled water here. Since then when anybody has come and asked for distilled water, we have got it out of the well. So all our drops have a milky colour now, because I make them up with well water instead of distilled water. And our Radix has broken off business relations with three firms already because he thinks they sent him adulterated oil and ether for the drops. You see, my lad, that's what one has to do. A chap must never lose his head, and the main thing is to make sure we diddle the boss, because we have to reckon that, when we in turn one day become bosses, someone may diddle us too. I'll take you down to the cellar, my lad, just so that you can learn where we keep the olive oil."

Mr. Tauben opened the wooden partition and said, pointing

to a metal drum, "Look, here's the olive oil, although it's labelled 'Linseed Oil'. When Radix sends you down to the cellar to fill a bottle with olive oil, fill it with this, because about half a year ago we broke the drum of olive oil. Sometimes people send the oil back to us, and the old man has written lots of letters to the firm from which he ordered it, asking them why they sent such a bad kind. Radix never comes down here himself to look. He's frightfully afraid of rats, so, sometime when you come back from the cellar, don't forget to complain that there are so many rats there that it's too awful. Now let's go up again."

When we were in daylight once more, Mr. Tauben went on:

"I've got just one more thing to tell you young man. Did you notice the sweet shop in the street behind this house? The apprentices from that shop come to us in the summer to get crude salt for making ice cream. Always give it to them *gratis*, then you can eat as much ice cream as you like. But don't eat it in front of the boss. We won't go up on to the loft today — we can do that tomorrow. I'm sure Radix will be mad enough as it is, because he's alone in the shop at this time when there's so much custom."

"Where have you been lazing about, Mr. Tauben?" Mr. Kološka asked angrily when we came back into the shop. "You just go off and leave me all on my own to sweat like a horse."

"Oh, do please excuse me, sir," Mr. Tauben answered. "I was showing the new apprentice round the establishment and teaching him his job."

"Ah, well, that's another matter," Mr. Kološka said mildly. "But see that you teach him everything and that you make something of him."

"Very good, sir," said Mr. Tauben. "I am quite confident that I'll make something of him."

Mr. Ferdinand, the messenger

AT THAT TIME MR. FERDINAND WAS ABOUT FORTY YEARS OLD. HE
had a high forehead, indicating an outstandingly developed intel-
lect, which was confirmed for me by Mr. Tauben when he said,
"He's a very cunning devil indeed."

He had kindly grey eyes, brown hair, and a slightly darker
moustache. But what struck one immediately about him was his
red nose, which was an infallible sign that he had once been a
messenger in a wine and spirits shop.

His suit was always filthy and greasy. You could see on it the
traces of all kinds of oil, spots burned out by acids, and various
stripes of floor paint and streaks of varnish were spread all over his
coat. His waistcoat sparkled with bronze dust which had firmly
settled on stains left by a solution of rubber and petrol. The left
sleeve of his coat reeked of essence of turpentine, the right sleeve of
powdered cinnamon. In short Mr. Ferdinand's clothes were a
mixture of every possible kind of drug and chemical, with the
result (as I found out afterwards) that when he went across to the
bar he sat in his customary place by the stove, where he was by
himself, and opened the stove door so that the smell from his
working clothes would not drive the other guests away.

But one thing was very peculiar: Mr. Ferdinand always wore
shiny shoes. And, as soon as he was finished with any piece of work,
he went to the storeroom and polished them so beautifully that
they shone like mirrors. Mr. Kološka used to say that Mr. Fer-

dinand only did this to kill time. Be that as it may, after every piece of work, however minor, he went off to clean his shoes.

And that was also the reason why, not long after starting my apprenticeship, I had a heart-to-heart conversation with Mr. Ferdinand. He had just returned from the yard, where he had been grinding cinnamon in a mortar. He then went to the storeroom, and was taking a box of shoe polish and a shoe brush out of a cupboard, when I came in.

"Come here, my lad," said Mr. Ferdinand.

When I had come close to him, he said, "Do you have a lot of saliva, young man?"

"Yes, I do."

"Good," he said approvingly. "Somehow my throat has got dry with pounding that cinnamon."

"Yes," I said, not knowing what he wanted.

"When you grind down polish with ordinary water, my lad," the messenger continued, "you can't get the shoes to shine brightly enough."

"You're right," I said.

"It shines best with saliva," said Mr. Ferdinand and added, "Fire ahead, then."

When I said nothing, he began again. "Would it put you to a lot of trouble, my boy, if you were to spit into the polish for me?

"You have to think of things like that right away yourself," he said, when I did what he wanted. "We must all of us help each other.

"Our sort must support each other," he continued, polishing his shoes. "That's how it is in the world, young man, and as long as the world goes on, it will always be like that. And the great lords" — he completed the sentence with an unexpected twist — "will do their best to stop the poor from supporting each other.

"You know, my boy, we are still very, very stupid," he said, pursuing his argument further. "We prey on each other. I see that best in Michle. Do you know where Michle is?"

"Yes, I do."

"Well, I live in Michle, and next door to me lives another messenger and he's angry because I earn four guilders a week more than he does and can spend four guilders more on drink than he can. And so he makes a noise all the time in the corridor at home to drive into my head once and for all that I'm going to pay for this until the day of my death. And not long ago he shouted out that I had, or so he said, cheated our boss at the customs point with the invoice, and that he knew how it was done. I got angry and said that everybody had a different method. I said, 'Plaček, not everybody steals so damned stupidly as you do, you filthy scum. When you worked in that factory, the porter only had to undo your waistcoat to see at once what you were carrying home, you thief.'"

Mr. Ferdinand exhibited considerable anger, as could be seen by the rapid way he polished his shoes. The brush moved about on the shoes with unbelievable speed and he wrinkled his high forehead and went on, "'Well, what have you got to say to that, Plaček?' I said, and Plaček stood in the corridor and began to shout, 'You chemist creature, they can smell you two miles off with those filthy concoctions of yours.' 'Now take it easy, Plaček,' I answered, 'I didn't say anything bad about you. All you can do is swear, you thief.' Plaček went out into the passage again and shouted out, 'You sold my boy's shoes and now the poor little fellow goes about barefoot. And you sold a kilo of pepper to a greengrocer — where did you get it from, tell me that? And you smashed your wife's face in from the jaw up, you brigand. And then at the inn you stole a salt cellar — all this in the course of this week.' And I answered, 'The cure for a foul mouth is a punch on the jaw.'"

Mr. Ferdinand paused. "And now that miserable bastard wants to take me to court because I slapped his face once or twice. Oh, my saliva's gone again! Spit, my boy, spit once again into the polish. Shoes won't shine with ordinary water. That's the way! Thank you. We must each of us help the other. . . ."

Returning to the shop I was stopped and addressed by Mr. Tauben.

"Doesn't Mr. Ferdinand smell rather too strongly of beer today?"

"I don't know. It's impossible to tell," I answered.

"You're quite right, those clothes of his . . . ," said the clerk. "But for safety's sake you'd better tell him to eat a lemon, because he's to come and see the boss. He's got to take his little trolley and fetch some varnish."

Mrs. Kološková

THE FIRST IMPRESSION I HAD OF MY CHIEF'S WIFE WAS THAT IT was no wonder Mr. Tauben called her "Acidum", the Latin for acid.

Only two days after my conversation with Mr. Ferdinand, she appeared in the shop at about nine o'clock in the morning.

The old clock on the wall had just rattled out nine when the door opened; the head of the automatic advertising doll with the inscription "Welcome!", drawn by a cord fastened on the door, gave a bow and the bell above the door tinkled. Then a tall, stout lady with a powdered face and features which were quite pretty despite her corpulence came into the shop with a purposeful stride reminding me of an abbot coming along to make sure that the monks in the cellar were not drinking up all the wine. She wore a gaudy hat and the rustle of her silk dress could be heard from a distance.

Mr. Tauben, who only a moment before had been joking, suddenly changed his expression to a very solemn one and hastily whispered to me, "That's the chief's wife," and he at once rushed to greet her, saying loudly, "I kiss your hand, Madam."

I ran forward and kissed her hand too.

Not deeming us worthy of an answer, Mrs. Kološková advanced towards the counter and demanded, "Where is the master?"

"In the counting-house, Madam," the clerk answered. And with unusual speed he ran along the narrow passage between the counter and the shelves, opened the glass door of the wooden partition, and called out, "If you please, sir, Madam is in the shop!"

The little husband ran out from behind the counter and brought a chair to his tall wife, welcoming her deferentially, "How are you, Mary, my dear? At last you've come to see us in the shop again."

"But of course you were asleep in your counting-house as usual," Mrs. Košková said furiously. "You take your nap and it never occurs to you that Mr. Tauben is lounging on the counter and yawning. . . ."

"But, Madam, pardon me," Mr. Tauben said in self-defence.

"Do you think I didn't see you?" Mrs. Košková snapped. "You were lolling on that counter, idling and yawning away. Of course people generally do yawn after a night on the tiles."

"Madam, I was at home last night," the clerk pleaded.

"And what about those bags under your eyes?" stormed the wife to our chief. "Why, isn't it plain as a pikestaff from your

appearance that you spent the whole night in debauch? And you go on tolerating this?" she added, turning swiftly on her husband. "What are you the chief for, if you do nothing to forbid such dissipation of youthful energies in the taverns."

"It won't happen again," Mr. Kološka answered miserably.

"But pardon me, Madam, I never went anywhere yesterday. I really didn't," Mr. Tauben protested. "I don't have any money left."

"So that's it!" said Mrs. Kološková in exasperation. "When you have money, you go and squander it, and I'm not surprised that after that you look like a corpse." (To tell the truth Mr. Tauben had been nice and red and rosy only five minutes before her arrival.)

"You fritter away your money," continued Mrs. Kološková, "and then after a night like that you're in a state where you cannot even serve the customers properly.

"But of course that doesn't matter a pin to you, Kološka," she said, turning on her husband who at that moment seemed even smaller than usual, "as long as you can have your nap next door in your counting-house. If it wasn't for me you'd have been bankrupt twenty years ago."

"My dear, if someone were to come in...," Mr. Kološka pleaded nervously.

"If someone were to come in" — Mrs. Kološková sneered — "I'd speak out just the same. What was it that saved you then? It was that fifteen thousand from my dowry and it's that that's still keeping your head above water. And if on top of everything else I didn't go on keeping an eye on the business, it would go to rack and ruin. And out of all this I get absolutely nothing for myself. The Bázas have a villa somewhere near Dobřichovice although they have a smaller income than we have. For how many years have I been telling you that you should have a villa built — but what's the use? Mr. Kološka prefers his own self-indulgence. At ten o'clock he orders Pilsner beer and a portion of anchovies. In the afternoon it's coffee with cream. But he doesn't care a rap about improving his wife's position although he knows very well that if it hadn't been for her he would have been bankrupt twenty years ago. That would have knocked all thoughts of Pilsner beer and anchovies out of your head, wouldn't it?" She went on scolding, refusing to abandon what was obviously her favourite theme. "Then you wouldn't have been getting any coffee with cream. How can you help being thirsty when you buy anchovies? And then you come to me and ask if you can send the servant for beer again in the evening, and when she's gone out you want to embrace me! Let me tell you that I could let myself be embraced by other people than you, Kološka. And if it hadn't been for my father and the money you owed him I would never have married you. Poor Papa thought that at least in this way he'd get his debt paid. Your father-in-law is still very good to you but he only does it for my sake, because he doesn't want me, your wretched victim, to suffer even more through squabbles and arguments in the family.

"I want to see the cash ledger for the last week," she commanded, when she had recovered her breath. "Bring it here at once!"

Mr. Kološka disappeared behind the wooden partition and shortly afterwards returned with the required object.

He put the book deferentially on the counter. Mrs. Kološková got up from her chair and Mr. Kološka pushed it towards the counter, after which his wife sat down again and began carefully to scrutinize the individual items of daily expenditure for the previous week.

It was pitiful to see Mr. Kološka at that moment. How different from his recent attitude when he had said to me, "My boy, from today on you are my new apprentice!" Then he had acted proudly and with dignity, and now he was pale and trembling. Supporting himself on the counter, an unusually humble and contrite expression on his face, he went through the items one by one with his wife. Great suffering was mirrored in his eyes.

I had the impression that he was making a vague attempt to cover with his elbow some item farther down in the book.

There was silence. One could hear the ticking of Mr. Tauben's watch and at one moment I thought I could hear the beating of Mr. Kološka's heart.

Mrs. Kološková pushed her husband's elbow away from the book and went on examining item after item. . . .

"What on earth is this?" she burst out, as her stern gaze fastened on the spot where a moment before her crushed husband had been resting his elbow.

"What's this? It says here: 'various disbursements 23 guilders 50 kreuzers'. What on earth are those 'various disbursements'?"

If the sight of Mr. Kološka had a moment ago been rather pitiful, it now became even more so. He opened his mouth, as though he were going to say something, but the words were stuck in his throat and his teeth began to chatter like those of a man who has just stepped out of a hot bath and has been suddenly exposed to an icy blast.

Mrs. Kološkova's penetrating eyes fastened inexorably on his chattering teeth, which emitted a tremulous "ta-ta-ta-ta-ta".

"What does this mean?" she thundered again. "Why these 23 guilders 50 kreuzers?"

There was no answer. Only Mr. Kološka's teeth emitted with incredible speed their tremulous "ta-ta-ta-ta".

"Are you going to explain this to me or are you not?" Mrs. Kološkova demanded.

"Sa-sa-sa-sardines and Pil-Pil-Pil-Pilsner b-b-b-b-beer," said Mr. Kološka, shaking all over, "and r-r-r-r-rolls and co-co-co-co-coffee".

"You're not going to get away with that," Mrs. Kološkova screamed. "You must be keeping some woman, some hussy. You're giving her money and robbing us at home. You're robbing us all."

Mr. Kološka recovered his breath and said, "It's not true, my darling, it really isn't. I — I must confess that I broke your antique vase in the drawing-room. Then I had to buy a new one and so that you shouldn't know I put the new one in place of the old. . . ."

At these words the cash ledger flew across Mr. Kološka's head in the direction of the counting-house, narrowly missing its human target. The chair by the counter was pushed aside and Mrs. Kološkova, red in the face in spite of her make-up, headed for the door uttering slowly and emphatically the following warning:

"Don't you dare come home to lunch, and this evening I'll make it hot for you — that's something you can look forward to, I promise you that!"

"You wait!" were her last words pronounced when she was already near the door, which she burst open. The bell tinkled, the advertisement doll over the door with the inscription "Welcome!" automatically bowed its head, and the train of Mrs. Kološková's skirt whipped up the dust in the street as though to demonstrate the violence of her rage.

At once Mr. Kološka began to breathe again — rather like a man restored to the fresh air after having been shut up in a foul atmosphere. Solemnly, with bowed head, he withdrew behind the wooden partition, addressing me again in managerial language: "Young man, you probably know that proverb 'Don't wash your dirty linen in public', and if you don't know it then you'd better learn it and fix it in your memory."

He disappeared into the counting-house from which his voice could be heard a moment later, "Mr. Tauben, come here!"

When Mr. Tauben came back from seeing his chief, he told me with a laugh, "He's really had a fright. He asked me whether I know of a hotel where he could stay overnight!" Then a serious expression came over Mr. Tauben's face and he added, "Watch out, young man! Ah, yes, it's only too true. 'Acidum' is *acidum* and *acidum* means acid."

The shop's customers

THE FIRST PERSON TO TURN UP EVERY DAY IN OUR PHARMACY was Mr. Brouček, the public carrier. Even before the shop was open he would be waiting in the street outside, and he was always the first one in, greeting everyone with a "God grant you a good morning — and two kreuzers' worth of schnapps please."

For old acquaintance sake we poured it out for him, whereupon he smacked his lips, and as he handed back the empty glass, he always said, "The brute certainly knows how to warm you up! You really ought to have a bar here." When he saw me for the first time he added, "Stick to it, my lad, so that you can be a credit to us."

A stout policeman who had his beat along our street sometimes waited with him for the opening of the shop. This gentleman, who aroused respect more by his corpulence than by his sabre and revolver, saluted as soon as he stepped into the shop and said, "Everything in order."

Mr. Tauben poured out a glass of schnapps for him too — *gratis* of course — and after the stout policeman had tossed it down he saluted and said again, "Everything in order." And then he left.

The carrier, Brouček, would stay on for a little while making critical remarks about the weather on the previous day like, "Yesterday it rained" or "I really can't recall any day as fine as yesterday, but it was cold". Then he would add, "Very well then, have a good time! I owe you two new kreuzers again", and leave.

After him the next visitor was always the old Jewess, Mrs. Wernerová, who owned the bar in the street next door. She brought with her a huge glass bottle, and every day we filled it up with the six litres of pure alcohol which she bought.

"*Um Gottes Willen*, Mr. Tauben," she would say, "just imagine it! There was another brawl at our place yesterday, and when I think that I was in the bar quite alone I'm really scared stiff that one day they'll beat me up as they did my late husband."

She never forgot to repeat that story at least once a week, especially if there was someone else in the shop, a story common in wine and spirits shops where the manufacturer of spirits gets beaten up by drunkards when it was he himself who made them drunk, perhaps on their last few kreuzers.

"And my late husband," she would add sorrowfully, "had such a good heart, *ein goldenes Herz*. He never diluted the schnapps and, poor dear, they set on him just because they found a fly in it. *Ja, ja, eine Fliege!* How could he help that?"

And every day, as she paid her bill, she complained and argued that she had read in yesterday's paper that the price of pure alcohol had fallen by two kreuzers a litre.

She was followed by the concierge, Mrs. Pazderková, who came to drink her usual ration of kümmel and at the same time to

explain to Mr. Tauben the meaning of his latest dream, her interpretation invariably concluding with: "Yes, that means they'll soon be taking you off to the churchyard." That rogue, Mr. Tauben, always used to tell her that he had been dreaming about white horses.

After Mrs. Pazderková had asked in a confidential tone about the health of Mr. Kološka, Mr. Tauben, and Mr. Ferdinand, she usually began to grumble about the behaviour of the tenants in the house. Then she would complain bitterly about the teacher who had kept Francek again in the previous day.

After she had gone, ginger-haired Francek came on his way to school to get a stick of liquorice, or a pipette to use as a pea-shooter in class, and he always assured us that his mama would pay for it. After that came young ladies and their maids on their way to the market, buying all sorts of necessities in our line, such as medicinal herbs against coughs or hoarseness, for or against vomiting, dietetic remedies from the mildest to the most violent, various ointments, toilet sponges, floor polish, stomach drops, face powder and other cosmetic requirements, and so on, and so on. . . .

The ladies used to haggle, especially the younger ones. Mrs. Voglová, the wife of the furrier, came for remedies to stop the spread of clothes moths. She was an elderly lady who always said, "Now hurry, hurry!" as though the moths would be increasing prodigiously in the course of those five minutes. And there was also young Mrs. Kroupková, the locksmith's wife, forever complaining that her husband suffered from indigestion. "Do the cooking for him yourself, dear madam," urged Mr. Tauben. "But that's just what I have been doing," the young lady replied naively.

Other people came who showed an insatiable desire to quarrel with Mr. Tauben. Among them Mr. Křečan took pride of place. He appeared every week, on Saturday morning when custom was at its busiest, and worked inexorably with his elbows until he had succeeded in forcing his way up to the counter. Then he shouted, "Last time you again gave me a load of rubbish. Do you call this lime tea? Why, it's nothing but dust from the road. You seem to forget that I've been a customer of yours for years and years. My good sir, this is not the way to do business. What have you got to say about it? Nothing? Then give me lime tea for forty kreuzers, but if it's the same old dust again I'll take it to the municipal authorities and show it to them."

Then he took out his snuff box, opened it and, leaning across the counter, said, "Try a pinch, Mr. Tauben. And may it do you good!" We called him crazy Mr. Křečan.

A farmer called Vlášek, who lived somewhere near Český Brod, always came to see us whenever he was in Prague. He used to place his hat on the table and solemnly take out of his pocket a piece of paper on which was written what he had to buy for everyone in the village — the teacher, the vicar, etc. . . . He would hand it to Mr. Tauben and begin to talk about farm work, "Now we're starting to mow the fields beyond the water," he would say, "Now we're going to harrow", or "The wheat is already starting to shoot". "Well, that's all," he would say when the goods marked on the list lay before him on the table, "and for myself, give me a packet of cattle herbs."

Another frequent customer was a tall gentleman with black glasses, of whom we only knew that he was the director of a minor orphanage. He always leaned across the counter and whispered to Mr. Tauben, "Could I have half a kilo of mercury ointment please?"

That mercury ointment! The very mention of it conjured up in my mind the memory of page 213 of Pokorný's *The Natural History of the Animal Kingdom*, and I saw myself as a small boy at school learning by heart: "C. Wingless insects. The Children's Louse (*Pediculus Capitis*) is greyish-yellow and wingless. It has short antennae, and a retractile proboscis with which it sucks blood. It is found only on the head, and most commonly in children." At the same time I remembered the words of our natural history teacher. "And so then they rub the heads of little children with mercury ointment. Don't laugh there at the back!"

Poor orphanage director! If only he had known that instead of mercury we put powdered graphite into the ointment. It was twenty times cheaper.

"It makes no difference," Mr. Tauben always said laughingly

after his departure. "At least the orphans will now have blacker heads and can play at being blackamoors."

Various people came into the shop and went out again — old people, young people, ladies, gentlemen, girls, and children; jolly people like the innkeeper from the Small Quarter who used to buy sneeze-weed from us, which he mixed with tobacco, afterwards offering a pinch of it to his guests with earth-shaking results; people who were miserable, like Mr. Wagner, a pensioner, who was always buying drops and medicinal herbs for his stomach until he completely ruined it, or like blind Josef, an old beggar, who struck the pavement with his stick and asked each day for a new kind of herb — such as dried cornflowers, peonies, and other plants — which he burned at home leaning over the smoke with his sightless eyes, in the hope that he might one day come across a herb which would help not only him but other blind people as well.

Then young ladies came for scent and powder, blushingly asking for various cosmetic preparations which did not do much good to their complexions but were considered "good tone". Violinists came for resin, boys from middle schools and secondary modern schools, enthusiastic about their chemistry experiments, came and bought chemicals which they bore carefully away with them. Twice a week the concierge from next door came in to buy rat poison. Servants arrived and laughingly asked for the lye they put into the washing without their mistresses' knowledge. A school porter came from a nearby secondary school and asked for various vessels and materials for school chemistry experiments. He was very fussy and always asked for them to be well wrapped up. "So that I shan't get blown to pieces one day," he said, putting cautiously into his pockets the things he had ordered.

And then it was the turn of the postman, who came and fetched the letters and price-lists which were to be sent out, and who was always treated to a glass of English gin. Representatives of various firms turned up in the shop and said, "Nothing today? We can offer very low prices." And every Friday the local beggars came one after the other to get the customary kreuzer. Sometimes too a travelling apprentice or a travelling pharmacy clerk appeared and asked for help or perhaps a job.

And it was all these people who came in to the shop and went out again, known to us, or quite new faces, who made up the shop's clientèle.

On the loft

YOU APPROACHED THE LOFT BY A WELL-TRODDEN WOODEN staircase and every step of it emitted a sound reminiscent of the twittering of birds waking early in the morning. It was at one and the same time a very gentle creaking and a whistling. Helping to produce this sound was one of the favourite amusements of the concierge's sandy-haired son, Francek, who whiled away his idle hours indulging in this particular game.

When I first went up onto the loft I did so on Mr. Kološka's orders to look for our messenger. These heights had remained a mystery to me until now. Two hours earlier Mr. Ferdinand had made his way up there to sieve bran, the main ingredient for our medicinal cattle herbs. When I climbed the staircase sandy-haired Francek was amusing himself half-way up it, hopping up and down from step to step and so forcing the stairs to emit that series of singular twitters and squeaks.

This otherwise quite inexplicable amusement of his was soon made clear to me by his own confession. "I've been jumping here for half an hour already and that old fool on the first floor by the stairway must be going crazy by now. He'll come out again any minute."

And so he did indeed. I had been following sandy-haired Francek's favourite sport for only a short while when the door of a flat off the staircase above burst open and an old gentleman in a dressing gown appeared on the stairs with a cane in his hand shouting, "You damned young rascal. I'm going to give you a hiding you won't forget. Keep quiet, or I'll...!"

He came down two steps, brandishing his cane, and sandy-haired Francek hopped three times again so that three times the steps emitted their soft but jarring squeaks, then he shot away down the stairs.

"Catch that rascal for me!" the old gentleman shouted to me. "Or better yet, leave it to me. I'll thrash the life out of him. You know it's terrible — like scraping a plate with a fork." He went back to his flat and I continued up to the unknown regions.

I made my way along the gallery of the two-storey house. On the balustrade washing was hanging out to dry and through an open window I could hear a woman exclaim, "That's the new apprentice." I looked down into the yard. Francek was returning from his mother's flat with his hands in his pockets. The concierge was standing in the doorway, screaming, "If that clerk dares touch a hair of your head, I'll teach him what's what." Francek disappeared in the direction of the staircase and after a while the familiar squeaking and twittering of the old wooden steps could be heard once more.

I went on to the end of the gallery and up the steps to the loft. In the passage where the steps led up to this highest part of the house, my eye caught an inscription drawn with black coal on the dirty plaster: "The apprentice Josef Kadlec came here for the last time on 29th February before his departure for Kladno, where he was going to complete his training. He had a good time here." Underneath this, in a less practised hand, was inserted the comment: "The apprentice Josef Kadlec was a dirty sneak and a stupid ass. Ferdinand." Underneath Mr. Ferdinand's gloss there was quite a clever sketch of a jug and some playing cards accompanied by the written confession: "That's the best thing in the world." I saw that it was in Mr. Tauben's handwriting. On the other side of the passage there was a sketch of a big barrel and below it half of a hideous scarecrow and the caption: "Radix bottling Malaga." And a little farther on, at the very door of the loft, a sentence shone out in blue chalk: "Mr. Ferdinand is running after the concierge." These humorous inscriptions ended with the notice carefully executed on the door in black spirit varnish: "Pharmacy Loft."

The door was half open. When I opened it fully an overwhelming smell of dried herbs met my nostrils, and my ears were assailed by the kind of snoring which fully justifies the popular Czech comparison with the noise of a saw-mill.

The semi-darkness of the loft had a mysterious effect on my imagination. As I went in through a door on the right, which was open, its enormous padlock hanging loose on the bolt, it seemed to me terrifyingly like the entrance to a prison.

Inside, a feeble light seeped through the skylights of the roof and faintly illuminated long rows of barrels with dusty lids, containing herbs of every possible kind. The barrels gave out a stupefying aroma. They were ranged in two rows and in between them was a kind of path strewn with empty bottles and straw from bottle wrappings which had not yet been swept away. In the midst of this mess were scattered handfuls of various drugs, and here and there broken pieces of glass and china.

Among the barrels one could just make out some long kegs containing powdered dyes — yellow and brown ochre, and red clay — which had left traces of their colour on their surroundings. Some barrels had been turned upside down and their spilled contents had produced on the paved floor of the loft a hotch-potch of dyes, chemicals, and dried plants. Here in this first section there were packing cases with lids which did not shut properly; crystals of alum, saltpetre, and other salts sparkled from inside them.

In one corner a narrow strip of light fell on large chunks of crude rock salt, its crystals glittering with all the colours of the rainbow. Here the ground was littered with sieves and large porcelain dishes for grinding dyes. Among the many packing-cases could be seen gleaming metal drums full of oil and stone jars of acids, which were sealed with clay stoppers, and like the jar of smoking nitric acid, were enveloped in a small cloud of fumes which circled around and made one cough.

This area of the loft gave off an acid odour. It reeked of ammonia from a huge, round glass hectolitre bottle, and nearby an open barrel of white chloride of lime caused further irritation to the respiratory organs. My eyes slowly got used to the semi-darkness and I found I was standing by a ladder. My object was, as I have already said, to find Mr. Ferdinand, but this was no easy task. It is true that the moment I entered the loft I heard those snores, and this sound, an infallible sign of the presence of our messenger, ought to have been my lode-star. But it was quite a difficult problem. I thought I could hear "Kchoo-poo-kchoo-poowoo-kchoo-poo" first from one corner and then from another.

"Mr. Ferdinand," I called in all directions, "you have got to bring downstairs the bran you've sieved!"

But I got no answer, only a muffled snore, "Kchoo-poo, kchoo-poo", which reverberated through the loft and confused me in my attempts to find the sleeping messenger.

"Mr. Ferdinand," I called out again, "you've already been here two hours. You've got to get up and bring downstairs the bran you've sieved!" Again not a word in answer.

Now I could hear a nasal sound, "Pfoo-pfoo-foo".

I climbed the ladder to the upper part of the loft, determined to have a look there too. Between the roof trusses and across the rafters of the loft, some boards had been laid and on them stood sacks of dried herbs which rattled each time I took a step. The light here was slightly better and I was able to look all around me.

My first momentary impression was that Mr. Ferdinand was sleeping on the left behind a barricade of various loaded sacks. But when I had climbed over the barricade I saw that behind it there was an empty space. So I began to look on the right and there indeed I found Mr. Ferdinand fast asleep on a bed of roses — literally bedded on a heap of dried ones. He lay comfortably stretched out with his coat spread over his face. It muffled his snores and made them less distinct.

"Mr. Ferdinand," I said, waking him and tugging at his leg, "you must get up and bring downstairs the bran you've sieved!"

At my third attempt Mr. Ferdinand woke up, pulled the coat from his head, drew himself up into a half-sitting position, yawned, and said, "Oh, it's you, is it, boy? I've just had a five-minute nap."

"You've got to bring down the bran you've sieved," I said. "You've been here two hours already."

"What, the bran?" was Mr. Ferdinand's shocked reaction. "My God, I'd clean forgotten about that. I just came up here to take a nap for five minutes and fell asleep. Well, a chap gets tired walking, you know. Well, there it is. Now I'll start doing the sieving."

He put on his coat, jumped up, and observed, "You can sleep beautifully here. If I had pulled the ladder up you would never have found me, young man."

As we were going down the ladder together, he turned round at the last step and said in a very low voice, "But you can sleep very much better in the summer, when the old women bring the fresh plants here, because then it's just as if you were in the country in fresh hay and you can stretch yourself out in it and have a really glorious snooze. Now go and tell our old man that I had a fit of nose bleeding and couldn't stop it."

When I left the loft, I found Francek still amusing himself by extracting sounds from the old steps.

"When shall I say you're coming?" I called, going up again into the semi-darkness of the loft.

"When it's done," answered Mr. Ferdinand.

His voice sounded from high above. I looked up to where he was speaking from and saw him going up the ladder towards his old place, where he had been lying on a bed of roses.

Literally on a bed of dried roses. . . .

The trolley

GRADUALLY I GOT TO KNOW THE WHOLE ESTABLISHMENT. I already knew the cellar, the loft, the vaulted storeroom behind the shop, and the shed in the yard, where Mr. Ferdinand ground the herbs and where, along with the huge mortar and heavy pestle, he kept his trolley — a pushcart which changed colour from time to time because he repainted it so often.

This little vehicle, which he used for fetching or delivering goods of various kinds, was his pride. No other shop messenger could boast such a beautifully kept trolley. Its wheels, its frame — in brief, its whole surface — were finely painted in variegated colours — blue, red, and green.

Although anyone who saw that trolley could not help praising it this was not good enough for Mr. Ferdinand. He continually overhauled it and painted it over with fresh colours, always choosing the afternoon hours of Saturday to do it, so that the trolley could dry properly overnight and all day Sunday.

And if he took it out anywhere on Monday people everywhere he went saw how it shone with a new coat of paint in a bold mixture of colours, never before used for painting a trolley like that. They saw it sometimes coloured like the rainbow, the cross-pieces picked out in blood red with stripes in shades of green and blue, or at other times they saw how the cross-pieces had been picked out in bronze and the trolley itself painted black with yellow and white stripes. Other Mondays would bring a new change: the trolley would be painted in zig-zag stripes of brown and white, the wheels yellow with black stripes. These daring combinations, these inventions of new and ever new colour schemes, could only have emanated from the brain behind Mr. Ferdinand's high forehead. He loved his trolley with paternal devotion — with the love of a foster-father who does his best to see that his adopted child always goes about beautifully dressed.

To insult it meant incurring Mr. Ferdinand's eternal wrath. When the cross-eyed Venca, a butcher's apprentice from the house, dared to say in the bar that it looked like a Red Indian covered with warpaint, Mr. Ferdinand used his favourite proverb, "The cure for a foul mouth is a punch on the jaw", and promptly practised what he preached. "I'll teach you for your Red Indian war-paint, you squinting fool!" he shouted, so loudly that he could even be heard outside in the courtyard.

From that time on the two became the bitterest enemies, openly displaying their hostility in looks and words. There was a chance that cross-eyed Venca would have made peace — particularly on that occasion when Mr. Ferdinand treated some of his friends to a tankard of beer in the bar. Then Venca came up to him and said, "I hope you're not still angry, Mr. Ferdinand." But that time Mr. Ferdinand only said very curtly, "I still am, you squinting fool." And when the tankards were carried round he said, "Not a drop for the squinting fool!" which showed how implacable he was to anyone who spoke contemptuously of his beautiful trolley.

And how carefully he checked every evening to see whether the shed in which it was kept was properly shut. And how often, as if not fully convinced, would he return and examine the lock once more. "Goodnight, dear little trolley," he always said. And in the morning his first visit was to the shed to make sure that nobody had stolen his trolley during the night.

"Good morning, dear little trolley," he would say, "Here I am back again. The daily grind starts once more!"

The trolley was his constant companion on his journeys. It was a joy to see him pulling it and solemnly smoking his porcelain pipe. When he stopped anywhere in a tavern along the way, it was a pleasure to see how he watched over it in the street with the anxiety of a father, how he continually kept his gaze fixed on it through the window, and how he immediately leaped up if anyone suspicious came near his charge.

This gaily-painted trolley brought him not only fame but profit. He used it to bring various goods from the railway or from the warehouses of big firms, and manoeuvred it so skilfully past the customs checkpoint that the dues on the wine, spirits, and other goods he transported, which should have gone to the city, went to him. He had adopted various tactics on these rounds to deceive the watchful eyes of the customs officials: the most common one was to pass the checkpoint very quickly, with the trolley carefully positioned between two big waggons. Of course you had to have a special gift for this sort of thing, a talent which consisted in waiting for just the right opportunity, exploiting the times when traffic was heavy, and choosing for your route streets where the waggons went in single file. Fast-moving carriages were no good to him. He had to wait for heavy freight waggons and nip in with his trolley at

the very moment that they passed the checkpoint after being given clearance. He had to move adroitly into the centre of the traffic, and, screened from the eyes of the customs officials, he would proceed at a carefully chosen pace — at first slowly and then faster and faster — eluding all prying eyes until his walk turned into a run and he was pushing his trolley along at the double. Passers-by saw nothing but the barrels and other goods bobbing up and down as the brightly coloured trolley flashed past them in an instant.

He would then turn off into side streets and there, far from the busy traffic, he would slow down until he was once more pushing his load leisurely and with dignity, calmly smoking his porcelain pipe and stopping from time to time to wipe the sweat off his brow or to consider by how much money he had cheated the city customs authorities to his own profit. Then he put the money earned through his admirable talent into his purse, anxious to try and spend it at the next opportunity in a tavern somewhere along the way. And at the tavern, sitting near the door, he would look gratefully at his trolley standing by the pavement — that good little trolley which never let him down.

Never let him down! What if at the most critical moment when he was crossing the checkpoint, screened by the waggons he had selected, the wheels of his trolley were to stick? What, if the axle, so beautifully polished, were suddenly to get bent. But no, his trolley would never fail him.

One day something very peculiar happened. Mr. Ferdinand returned towards evening with his trolley and the goods, but you should have seen the state of the trolley. It was spattered all over with dirt, the wheels were choked with mud, and its bright colours were completely covered in filth. Mr. Ferdinand himself was pale and mud-stained. It was as though he had intentionally picked out the biggest puddles he could find for his trolley. It was the first time we had ever seen it in such condition.

And wonders would never cease! Mr. Ferdinand put away the goods and shut the trolley up in the shed without cleaning it. Indeed he gave it a very rough shove.

And when he had shut up the shop he did not make his usual

trip back to the shed to check that the lock was securely fastened. He did not say, "Goodnight, dear little trolley," but instead he showed Mr. Tauben a yellow ticket and said to him, "Well, they caught me for the first time. Just at the very moment when I was passing the checkpoint that brute of a trolley wouldn't budge. Its wheels got stuck somehow. So I took it into a puddle and spoiled its colours for it."

And Mr. Ferdinand never again repainted his little trolley with new and fancy colours.

Mr. Kološka's father-in-law

THERE WAS TALK ABOUT HIM ONE DAY AT NOON. MR. KOLOŠKA
had gone off to lunch, there were no customers coming into the
shop, and Mr. Tauben was sitting on the counter with his back to
the door at one corner and Mr. Ferdinand at the other. That was
the time when they always started gossiping.

"Radix has to put up with a lot from his father-in-law," Mr.
Tauben remarked suddenly, lighting a cigarette.

"Even with a mother-in-law he wouldn't have had to put up
with so much," Mr. Ferdinand said gravely. "It's true that people
say 'From women's tongues Good Lord deliver us!', but when his
father-in-law starts talking all hell's let loose."

"And the older his father-in-law gets, the worse it is," said
Mr. Tauben. "Recently Radix told one of his friends here that his
father-in-law suspects him of having taken out a licence for the sale
of poisons for the express purpose of poisoning him. When he
requires any medicine the father-in-law has it made up in a
dispensary and not by us. When Radix comes home, his father-
in-law even goes through his pockets to see that there isn't any
poison there. Mr. Ferdinand, it's a damned curse to have a
father-in-law like that."

"It's very sad indeed, Mr. Tauben," said Mr. Ferdinand.
"Indeed far too sad when in the evening the father-in-law throws
his shoe at his son-in-law's head as happened recently according to

what their maid told me. But he missed him. He's an old man, and you know, his hand shakes. Fancy his having the nerve to do that, Mr. Tauben! Only a very wicked man could have the nerve to do it. And then you must take into account that Radix can't say a word, because he has Acidum at home. A wicked wife and a wicked father-in-law. Both of them very peppery! I tell you, Mr. Tauben, it's a very great trial."

"And all the time, Mr. Ferdinand," said Mr. Tauben, "he throws it in his son-in-law's face that he put money into his business. Do you know, Mr. Ferdinand, how it came about that Radix married Acidum?"

"No, I don't really know," said the servant. "Mrs. Kroupová, the cooper's wife, says she once heard that they shut Radix up in the drawing-room and forced him to ask for her hand."

"That's not quite correct, Mr. Ferdinand," said the clerk. "It actually happened like this. Radix already owned this business before he was married, and Mr. Vaňous, who later became his father-in-law, had a wholesale drug business then. Radix got all his goods from him. But in those days he didn't buy for his elevenses just a portion of anchovies, a roll, and a glass of beer. He liked to give himself a proper treat. He guzzled tasty things in the shop and in the evening after closing-time he went and guzzled again. Like a young bachelor he flitted from one place of amusement to another, and spent money on others so that his business fell more and more into debt. In the end Radix frittered away all the money he made from goods bought on tick from his future father-in-law's whole-sale business. He then went on ordering more and more goods without paying him a sou. Mr. Vaňous reminded him about this and one day Radix went to see him to beg him not to press him for payment. He went straight to his home and there he saw for the first time his future wife, Acidum.

"Old Mr. Kraus, Mr. Ferdinand — you know, that fellow who was here before you — said that when Radix was young he was a good-looking man and knew how to run after the girls and talk persuasively. And so it happened that at that time Mr. Vaňous took a fancy to him and apologized for having reminded him about the payment. He even invited him to come and see him again. Well then, Radix went to see Mr. Vaňous quite a lot, and whenever he did so he took more and more goods from his storeroom and always on tick, instead of paying for them. And when the debt had grown to enormous proportions, Radix stopped going to visit him, which of course, as was to be expected, infuriated Mr. Vaňous who wrote him a letter threatening to sue him and get the court to declare him bankrupt. Old Mr. Kraus told me that Radix then said, 'Tomorrow I'll go there and settle things with him. There's no help for it, Kraus. If Mr. Vaňous makes me bankrupt, they'll sell my business and after that I'll have to start afresh.'

"Old Mr. Kraus also told me how Radix described his visit to Mr. Vaňous. 'I felt pretty small,' he told him, 'when I walked up the steps to Vaňous's. My legs trembled and an electric current went through me. I went there without any money, without any hope that Mr. Vaňous would have pity on me and agree not to take me to court. When I arrived, Mr. Vaňous said, 'Very well, let's go in here.' He led me into a room, locked the door, and started off, 'You haven't a sou in the world, young man. You're a rogue and a spendthrift. You take goods from me on tick. You make promises without ever keeping them.' 'Please have mercy,' I said. 'I'll try and improve.' Mr. Vaňous flew at me and said, 'Fiddle-de-dee! I'll never get my money back that way.' He walked furiously up and down the room and suddenly turned round and demanded,

"'Mr. Kološka, are you in debt anywhere else?'

"'Yes, in Ústí nad Labem.'

"'How much?'

"'About five hundred guilders.'

"You should have seen how Mr. Vaňous stormed around the room shouting, 'Well, that means I shan't get my money back at all. That means I shan't get my money back at all.' Then suddenly he calmed down a little and asked, 'I thought you were an honest man. Did you come and see me for my daughter's sake or did you only want to entice me into giving you further goods on tick?'

"I was astonished. I'd never given a thought to his daughter. But taken by surprise I told a lie in the hopes of winning him over and blurted out, 'Because of your daughter, Mr. Vaňous.' Then I was quite astounded. Mr. Vaňous unlocked the door and called his daughter. When she came in, he said to her, 'Mary, Mr. Kološka has just asked for your hand. I have nothing against it, if you agree.' And before I could pull myself together that woman sprang at me and hugged me so tight that I thought she would choke the life out of me."

"Old Mr. Kraus always used to say, Mr. Ferdinand, that when Radix told him this the following day, he opened his mouth and kept it open for a whole quarter of an hour. That's how it was, Mr. Ferdinand. On that day Radix acquired a wife and a father-in-law, and his father-in-law imagined he would recover his money that way."

"It's frightful," Mr. Ferdinand gasped. "On that day Radix ruined his whole life. It's absolutely terrible to have a father-in-law like that."

"Mothers-in-law are already outdated," Mr. Tauben reflected, "but every mother-in-law is an innocent babe compared with old Vaňous. Once I came to see Radix in his home at about

noon. His father-in-law sat with his glasses on next to Radix and watched him to make sure he didn't help himself to a second portion. They were having fillet of beef in sour cream sauce, which Radix liked very much, so he made a timid attempt to take a second helping. His father-in-law noticed and got angry. 'Put it back, will you? Didn't we give you a large portion and haven't you still got some dumplings left? And now he's helping himself to another portion! When it comes to good things you're as voracious as a fox terrier is with rats. It would be a good punishment for you to let you eat nothing for a whole week.'"

"On Sunday he has to spend the whole afternoon reading the newspapers aloud to his father-in-law," said Mr. Ferdinand. "In the meantime his wife goes for a walk or pays calls."

"Altogether his father-in-law treats him very badly," said Mr. Tauben. "When he gets angry with him, he locks up his pipe in a cupboard and Radix is not allowed to smoke for perhaps a whole week. And on top of it, his father-in-law has already broken several of his pipes."

"And his maid told me," the servant went on, "that Radix once came home in the evening and absent-mindedly greeted them with 'Good morning!' 'What did you say? Repeat that!' said his father-in-law. Radix became scared and in his fright stammered out, 'Good morning, papa.' So his father-in-law took his pipe, which was on a stand, and dashed it several times across his head.' I'll teach you to make a fool of old people. The hooligan!' the father-in-law said angrily. In the evening he says to me 'Good morning'!"

"It's a certainty that he beats him," said the clerk. "It's a trial, and a very terrible trial."

"And when Radix had those little trees planted in the garden at home," said the messenger, "his father-in-law cut them down. I think that Radix can hardly wait. . . ."

"For what, Mr. Ferdinand?" Mr. Tauben asked.

"Well, until one afternoon we shut the shop and hang out a notice which Radix painted two years ago, when his father-in-law fell seriously ill," answered Mr. Ferdinand.

"Ah," said Mr. Tauben, "you mean 'Because of my father-in-law's funeral the shop will be shut today'."

"Exactly," said the messenger. . . .

This conversation was suddenly terminated by a gentleman coming into the shop, requiring something for toothache. . . .

STORIES FROM THE WATER BAILIFF'S WATCH-TOWER AT RAŽICE

INTRODUCTION

A fascinating feature of Southern Bohemia is its chain of some 270 fish-ponds or lakes, in which the carp, so much prized in Catholic lands, are bred and fished. The system of interlocking lakes, held by dams and linked by narrow canals and conduits, is of great antiquity, dating back to the sixteenth century, when the Rosenbergs, the mighty "Lords of the Rose" who were the largest landlords in Bohemia, laid out this enormous complex of water. Every three years these lakes are still drained and the carp brought in by a wide sweep of drag-nets. The fisheries had to be protected from poachers, and the level of the waters and the state of the dams controlled. From the first this was done by water bailiffs or so-called "fishmasters", of whom Hašek's grandfather was one.

HAŠEK'S INTRODUCTION

Jareš, the water bailiff, was my grandfather. By now his bones and his wife's have long been mouldering in their graves. Once I went to see his former work-place, the water bailiff's watch-tower at Ražice. It lay in a picturesque valley, through which the river Blanice flows on its way from Vodňany and Protivín. All around in a semi-circle stretch the forests of Písek, and the old watch-tower is surrounded by the villages of Putím, Heřman, and Ražice which are about a half-hour away.

There are two lakes nearby — Ražice and Prkov. On the other side of the watch-tower are wide stretches of fertile land, and beyond that runs a white road which skirts the black woods of Háj. It is one of those many very picturesque corners of Southern Bohemia.

But today the former water bailiff's watch-tower, in which life was often so merry, houses one of the fishery keepers from the estate. The building is falling to pieces, and through a window, which is pasted over with grease paper, the old keeper watches the dam, which shows serious cracks. And beyond it he can see the lake, the upper part of which has now been changed into fields, where a ploughman, striding behind his plough, turns up here and there roots of water plants, which once rippled the surface of the water and gave cover to wild ducks. . . .

From the dam I gazed at the watch-tower and remembered how my late grandfather used to tell me of the many evenings when they sat in it and told stories of poachers, of Behalt, director of the estate, of the hollow oak on the dam, of Matěj, the stable boy, and of the final demise of the watch-tower itself.

The stories they told one evening

IN THE ROOM WERE SEATED ROUND THE TABLE THE WATER
bailiff from Ražice, the fishery keepers from Řežabinec and Štětice,
and a young assistant from Kestřany. They were waiting for it to
get quite dark.

Outside, the autumn evening was gradually descending.
Wisps of mist circled over the lakes and revolved between the
tree-tops in the woods beyond the white road. Through the
window one could see how in the mist above the meadows
will-o'-the-wisps rose out of the pools, bobbed up and down a little
while, and then vanished among the thickets.

"Those will-o'-the-wisps roam over the countryside like the
late-lamented Hanžl," said the keeper from Řežabinec.

"Why the late-lamented Hanžl?" asked the young assistant
from Kestřany, who was sitting at the table at the very window-
ledge and peering into the autumn mists.

"Yes, the late-lamented Hanžl," the keeper repeated. "He
was a farmer from these parts, from Ražice in fact. He had a fine
farm, but he mortgaged all of it. He loved to drink and play cards.
At that time, when he was still alive, there were three dangerous
poachers in this region who did a hell of a lot of damage to our
fisheries. Their names were Kalous, Špačík, and Šrámek. They
knew every path there was and could find their way even at night
and in the worst mist. No one ever managed to catch them.

"Well to go on — one day Hanžl went to Protivín to sell a cow at the fair.

"'If you don't bring back a hundred guilders,' his wife said before Hanžl left, 'don't you dare show your face at home!'

"And so Hanžl went on his way and managed to sell the cow. He got a little more than a hundred guilders for it. It was then that same autumn weather, like today, and very cold.

"'Why shouldn't I go and have a glass of something to warm me up?' Hanžl thought to himself. And so he went into an inn, and being the sort of chap he was, started drinking and playing cards. In the end he lost twenty guilders. 'What am I to do now?' he wondered. 'I've got to bring home a hundred guilders or else my wife will throw me out.' And you know, his wife was a masterful woman.

"And so Hanžl decided to stay the night at the inn, and spent the whole of the following day and evening playing cards until he had made up the hundred guilders again. But next evening he lost all his money once more, the whole hundred, and when he had none left to pay his bill with they threw him out.

"He was tipsy, and on his way home he fell into the lake somewhere. This sobered him up a bit and as soon as he got home he said to his wife, 'Don't stare at me like that! I fell into the lake. My goodness, in that mist it's easy for a chap to lose his way. Now I must go and change, and then I'll tell you everything. Old girl, it went absolutely splendidly.'

"Meanwhile Mrs. Hanžlová began to recover from her initial shock and said sternly, 'Have you brought back all the money?'

"'No, I haven't brought any,' Hanžl replied calmly. 'But it's all in good hands.'

"'You dirty villain!' said Mrs. Hanžlová. In short, she didn't half swear at him and said she would throw him out, but God she would.

"'Wife, don't take the name of the Lord in vain,' Hanžl said solemnly. 'I've deposited the hundred guilders at the law courts at Písek as a security. It's a long story. In Protivín I learned something very interesting. You know of course that Kalous, Špačík, and Šrámek poach fish hereabouts?'

"'Lord love us,' wailed Mrs. Hanžlová, 'you haven't surely been making friends with them?'

"'Oh, it's difficult to make you understand,' said Hanžl seriously, 'but, to cut a long story short, the noble Prince Schwarzenberg's estate has offered a reward of three hundred guilders to anyone who catches those three. Well, I thought to myself, 'Good heavens! I've got plenty of courage, so why shouldn't I try?' But the snag is that anyone who applied had got to deposit a hundred guilders at the Písek law courts as a security, to ensure that no one makes a fool of the estate. All right, then, I deposited the money and went home. And as I was coming from Písek, it was so dark that I couldn't see a single step in front of me. Then suddenly I heard a voice. And, can you imagine it? It was Šrámek, Kalous, and Špačík. I recognized them by their voices and followed them as far as Sukov lake. There in the mist I fell into the water and, before I could manage to climb out, the rascals were gone.'

"'Dear heaven,' sobbed Mrs. Hanžlová, 'think that there were three of them and you only one! If they do anything to you, what'll become of me?'

"'Yes,' said Hanžl, 'it's true that I'm only one, but I'm pretty tough you know. Or do you want me to give the whole thing up? Then I'll lose the deposit and we shan't get anything.'

"'No, for heaven's sake, don't do that!' said Mrs. Hanžlová in a frightened voice. 'I'm only saying that one day that boldness of yours will be the death of you.'

"You can easily imagine that he probably hardly slept a wink the whole night, being so afraid that his wife might jump to the truth. She didn't, however, because she said to him next morning, 'I dreamed that Šrámek threw you into the lake.'

"'I'll get the better of them,' said Hanžl. 'This evening I'll be on the watch, to see whether they go after the fish again.'

"And that evening he went out. You can understand how he felt. He couldn't come home until night, in case the truth became obvious to his wife. In the autumn it's not pleasant to wander about the countryside at night in the mist. We all know that very well.

"Well, it went on like that for three days. Hanžl wandered

about the countryside at night, caught a cold, and his wife began to grumble that he had still not caught anyone and that in the end he would lose the deposit. And so he went out into the mist for a fourth day, swearing and telling himself that he had been an awful ass to tell lies like that to his wife, all because he had been afraid of confessing the truth.

"But one day it all came out at last. Hanžl went out once more in the evening into the mist and during that time his wife went to see some neighbours. They happened to have their son Vincek with them and, as luck would have it, he kept the inn at Protivín, where old Hanžl had lost that wretched hundred guilders. One thing led to another and they started talking, just as we're talking now, until the conversation turned on the fair. And Mrs. Hanžlová pumped Vincek so long until she wormed out of him that Hanžl had lost that hundred guilders playing cards.

"That night all hell broke loose at the Hanžls. When Hanžl returned home numb with cold from his wanderings, he knocked on the window and waited.

"Not a sound. Silence over the whole building. He knocked again. Once more no sound, silence. And when he knocked a third time, he heard the voice of his wife from the room, 'You low-down scoundrel, they ought to offer those three hundred guilders for catching *you*, throwing away those hundred guilders playing cards. Go and sleep at those law courts in Písek or in the lake, but I'm not going to have you here, you dirty crook!'

"There was nothing for Hanžl to do but go away and continue his wanderings in the countryside in the cold and misty night. In the end he came to see us at the water bailiff's watch-tower at Kestřany, where I was then apprenticed. He told us about his sufferings and slept the night with us. From that time on, we called him Hanžl, the will-o'-the-wisp, because he roamed about at night like the will-o'-the-wisps from the marshes."

"Yes, I remember that too," said the fisheries keeper from Štětice. "At that time there was only a water bailiff at Kestřany and not a head fisheries overseer as there is now."

"Alas, those times are gone," said the water bailiff. "It was quite different then."

But that's exactly what they used to say in those days," said the keeper from Řežabinec. "When they remembered the old times, they always said, 'And think of what it's like today!'

"Yes, certainly, it was jolly in the watch-tower at Kestřany," he went on, "especially when they drained the lakes of the fish. Then all the gentry came. All the free beer was drunk up at once; there was a lot of baking, cooking, and singing. The servants had a good time too. When I was an apprentice there — I remember I was about seventeen — I hadn't been there longer than a few months, when I took part for the first time in the catch and had the job of counting the fish they caught.

"I counted up to twenty. Then I suddenly realized that when you count fish, instead of 'twenty' the fisherman say '*mecítma*'. But I counted 'one and *twenty*'. Suddenly I got a terrific clout on the ear from the water bailiff, who shouted in my ear, '*Mecítma, mecítma, one and mecítma!*'"

"'Why do you hit me, master?', I asked. And he replied, 'You must say "one *mecítma*" and then go on counting "two *mecítma*, three *mecítma*" and so on.'

"But I went on counting, 'One and twenty, two and twenty.' And once more I got a great clout on the ear. The water bailiff shouted, 'One and *mecítma*, two *mecítma*.' But this was too much for me and I said, 'But, master, I can't speak that language.' And after that they laughed at me for a whole week. Fortunately the water bailiffs came up and took over the counting and I helped them draw in the net."

"It was not only in the water bailiffs' watch-towers that we had fun," said the keeper from Štětice, "but we had it in the keepers' lodges too. Like, for example, once in the lodge at Telín, when they were fishing out Telín lake. The water bailiffs came there from all over the region. They ordered food at the village inn but it's a long way from Telín to the lake's edge. So they went to the keeper's wife. 'Missis, here's a nice carp. Cook it for us *au bleu* — blue.' 'Of course I will, however you like,' she replied. That was in the morning.

"When you're fishing you get pretty hungry, and the water bailiffs were longing for the moment when they could sit down to their meal that evening.

"'I think we ought to have one more carp cooked *au bleu*,' said one of the water bailiffs. And so they had another one cooked, and talked about how they would enjoy it. Their mouths watered at the thought of that carp *au bleu*.

"Whenever the keeper's wife appeared, they asked her how the carp was getting on.

"'You're going to enjoy it,' she replied.

"'It had better be good,' the water bailiffs said. 'You'll be well paid for your trouble.'

"At last came the evening after the catch. The water bailiffs came into the room starving and sent for some beer.

"'Now, Missis, let's have that "blue" carp.'

"'Missis, you're taking a long time over that carp.'

"Finally she came in carrying a huge steaming dish and with it a small paper bag.

"'Here you are, gentlemen, here's that carp, and if some of you, gentlemen, think it's not "blue" enough, please add a little "blue" yourselves. I'm a simple woman and I don't know how exactly you gentlemen like it,' the keeper's wife said.

"'Oh, you Godforsaken woman, you, you've put washing blue in it,' the water bailiffs groaned and went off hungrily to the village to get some food there.

"The keeper's wife said afterwards, 'Well, well, it's not easy to please important gentlemen.'"

"It was marvellous fun, and it still is to be there when the fish are being counted," said the water bailiff Jareš. "But once that fun cost me dear. When we had finished counting — it was at Kestřany before Christmas — we had a drink or two, as was our custom. I drank too and when we left I was not perhaps drunk but a little 'squiffy', as they say.

"And so I walked home to the Ražice water-tower at midnight. It was snowing and the wind blew in my face. My waders sank deep into the snow. The wind made snow drifts and you couldn't tell the road from the ditch. It was blowing everywhere and snowing all the time.

"I might have frozen. I wanted to have a rest. I was hot because I had a heavy fur coat on, and so I sat down on a small slope. At home they organized a search party for me and in the meantime I fell asleep in the frost and blizzard. I don't know how it happened, but all at once it was as if something fell on me.

"Suddenly I woke up and found myself in bed at home. I should certainly have frozen outside, if it had not been for the dog Pinčl.

"He scented me just outside Ražice. Then he barked, and ran out onto the dam. Then he rushed back again and went on barking and running until people came out, went to look for me and brought me home.

"Pinčl was the first to find me and he saved my life. Alas, the poor creature had a sad end. He was an excellent dog, but unfortunately he caught rabies. One day he ran after us the whole morning, licked the hands of every one of us, rubbed up against us, licked our hands and whined. We looked for him in the afternoon, but he was nowhere to be found. We called him, but he didn't come. Only in the evening one of the servants found him hidden in a corner. He was motionless and quite cold.

"We thought it was all over with him, and the servant carried him out into the yard to bury him the next morning. We were very cut up about that dog. Next morning we went out into the yard to look at him — and he was gone! He'd recovered outside and run away. But after he'd bitten three dogs, the hunters from Písek shot him. It was confirmed that he had got rabies.

"Then Tonda Koštěl, from the hospital at Skočice, treated us all to a crust of bread basted with something like ink. We had to cook it in unsalted water and drink the brew for nine days. Just think of it, we weren't allowed to eat anything salt for nine days. Nothing but unsalted food!"

"Tonda was a good medical assistant," said the keeper from Štětice. "In the late Princess Eleonore Schwarzenberg's time a mad dog bit the prince's hunting dogs. They called in Tonda and he cured them all.

"The doctors took him to court in Písek and tried to get out of him how he did it, but he wouldn't tell."

"He ought to have told them," said the gamekeeper from Řežabinec. "As it was, no one had any benefit from it."

"They say his father made him promise not to tell it, when he confided the secret to him," said the keeper from Štětice. "His father learned it somewhere in France where he was fighting during the Napoleonic wars there."

"Well, it's time for us to go and wait for the poachers in the lake at Řežabinec," the gamekeeper said, interrupting Jareš's story. "It's nearly ten o'clock."

All of them rose from the table and went out into the foggy autumn night, the water bailiff, the two fishery keepers, and young Hynek from Kestřany.

While Jareš was water bailiff at Ražice, most of the poachers were in Putím and poached fish, sometimes in one lake and sometimes in another.

And of all these Putím poachers the most famous were the Vejr family, which consisted of father, son, and daughter. As for the daughter, Anna, she only sold fish which had been poached by her brother or father.

At the age of twenty, Josef Vejr went one better than his father, when he once actually tried to drain Prkov lake.

He pulled out the plugs which keep the water from running out of the lake into the conduits, and then in the shallow water he caught a huge creelful of carp.

That was young Vejr's method. Old Vejr usually stuck to the traditional methods, catching fish in a net with a long handle. "It makes less noise," he said, justifying his traditional technique, but the young man, imbued with new and advanced ideas, objected. "It doesn't yield half as much as when you drain the lakes."

This often disturbed the family harmony, because both of them, the younger and the elder, obstinately defended their own ideas, and once it even happened that young Vejr went off to live with his uncle Holoubek, who was a poacher too.

But he did not stay with him for long. You see, he didn't get on with his uncle either, because of his technique of "draining the lake". Uncle Holoubek said to him one day, "If you have to poach, then do it decently. New tricks like that are neither decent nor honest. Look, yesterday, with the net, my godfather and I caught four fully grown carp in the Ražice lake."

And so young Vejr moved back to his father again. That was the time when the following song was going the rounds of Putím:

> Young Vejr from Prkov,
> Drained the lake at night. . . .

It ended:

> And so that young devil
> Flooded all the meadows
> Until Ražice's water bailiff
> Drove the plugs in again.

Young Josef was mortally offended by this song and swore that he would take vengeance on its author.

From the earliest times the history of the human race offers us abundant examples of how in various peoples and communities traitors can be found, who, driven partly by a lust for revenge and partly by a desire for fame, have basely betrayed the plans of their fellow-citizens to the enemy. Just such a traitor was young Josef Vejr in Putím. When he learned that his uncle Holoubek had composed the above-mentioned insulting song, he came one day to Kestřany and told the fisheries overseer that Holoubek planned to poach fish in the Řežabinec lake the following Saturday.

The fisheries overseer at Kestřany was an old man, but it was well known all over the district that he was very fond of girls, if they were the least bit pretty.

His old wife was consequently very careful when it came to choosing maids for the household. She refused to accept any that were even a tiny bit pretty, and so all those who worked in the old overseer's house were notorious for their ugliness. Consequently he sought compensation among the girls of the nearby villages, to the considerable fury of his wife, who was madly jealous of her husband and just as ugly as all the maids who worked for her.

"You're young Vejr, aren't you?" the overseer said, when Josef confided to him that his uncle was going to poach fish in Řežabinec lake, "and you have a sister called Anna?"

"Yes," Josef replied.

"She has dark hair," the old overseer, who knew all the girls in the neighbourhood, went on, "and it was you who drained the lake at Prkov?"

This came as a thunder-clap to young Vejr.

"Confess it now!" said the overseer in a severe voice. "You'll go to gaol for that."

Then he altered his tone and said familiarly:

"Well, tell the truth to me now. Who else is going poaching with your uncle?"

"Papa," Josef blurted out. A vision of gendarmes and the gaol rose up before his eyes and in his ears rang out the refrain of the song:

And so that young devil
Flooded all the meadows,
Until Ražice's water bailiff
Drove the plugs in again.

"And old Vejr too?" the overseer replied. "Then you must send your sister Anna here, so that I can investigate the matter properly."

Young Vejr pulled himself together and said, "Yes, but please don't tell that I've been to see you."

"In that case I'll send a boy to fetch Anna," said the overseer in an affable tone, because he already saw Anna in front of him and visualized how he would clasp her round the waist and pinch her cheek.

And so he sent Hynek to fetch Anna. The young assistant had danced three times with her not so long ago at the country fairs at Putím, Štětice, and Ražice.

"My young lass," the overseer said to Anna, when Hynek brought her to him, "this is an official matter, so sit here close by me! I've just heard that your father poaches fish. Now, come on, sit closer to me — much closer! This is what I've heard and I think that it's sometimes better to settle things in an amicable fashion. Come on, do sit closer to me! You know, my lass, that I'm a good man, but duty is duty. There's the gendarme, prison, and so forth, but all sorts of things can be arranged."

And as he spoke these words he seized Anna round the waist with one hand and pinched her cheek with the other, smiling very amiably as he did so. "Give me a kiss," he whispered.

Anna was furious and jumped away. "Kiss your old missis, grandpa!" she said. "If you dare to try that again, I'll tell your wife straight away. Goodbye."

She rushed out of the room, flushed wth anger.

"Dear little Anna," Hynek called after her, as he stood on the dam, "don't run so fast! I'll see you home. What's happened to you?

And he went with Anna as far as Putím and, when they parted, he said, "Don't be afraid. I know our old man's going to take his revenge, but I'll put it right somehow."

The old overseer did indeed take his revenge. He informed the water bailiff Jareš that on Saturday the poachers were going to take fish from the Řežabinec lake and that he should take strict counter-measures. He sent young Hynek off to help him.

As they all went out into the dark autumn night the water bailiff, Jareš, the fishery keepers from Řežabinec and Štětice, and young Hynek from Kestřany. The water bailiff warned, "Quiet! None of you are to utter a word!"

The expedition walked over the meadows, jumped over the ditches, and strode along the narrow track between the fields.

They strode confidently, although they could not see a step in front of them, confidently and silently, so that they could hear how the water gurgled in the canals and somewhere in the distance the carrier's cart rattled along the road.

It was so dark that, although they walked in single file, they could not see each other.

In this way three-quarters of an hour passed until they came near the dam of the Řežabinec lake. But before they actually reached it, they heard a suspicious splashing of water, a continuous splashing, quite unlike the single ripple made when a carp jumps.

The suspicious splashing and murmurs went on and now it sounded more definitely as though they came from the other side of the lake.

"And so the overseer was right," they all thought to themselves. "We've got them," said Hynek, remembering Anna.

They separated on the dam. They wanted to encircle the poachers.

"Absolute quiet!" the water bailiff whispered into their ears, "and you, Hynek, go round the dam on the other side."

But just as they were encircling the unsuspecting poachers, a shout suddenly rang out through the quiet misty night: "Help! Help! I'm in the water."

It was Hynek's voice and the result was that from the other side of the dam the irate voice of the gamekeeper from Štětice rang out: "You ass, can't you at least keep your mouth shut?"

Another result was that the suspicious splashing stopped and that when old Vejr and Holoubek trudged their roundabout way across the meadows to Putím with empty nets they congratulated themselves, "It was a good thing that that ass fell into the water."

Hynek, assistant at the water bailiff's watch-tower at Kestřany, remember that a prophet is never honoured among his own people — especially if the people don't know about him. . . .

I am afraid that in the eyes of both parties you made a perfect ass of yourself.

Director Behalt

AFTER THE RETIREMENT OF THE GOOD DIRECTOR OF THE PRINCE'S estate at Protivín, a new one came, by the name of Behalt. He was a German. It was true that he had already learned Czech, but he never missed an opportunity to introduce into his Czech conversation the German expletive "Himmel, Herrgott!"

What was remarkable about his person was that wherever he went there appeared in the doorway first his waistcoat and only afterwards his face, because he had a belly of enormous proportions which might have resembled many other round objects but least of all a human belly, if the saying is true that the most perfect creature on earth is man.

It is rather sad that when describing Mr. Behalt's person one has to start with this part of his anatomy. But it is very necessary to describe it because throughout his life, and during his time as director at Protivín, it played the most important role.

His digestive organs were in good shape, as was self-evident, and they too played an important part in his life.

One can safely say that Mr. Behalt gorged his way through life and I am sure that when he was sleeping he dreamed he was sitting at a table groaning with food, and if he had nightmares they would certainly have been that a famine had descended upon Bohemia.

Some directors have a habit of making a small fortune for themselves during their term of office, neglecting other vital questions, and Mr. Behalt certainly not only tried to amass a fortune, but wanted to enlarge the circumference of his belly as well.

Different people have different foibles, like the former director, for instance, who was fond of remembering the years he spent in the army and used to talk about them wherever he went: "Ah, yes, yes. . . . At that time. . . . Our captain. . . . And there were many like him. . . . The whole company stood as though they were on guard. . . . He winked his eye. . . . But the army now. . . ."

But in whatever company Mr. Behalt found himself he would say, "And you say that piquant sauce with goose. . . . What? Crisply roast goose. . . . Yes! That's the best. . . . What about sirloin of beef with dumpling? Roast mutton, sir, that's something, only it must be swimming in sauce."

I can picture him quite clearly from my late grandfather's account of him. I can see him going home after a visit somewhere, pleased that they had helped him into the carriage, which had been specially built for him, delighted with his good lunch, stroking his waistcoat, patting his belly, and saying, "Now, all praise to the Lord, and render unto Caesar what is Caesar's."

I can imagine how he contentedly panted and puffed, until the coachman, who did not yet know him very well, looked round on his driver's seat thinking that the director was trying to give him a sign to turn to the left or the right.

I can also see how after an hour's driving he would start to stir uneasily, because he was beginning to feel hungry again, and how he would stroke his waistcoat once more and speak to himself in a fatherly tone, "Just keep calm. We'll be home in a minute."

The journey continued to the accompaniment of his sighs: "Oh, it's a nightmare, when a chap is always hungry."

Yes, it was true. He suffered from everlasting hunger: it woke him up even at night; he felt it ten minutes after he had had his breakfast, soon after he had had lunch, and after dinner too. In short, there had never been in Protivín a director like that, so fat and so everlastingly hungry. When after taking up his post he gave a lunch to the staff of the Protivín estate, he ate a whole goose and two hens, and after the guests had gone he said to his wife, "For the first time I could not eat very much. Everyone of those people kept staring at me. A chap feels he has to restrain himself. But I'll make up for it in some other way."

And make up for it he did, by driving round the various water bailiffs' watch-towers.

The wives of the water bailiffs on the Protivín estate kept up the custom of bringing to the director's kitchen geese, chickens, ducks, eggs, butter, and various other requisites.

It was a custom of unknown provenance, observed by all the wives except the wife of Jareš of Ražice.

It was a form of bribery which could have had its origin in the bad conscience of some of the water bailiffs, because Jareš used to say, "Anyone who does his job honestly doesn't need to deliver anything. A director like that, who has six times my salary, is an employee of the Prince, just like me. Why should I have to give him anything, when I earn six times less than he does and do my job honestly and well?"

And so his wife never brought anything to the kitchen of any of the directors.

But now the new director, Behalt, to appease his everlasting hunger, drove round the water bailiffs' watch-towers under the pretext of getting to know the people personally. He made them arrange lavish feasts for himself and later, on the excuse that he had to keep an eye on how they were carrying out their duties, he drove round again and sampled their tables.

The wives of the water bailiffs entertained him royally. After he had eaten his fill and cleverly hinted during the meal that it would do no harm if he could take home with him some of their poultry, he drove a little further to another water bailiff's watchtower, where he had another meal and where the wife not only set food on the table but before he departed put some poultry into his carriage as well.

Mr. Behalt looked forward most of all to visiting the watchtower at Ražice, because he had heard it said in all the watchtowers what an excellent cook Jareš's wife was.

Above all, it was common talk how exquisitely she could cook game, and this filled him with enthusiasm. People also talked of her roast mutton, which sounded to the director like the loveliest poetry, assuming of course that he ever read any.

And so he was not slow to visit the watch-tower at Ražice. He had the carriage prepared — to the back of which he had fitted, after he had taken up his post, a sort of trunk, into which the coachman stored away the eatables — and then he drove off, looking forward very much to the meal which the wife of Jareš would have prepared to welcome him.

His reception by Jareš was quite formal. Neither the water bailiff nor his wife bowed very deeply.

"I've come," said the director, when he had sat down on a chair (after having first carefully examined it to see whether it would bear the weight of his body), "to meet you and get to know you personally."

"Would you like something to eat first, sir?" the wife asked.

"Well, hm, something to eat, well, to tell the truth, I certainly wouldn't reject it," he answered hungrily, looking with peculiar pleasure through the window, where geese and ducks could be

seen wandering about, as well as various poultry — from crested
Houdan to guinea fowl — which he also very much enjoyed eating.

"You've got a lot of poultry, geese, and ducks here," he said
to the water bailiff, as though in a reverie. "I love a good roast
goose. I've heard that you're marvellous at cooking game. Ah, there
I see guinea fowl. I adore them with noodles. Also hens with
noodles. . . ."

"Take it easy, now," the water bailiff thought to himself and
went on listening to what the fat director had to say. "On the estate
where I was director before," he said, "the bailiffs also kept guinea
fowl, geese, ducks, and poultry of all kinds. Wherever I went they
entertained me and, when I went home, the coachman said, 'Your
Honour, I can't sit properly on the driving seat, I am so cluttered
up with geese and ducks. I believe they're for Madam's kitchen, for
your good lady.' And the bailiffs' wives came themselves and
brought all sorts of things. Of course I said to myself, 'I'll show
myself considerate in return.' And so I never harried anyone
unnecessarily. And you should have seen how popular I was."

"I see," thought the water bailiff to himself, "but you're not
going to catch me quite so easily," and he went on listening to what
the director was saying; he was speaking in dulcet tones, like
someone recalling lovely moments. "And wherever I went they at
once asked me, 'What do you like to eat best, sir?' 'I like this and
that,' I replied, and after a time they set before me on the table just
what I had said."

The director patted his belly and sighed. "They forced me to
help myself to more and more. 'I've had too much to eat,' I told
them. And believe me, I had to loosen my waistcoat very often,
and, when I left they again gave the coachman things for my
kitchen.

"In Kestřany," he continued after a pause, "I heard that your
wife knows how to roast a joint of mutton like venison, and that
few people can do it so well."

Again he was silent and then, stroking his waistcoat, he went
on, "Mutton prepared like venison is my weakness, but of course a
chap has to give prior warning. At home I say, for example, 'I'd like

mutton done in venison style.' And in a week's time I have a delicious leg of mutton.

"You don't hapen to have any sucking pigs?" he asked suddenly. "If you do, you could perhaps sell me some for my kitchen. I love sucking-pig. When a chap sees a finely roasted sucking-pig, then — if I may put it like that — everything inside a chap sings with joy. I'll tell you something. On the estate which I ran before, I once said to a bailiff, as I said to you just now, 'Could you sell me a sucking-pig?' 'I can't, Your Honour,' he replied and made some excuse or another. But after a few days he came to my kitchen in person and brought two sucking-pigs. 'You sly rogue,' I said laughingly, 'why, you said you couldn't sell them. How much do they cost?' And, do you know what he said? 'For Your Honour nothing at all.'"

The director expected that the water bailiff would laugh, but it produced no such reaction.

Jareš said, "Will you allow me, sir, to show you over the watch-tower and the dam? Some repairs are needed."

"Oh, some other time," the director replied, and went on in dulcet tones. "But here too on the estate it's not so bad either. The water bailiffs are appreciative people, I think."

"They do their job," said Jareš.

At that moment his wife came in and set in front of the director a dish of fried chicken and a bottle of beer.

"This is a good beginning," he thought to himself, as he ate the chicken. "Fried chicken always provokes the appetite. It's strange that they serve chicken before the other courses, but perhaps that's the custom hereabouts."

When he had eaten the chicken and drunk up the bottle of beer, they took away the empty plate and bottle, and cleared the table.

"They're perhaps going to change the table-cloth," the director thought to himself, as he stroked his waistcoat. "Judging by that chicken the wife is really an excellent cook. I've got something to look forward to when the other courses follow."

If he had gone on looking forward until evening, he would

still have been waiting in vain, for he sat at the empty table for another half hour and the table had still not been laid again. "They haven't got it ready," he decided and interrupted the half-hour's silence with the words, "The chicken was really delicious."

"We've given you what we have," answered the water bailiff, "but we gave it with all our hearts. I, for example, don't really care about a chicken like that. I prefer a good piece of smoked pork with peas and cabbages, which we're going to have for lunch. If you'd like to wait and share our simple lunch with us, please do so. Now I must go and see if the reapers are doing their job properly. If you would care to come with me...."

"Smoked pork with peas," the horrified director burst out. "I thought — very well then, if you have work to do — now I think about it, I too have got some other visit to make."

And he went on without even saying goodbye. When he climbed into the carriage and was a little way away from the cabin, he said to the coachman, "Volešník, didn't the wife of the water bailiff give you anything for the kitchen?" "No, she didn't," answered Volešník. "Where do you wish me to go now, sir?"

"To the water bailiff's watch-tower at Sudoměř," the director ordered, looking at the notes he had made the day before. "Sudoměř, three ducks for the kitchen."

And now he wrote: "The cabin at Ražice. Water bailiff a rebel." This brief note meant, "Wait, I'll teach you to do what your betters require of you!"

He was beside himself with rage, because nothing like that had ever happened to him before.

"I'll teach you to talk to me about repairs," he thought to himself, remembering the water bailiff's words — "Will you allow me, sir, to show you over the watch-tower and the dam? Some repairs are needed."

"One fried chicken and a bottle of beer, and they didn't even say 'Your Honour!' Repairs needed, indeed! I'll teach you who I am. Why, to me you're just a nobody! Never mind, we'll see each other again soon."

And the director came again a week later and from that time

on he drove to the Ražice watch-tower at any hour, surprised the water bailiff with his visits in the morning or afternoon, and always found something which did not please him.

"I definitely forbid you to keep geese and poultry here," he said one day during his visit. "They do a lot of damage."

"Excuse me, sir," the water bailiff answered, "His Highness gave me permission to keep them, and as far as the damage is concerned, if they do any, it's only on my meadow, which I receive in kind in lieu of part of my wages, and I have a herdsman to keep an eye on them."

"They do a lot of harm to the fields," said the fat director. "The fields belong to the farmers," replied the water bailiff, "and if they did any damage, I'd settle it with them."

"They eat the fish and small fry," said the director, falling back on his last objection, which was in his opinion unassailable.

"Excuse me, sir, geese don't eat fish or small fry. I've certainly never taught them that," replied the water bailiff.

On another visit of inspection the director looked at the ricks near the cabin. "You're a real landowner," he said, with a malicious smile.

He tried to find any way possible of getting his revenge. He forbade now this, now that, waiting for the water bailiff to send something to his kitchen at last. But nothing of the kind happened. The director's wife said, "It's a funny thing, but I know all the water bailiffs' wives except that one at Ražice."

And the director drove again and again and again to the watch-tower at Ražice, always on the look-out for some opportunity of revenging himself.

And one day the news spread over all the watch-towers on Protivín estate that the director had died and that the water bailiffs must go to his funeral.

When the Božov water bailiff returned home, he gave an account of it:

"There hasn't been such a funeral for a very long time. All the officials, the director, the water bailiffs, the fishery keepers — in short, masses and masses of people. And lots of ordinary folk. You know, he hasn't been director for as much as half a year and then he dies. According to custom we water bailiffs ought to have carried the coffin. But something happened which won't happen again soon. The late director, as you know, was a fat man, and because of that fatness, he burst while in his coffin. And the coffin got soaked, and the stench was appalling. No one wanted to take it on his shoulder, until Jareš said to me, 'Josef, we'll take him on our shoulders.' And we did and carried him off. The others found this extraordinary and said, 'Hallo, look at Jareš! Behalt couldn't see any good in him and they were always at daggers drawn. Now, see how splendidly he has behaved.'"

People all over the region went on talking for a long time about that strange funeral, until another event completely brushed aside the story of Director Behalt.

Another event

THIS IS HOW THEY GOT TO KNOW ABOUT IT ON THE ESTATE AT
Protivín. The director mentioned it to the officials, the officials to
their wives, the wives to their married lady friends in Protivín, and
they in their turn told other people, until it spread to the village and
the water bailiffs' watch-towers. Something quite unheard of and
unprecedented had happened to the director, who was the main
person on the estate after the Prince himself, and this was what it
was.

The director had set out on a tour of inspection and a survey of the
water bailiffs' watch-towers and the dams only a few days after the
great autumn rains.

In the part of the country where the lakes are situated the
rainy season keeps the water bailiffs busy. They have continually to
walk on the dams in the rain, see how far the water is rising and
whether the plugs controlling the outflow are properly released, so
that the superfluous water can escape through the conduits onto
the meadows. They must see whether the water has not seeped out
through the dam somewhere and that the dam is not leaking.

God forbid that it should! If it does, a great quantity of water
begins to undermine a stone and seeps out through a small opening,
which grows gradually wider. The enormous pressure of water

forces itself through the opening, undermines another stone, and begins to erode the masonry of the dam. And all this happens so quietly, without any noise, perhaps without even any pounding of waves or the surface of the lake being rippled.

Watch the lake. The rain makes infinitesimal rings on the surface, which begins to seethe slightly and all at once a torrent of water spurts out of the dam, a small torrent which becomes larger and larger, and after that the harm is done.

If this torrent is not noticed, the dam soon begins to break. As though at a given sign, huge boulders overgrown with grass begin to break out of the dam. It starts to rock and torrents of water begin tumbing out, foaming, and carrying with them stones, grass, and clay from the dam. The force of the whole lake seems to be concentrated here on this opening, which goes on and on widening with terrifying speed to the accompaniment of the terrible thunder of the waters, that hideous force, which only a short time before was lying so still and whose roaring muddy torrents are now bursting out on to the meadows below and destroying everything in their path.

A water bailiff's life seems to be nice and peaceful, but in reality it is nothing but a series of anxieties. He must continually watch the dam and see that the stones are firmly seated and the dam nowhere undermined. And if there are rains and the water in the lake rises, he has to pay careful attention and see that no tiny spring is trickling out of the dam. If it is, then the most important thing for him is not to lose his head. Clay must be thrown on both sides of the opening so that it is stopped up. All this has to be done very quickly, because if the opening is a large one no one will be able to stop the torrent of water, however many cartfuls of clay are thrown into the lake in front of the opening.

And now, when the rainy season had come and the surface of the lake had risen, the water bailiff Jareš watched the dam vigilantly throughout the night, testing the level of the water and seeing that the overflow plugs were removed so that the water could safely flow out.

The state of the dam of Ražice lake was good, but it was always necessary to keep a sharp look out none the less.

The water was now higher, but it was flowing out through the conduit, and when it rose still higher, the water bailiff had the sliding beams raised so that it flowed out along the conduit onto the meadows below the dam, where it flooded the grass.

Then the rains ceased. The surface of the lake returned again to its normal level, the plugs were firmly fastened, the dam had dried out, and only the grass below the dam, which had been under water during the rains, was beaten down — a sign that there had been a flood.

And it was just then that the director elected to come on a visit to the water bailiff's watch-tower at Ražice. He examined the entries in the book and went to inspect the dam, accompanied by the water bailiff.

The director noticed that the grass below the dam was beaten down and covered with mud.

"The dam must have leaked," he declared. "This is a very strange state of affairs."

"Excuse my saying so, sir," Jareš answered, "but there has not been any leak. Please come and look here."

"There's no doubt about it at all," the director said. "Do you think I'm blind? Do you really imagine I can't see that the grass is beaten down?"

"But please believe me, sir, that the dam has never leaked while I've been employed here."

"Of course it has," said the director. "Look, the grass is covered with mud."

Jareš began to get angry. "Please, I would have you understand, sir, that I know very well whether a dam has leaked or not. The grass is flat because there has been a flood and the water from the conduit has flowed out onto the meadow."

"The dam *must* have leaked," the director declared decidedly, although he understood very little about it.

Then Jareš became angry in earnest. "And I tell you, sir, that it has *not*. Look at it! You would know by the stones, if it had. It's the dam, not the grass, which shows whether there has been a leak."

As he said this, they were both standing on the dam above the sluice-gates, and the director, looking back into the black pools of water, repeated, "I tell you that it has leaked."

His obstinacy maddened the water bailiff to such an extent that he shouted out in fury, "If you say that once again, I'll throw you into the water!"

The director turned deadly pale, jumped away from the dam and stammered out, "Well, it's not quite as bad as all that. I'm only asking. I like things to be in order, you know." And he added as an afterthought, "How many days did it rain for?"

"Three days in succession," replied the water bailiff.

"Three days! Hm, that's quite a while," he said, jumping off the dam. "Well, I think I've seen everything now."

Jareš' wife, who was in the courtyard and had listened in horrified astonishment to their dispute, watched them coming to the cabin in perfect calm, as though nothing had happened.

From that time on, whenever the director paid a visit to the Ražice watch-tower, he made himself as amiable as possible, never giving any sign that he was angry with the water bailiff, because he was so afraid of him.

However he did not fail to mention the incident to his staff; the staff then told their wives; the wives told their married lady friends etc., etc., until it got around the whole estate that the Ražice water bailiff had threatened to throw the director into the water.

But everyone said, "Don't tell anyone, whatever you do."

The end of the water bailiff's watch-tower

IT HAPPENED VERY SUDDENLY. IT WAS NOT PERHAPS A NATURAL calamity, but the will of the all-powerful director of the estate, to whom the water bailiff at Ražice appeared to be a rebel, all because he would not humble himself as he would have liked him to do.

Not far away at Talín they were once fishing out a lake and Jareš was there.

The lake had been drained in the evening, until water was left only in the middle, and in the falling waters heaps of fish had collected, which must be caught next morning by drawing in a net over what remained of the surface of the lake. Then an unknown miscreant opened the flood gates, and the remaining water escaped out on to the meadows so that the fish remained high and dry.

In this critical moment, Jareš appeared, roused up the other men and then, but only with tremendous exertion, brought water from a neighbouring lake in barrels on carts and poured it into the empty lake, where the fish were lashing about in the mud.

If that had not been done, all the fish would have perished but although Jareš, by his vigilance when all the others were asleep, saved the whole shoal of fish, the director, when he heard of it next morning, rebuked him for his carelessness.

And when Jareš, conscious of the correct way he had discharged his duties, tried to defend himself, the director shouted at him, "Get away from the tub and clear off!"

Then Jareš pulled off his waders, threw them at the director's feet and said, "All right, then, you can damn well get the fish yourself!"

And he went home to his watch-tower at Ražice.

The director left word that Jareš must come and apologize.

He left word once, twice, three times, but the water bailiff said each time, "Because he drove me away from the tub, am I to beg his pardon and perhaps kiss his hand?"

Then the director finally summoned Jareš to his office. When the water bailiff came home afterwards, he said quite simply to his wife, "Well, from this autumn we're retired."

"I'll get two hundred guilders a year," he went on. "'We're going to abolish the water bailiff's post at Ražice,' the director told me. 'We've been thinking of doing so for a long time. We shall just have a fishery keeper there and the watch-tower will become a keeper's cabin.'"

And that was the end of the water bailiff's watch-tower. . . .

A HOUSE SEARCH
Jarmila Hašková

INTRODUCTION

During the period that Jaroslav Hašek was associated with the Anarchist movement he was won over to anti-militaristic ideas. The Anarchists spat on the Austrian uniform and refused to do military service for "the enemies of the Czech people". It was only natural, therefore, that the Austrian police should get onto his tracks, particularly when he was found to be visiting military barracks and contacting suspicious elements there. His wife, Jarmila, who was a journalist herself and often wrote stories in Hašek's vein, describes here how a year or two after their marriage the police carried out a search of their flat.

A house search*

...ONE DAY IN 1910, AT THE TIME OF THE ANTI-MILITARIST trial, Míťa [Hašek] returned home in the early hours of the morning.

"Has no one been looking for me, darling?"

"No, no one."

"Listen, they took me round the barracks and confronted me with some soldiers. Tomorrow we'll probably have a house search."

"My God!"

"Don't be an idiot, darling. A house search like that is just a bit of a lark. You'll see."

Dawn was breaking when we fell asleep. We were suddenly awakened by a loud ringing.

"They're already here," said Míťa, getting up.

He put on his dressing gown and went to open the door. I remembered that my own dressing gown was in the dining room on the chair and I wanted to make a quick dash to get it, but it was too late. A number of footsteps sounded in the hall and I heard the door of the dining room fly open.

"Sit down, Mr. Hašek, and be quiet!" said a strange male

* From *Drobné příběhy* (1960) with the permission of the Estate of Jarmila Hašková.

voice. "We are only going to look through your flat and take away your correspondence."

Some footsteps approached the door of my bedroom.

"Excuse me, Commissioner," said Mîťa, "that's our bedroom and my wife has not got up yet. Surely you're not going to be so unmannerly."

Someone knocked at my door. "Madam, may I request you to come out to us immediately. Please don't remove anything or touch anything at all!"

"I can't, Commissioner, I'm just getting up and I haven't even got my dressing gown here."

"Mr. Hašek," said the Commissioner," you may get up from your chair, half-open the door, and hand Madam her dressing gown. Please let Madam put it on as quickly as possible."

Everything took place as quickly as the Commissioner had ordered. I came into the dining room, unwashed and uncombed.

There were four people dressed in black there besides my husband. The Commissioner offered me a seat and another man a cigarette.

"Please sit down quietly and don't interfere with the execution of official business," the Commissioner said to me.

"Yes, darling, please let these gentlemen root about in our love letters, because there's a policeman standing behind the door ready to protect them if we should think of breaking their heads in or shooting."

While we sat at the table in the company of two of the gentlemen, who watched our every movement, the other two rooted about in the bookcase. They worked very thoroughly but after long and vain efforts they shut the glass doors of the bookcase with a sigh, only to throw themselves onto the writing desk. Here they opened one drawer at random. It was empty. Then they opened another. That, too, was empty. They half opened a third, and looked disappointedly and questioningly at the senior Commissioner.

"If I were you, I'd go on looking," said Mîťa. "The devil never sleeps, and it was Christ who said 'Seek, and ye shall find'."

At that moment one of the gentlemen opened the first

drawer on the left, and Mít̆a commented, "You see, gentlemen, the Bible speaks the truth." The drawer was stuffed with correspondence. They opened a second drawer and a third, and all my files were revealed to their wide-open eyes: sighs of my friends, who wanted to go, at the age of fourteen, to a convent because they had *Weltschmerz*; maternal counsels and precepts; vows of undying love — my whole collection, all my treasures, preserved from the time I was six to twenty-two and beautifully tidied up. They took the letters in handfuls and carried them to the table.

"Gentlemen," said Mít̆a, "I think you came here to confiscate the suspicious correspondence of Jaroslav Hašek. I am he. The letters, which you are dragging out of the drawer, don't belong to me, but to my wife. There's a great difference, you know."

"You're mistaken, sir. We have the right to confiscate all the correspondence we find here. We shall read it, and, provided there's nothing irregular about it, Madam will get it all back again in perfect order. Please take it calmly."

Meanwhile the official ardour of the gentlemen, who had made that gigantic find of a thousand letters and cards in the writing desk, began to cool. *Pro forma* they had gone on to open the drawers in the sofa, the table, and the wash basin, and it was obvious that they were already getting tired. It was Sunday, and the gentlemen were in evening dress. Mít̆a's eyes were sending out sparks.

"If I were you, gentlemen," he said, "I would root about in the stove. You must concede that I've had enough time to burn the suspicious things, while you were coming to a decision as to whether or not you would carry out a house search in my home."

Reluctantly they went and rooted about in the stove and in the kitchen.

Unprompted, Mít̆a took the lead.

"I should turn the carpet upside down," he said, "to make sure that there's nothing hidden underneath."

Looking very angry indeed, they went and lifted up the carpet.

"I'd take the mattresses off the beds and look into the basket with the dirty linen."

They did that as well.

"I'd search through the drawers in the wardrobes."

They knelt on the ground and rummaged about in them.

Just before midday, they asked me for string and packing paper. It didn't matter what I offered them, Míta was against my doing it. Finally he gave them some pieces of old newspaper and tangled cord. The four packages packed in this way were not at all elegant and that was perhaps why, when they finally went away quite dishevelled, one of the gentlemen forgot his packet on the dining room table. Loyal Míta went to the window, opened it, and shouted after them, just as they were getting into the car, "Gentlemen, you've forgotten a packet of correspondence. Shall I throw it out after you?" But the gentlemen pretended not to hear.

Some time later I met one of them in a tram.

"Would you please tell me, Commissioner, when I'm going to get my correspondence back?"

"It's already prepared for you, Madam. But, my goodness, if you only knew what a trouble we had with it! Everything had to be translated into German and I went with it personally to Vienna. It was a confoundedly large consignment, Madam."

"Well, so you see, that's exactly what you deserve. By the way you had left behind one packet."

"Thank the Lord, Madam, only please don't tell anybody."

I burned all my correspondence when after half a year I saw it again. I burned everything except the package which they had left behind on that occasion, because it had not been translated into German or kept in their archives. And it happened to be the most interesting of them all.

THE GOOD SOLDIER ŠVEJK

INTRODUCTION

It was in May 1911 that Hašek first hit on the idea of creating the character which made him famous throughout the world, the Good Soldier Švejk.

Hašek's son, Richard, who is still alive, recalls being told by his mother, Jarmila, how his father first came to invent the Good Soldier. This is how she remembered the event:

"One evening in May Hašek returned home very exhausted. But he still had enough strength and will at that hour to set down in a few words an idea which was continually haunting him. Hardly had he woken up next morning, however, than he started searching for a small scrap of paper, on which, as he maintained, he had noted down a brilliant idea, which to his horror he had forgotten by the morning. In the meantime I had thrown that scrap of paper onto the rubbish heap. Hašek rushed to look for it and was enormously happy when he found the crumpled paper at last. He picked it up, carefully read its contents, crumpled it up again, and threw it away. I rescued it once more and preserved it in safe-keeping. On it was clearly written and underlined the headline of a story: 'The Idiot in the Company'. Underneath came a sentence which was just legible: 'He had himself examined to prove that he was capable of serving as a regular soldier.' There then followed some further words which were illegible." Obviously any Czech who tried to prove that he was fit to serve in the Austrian army must have been an idiot!

In that same month Hašek wrote his first five stories about Švejk and published them in Caricatures, *a weekly,* edited by the cartoonist Lada who was later to contribute the illustrations for the final book, The Good Soldier Švejk. The first of his stories was called "Švejk Stands Against Italy". It was followed by four others.

Švejk stands against Italy

ŠVEJK JOINED UP WITH A HAPPY HEART. HIS OBJECT WAS TO HAVE fun in the army and he succeeded in astonishing the whole garrison in Trient including the garrison commander himself. Švejk always had a smile on his lips, was amiable in his behaviour, and perhaps for that reason found himself continually in gaol.

And when he was let out of gaol he answered every question with a smile. And with complete equanimity he let himself be gaoled again, inwardly happy at the thought that all the officers of the whole garrison in Trient were frightened of him — not because of his rudeness, oh no, but because of his polite answers, his polite behaviour, and his amiable and friendly smile, all of which anguished them.

An inspecting officer came into the men's quarters. A smiling Švejk, sitting on his camp bed, greeted him politely: "Humbly report, praise be to Jesus Christ."

Lieutenant Walk ground his teeth at the sight of Švejk's sincere, friendly smile and would have relished knocking Švejk's cap straight on his head to make it conform with regulations. But Švejk's warm and fervent look restrained him from any such display.

Major Teller came into the room. Lieutenant Walk sternly

eyed the men, who stood at their camp beds, and said, "You, Švejk, bring your *kver** here!"

Švejk carried out the order conscientiously and, instead of bringing his rifle, brought him his pack. Major Teller looked furiously at his charming innocent countenance and flew at him in Czech: "You do not know what is *kver?*"

"Humbly report, I don't." And so they took him straight away to the office. They brought in a rifle and stuck it under his nose: "What's this? What's it called?" "Humbly report, I don't know." "It's a *kver.*" "Humbly report, I don't believe it."

He was put in gaol and the prison warder considered it his duty to tell him that he was an ass. The rank and file marched out for heavy exercises in the mountains, but Švejk sat behind bars smiling placidly.

As they could do nothing whatsoever with him, they appointed him orderly to the one-year volunteers. He served at lunch and dinner in the officers' club.

He laid the knives and forks, brought in the food, beer, and wine, sat down modestly by the door, and uttered from time to time: "Humbly report, gentlemen, Lieutenant Walk is a nice gentleman, yes, a very nice gentleman indeed." And he smiled and blew his cigarette smoke into the air.

Another day there was an inspection at the officers' club. Švejk was standing modestly by the door and a new officer was unlucky enough to ask him which company he belonged to.

"Humbly report, if you please, I don't know." "Hell's bells, which regiment is stationed here?" "Humbly report, if you please, I don't know." "For Christ's sake, man, what's the name of the garrison town here?" "Humbly report, if you please, I don't know."

"Then, man, how on earth did you get here?"

With an amiable smile and looking at the officer in a sweet

* The Lieutenant and the Major both speak a kind of pidgin Czech. "Kver" ("Gewehr") is not a Czech word and Švejk is fully justified in not understanding it.

and extremely pleasant manner, Švejk said, "Humbly report, I was born, and after that I went to school. Later I learned to be a master joiner. After that they brought me to an inn, and there I had to strip naked. A few months later the gendarmes came for me and took me off to the barracks. At the barracks they examined me and said, 'Man, you're three weeks late in beginning your military service. We're going to put you in gaol.' I asked why, when I didn't want to join the army and didn't even know what a soldier was. All the same they clapped me in gaol, then put me on a train and took me all over the place until we reached here. I didn't ask anyone what regiment, company, or town it was, so as not to offend anyone, but immediately during my first drill they gaoled me because I lit a cigarette in the ranks, although I don't know why. Then they put me in gaol whenever I appeared, first because I lost my bayonet, then because I nearly shot the Colonel at the rifle butts, until finally I'm serving the one-year volunteer gentlemen."

The good soldier Švejk fixed the officer with the radiant look of a child and the latter did not know whether to laugh or get angry.

Christmas Eve was approaching. The one-year volunteers had decorated a Christmas tree in the club and after dinner the Colonel gave a moving address, saying that Christ was born, as all of them knew, and that he was delighted in having good soldiers and that every good soldier should be delighted with himself. . . .

And at that moment, in the midst of this solemn address, a fervent voice could be heard: "Oh yes, indeed! That's so."

It came from the good soldier Švejk, who stood with a beaming face, unobserved among the one-year volunteers.

"You, volunteers," roared the Colonel, "who was it who shouted that?" Švejk stepped forward from the ranks of the one-year volunteers and looked smilingly at the Colonel: "Humbly report, sir, I serve the one-year volunteer gentlemen here and I was very happy to hear what you kindly said just now. You've got your heart and soul in your job."

When the bells in Trient rang for the midnight Mass the good soldier Švejk had been sitting in clink for more than an hour.

On that occasion he was locked up for a pretty long time. Later they hung a bayonet on him and assigned him to a machine-gun section.

There were grand manoeuvres on the Italian frontier and the good soldier Švejk marched after the army.

Before the expedition he had listened to a cadet's speech: "Imagine that Italy has declared war on us and we are marching against the Italians."

"Good, then, forward march!" Švejk exclaimed, for which he got six days.

After having served this punishment he was sent after his machine-gun section together with three other prisoners and a corporal. First they marched along a valley, then they went on horse-back up to the mountains, and as could have been expected, Švejk got lost in the dense forest on the Italian frontier. He squeezed his way through the undergrowth, searching vainly for his companions until he safely crossed the Italian frontier in full equipment.

And it was there that the good soldier Švejk distinguished himself. A machine-gun section from Milan had just had manoeuvres on the Austrian frontier and a mule with a machine-gun and eight men got up onto the plateau, on which the good soldier Švejk was making his reconnaisance.

The Italian soldiers, feeling confidently secure, had crawled quietly into a thicket and gone to sleep. The mule with the machine-gun was busily pasturing and straying further and further away from its detachment, until finally it came to the spot where the good soldier Švejk was smilingly looking at the enemy.

The good soldier Švejk took the mule by the bridle and went back to Austria together with the Italian machine-gun on the back of the Italian mule.

From the mountain slopes he got down again into the valley from which he had climbed up, wandered about with the mule in a forest for the whole day, until at last in the evening he caught sight of the Austrian camp.

The guard did not want to let him in, because he did not

know the password. An officer ran up and Švejk smilingly assumed a military posture and saluted: "Humbly report, sir, I've captured a mule and a machine-gun from the Italians."

And so they led off the good soldier Švejk to the garrison gaol, but we now know what the latest Italian machine-gun type looks like.

The good soldier Švejk provides wine for the mass

THE ARMY VICAR APOSTOLIC, KOLOMAN BELOPOTCZKY, BISHOP of Trical, appointed Augustin Kleinschrodt chaplain of the garrison in Trient. There is a great difference between an ordinary cleric, that is to say a civilian priest, and an army chaplain. The latter perfectly combines religion with soldiering so that two utterly distinct castes are compounded together in him and the difference between the two types of clergy is as great as that between a lieutenant in the dragoons who instructs at a military riding academy and the owner of a riding school.

An army chaplain is paid by the State. He is a military official with a certain rank and has the right to carry a sabre and to fight duels. It is true that the civilian priest also gets pay from the State but he has to try to get money out of the faithful as well so as to live in comfort.

A soldier need not salute an ordinary priest, but must pay an army chaplain the appropriate honours, otherwise he will be sent to gaol. And so God has two representatives here, one civilian and the other military.

The civilian priests must look after political agitation whereas the military chaplains have to confess the soldiers and send them to gaol, which certainly is what the Lord had in mind when He first created this sinful world and later Augustin Kleinschrodt too.

When this reverend gentleman rolled about the streets of Trient, he looked from the distance like a comet which a wrathful god was resolved to visit upon this unfortunate town. He was awful in his majesty, and rumour had it that in Hungary he had already fought three duels, in which he had cut off the noses of his adversaries from the officers' club, who had been too lukewarm in their faith.

After having so voluminously reduced unbelief he was transferred to Trient just at the time when the good soldier Švejk had left the garrison gaol and returned to his company, to continue the defence of his fatherland.

At this time the spiritual father of the garrison in Trient was looking for a new servant and personally went to choose one from among the men of the garrison.

No wonder that, when he walked through the rooms, his gaze fell on the good-natured face of the soldier Švejk and he patted him on the shoulder and said, "You will come with me!" The good soldier Švejk began to make excuses, saying that he had done nothing wrong, but the corporal gave him a push and led him away to the office.

In the office, after prolonged excuses, the NCO told the chaplain that the good soldier Švejk was a "dirty beast" but the Reverend Kleinschrodt interrupted him: "A dirty beast can have a good heart all the same." To this the good soldier Švejk meekly nodded his head. His smiling rounded face with its honest eyes beamed from the corner of the room and the army spiritual pastor, after seeing this good-natured head, refused even to look at the good soldier Švejk's punishment book.

From that moment Švejk began to lead a life of bliss. He secretly drank the wine for the mass and cleaned his superior's horses so beautifully that once the Reverend Kleinschrodt praised him for it.

"Humbly report," the good soldier Švejk put in, "I do everything possible to make him just as fine as you, sir."

Then came the great days when the garrison lay in camp at Castelnuovo, and a drumhead mass was to be served there.

For church purposes Augustin Kleinschrodt never used anything else but wine from Vöslau in Lower Austria. He could not
stand Italian wine, and so it transpired that, when supplies ran out,
he called the good soldier Švejk to him and said, "Tomorrow
morning you will go to the town for wine from Vöslau in Lower
Austria. You'll get money in the office and you'll bring me an
eight-litre cask. Come back at once! Now, remember, from Vöslau
in Lower Austria. Dismiss!"

The next day Švejk received twenty crowns, and to forestall
the sentry stopping him from entering the camp on his return a
permit was made out for him: "On Official Duty for Wine."

The good soldier Švejk went off to the town, conscientiously
repeating to himself throughout the whole length of the journey
"Vöslau, Lower Austria". He said the words out loud at the station
too, and in three-quarters of an hour he was travelling contentedly
in the train to Lower Austria.

That day the dignity of the drumhead mass was only marred
by the bitterness of the Italian wine in the jug.

By the evening Augustin Kleinschrodt had convinced himself
that the good soldier Švejk was a scoundrel, who had forgotten his
military obligations.

The frightful oaths of the chaplain could be heard all over the
camp and were carried up to the giant Alps and merged into the
valley of the Adige in the direction of Merano, where a few hours
previously the good soldier Švejk had been travelling on his way
with a smile of contentment and in the blissful knowledge that he
was honestly performing his duty.

He sped along the valley, passed through tunnels, and at
every station asked impassively, "Vöslau, Lower Austria?"

At last the station at Vöslau received its first sight of the
good-natured face, and the good soldier Švejk presented to a man
in an official cap his official military permit: "On Official Duty for
Wine."

Smiling sweetly, he asked where the barracks were.

The man in the cap asked him for his itinerary. The good
soldier Švejk averred that he did not know what an itinerary was.

And then two more men in caps came and they started to explain to him that the nearest barracks were in Korneuburg.

And so the good soldier Švejk bought a ticket to Korneuburg and travelled on further.

In Korneuburg there was a railway regiment and at the barracks they were very astonished when the good soldier Švejk appeared at night at the gates and showed the sentry his permit: "On Official Duty for Wine."

"Let's leave that until the morning," said the sentry. "The inspecting officer has just gone to sleep."

In the happy knowledge that he was doing what he could for the State the good soldier Švejk lay down on a bunk and fell contentedly asleep.

In the morning they took him to the office stores. There he showed the quartermaster NCO his permit: "On Official Duty for Wine", a pass with the official stamp: "Camp — Castelnuovo Rgt. 102, Bat. 3", and the signature of the orderly officer of the day.

The NCO, his eyes agape, took him to the regimental office where he was subjected to cross-examination by the colonel.

"Humbly report," said the good soldier Švejk, "I have come from Trient on the orders of the Reverend Chaplain Augustin Kleinschrodt. I am to bring back an eight-litre cask of wine for mass from Vöslau."

A great council followed. His good-natured, simple face, his frank military bearing, and his permit "On Official Duty for Wine", with its properly verified stamp and signature, all made a most favourable impression and rendered the whole affair even more confused.

A major debate took place and the opinion was expressed that the Reverend Chaplain Augustin Kleinschrodt had probably gone mad and there was nothing to be done but send the good soldier Švejk back with an itinerary.

And so the NCO prepared an itinerary for him. He was a decent man and did not worry about a kilometre or two, so he drew up a journey for him via Vienna, Graz, Zábřeh, Triest, and Trient. His journey was reckoned to last two days. They gave him 1 crown 60. The NCO bought him a ticket and out of fellow feeling the cook put three loaves of army bread into his hand.

Meanwhile in Castelnuovo the chaplain was walking up and down the camp, grinding his teeth and saying nothing except "Seize him, bind him and shoot him!"

The good soldier Švejk had been entered in the records as a deserter, and imagine the surprise when on the fourth day at night he appared at the entrance to the camp and with a smile handed over to the sentry his itinerary from Korneuburg and his permit from the camp, "On Official Duty for Wine".

They immediately took hold of him and to his utter astonishment put him in irons and led him off to a hut, where they locked him up. In the morning they took him off to the barracks in the town.

At the same time there came a communication from the railway regiment at Korneuburg, in which the colonel enquired why the Reverend Chaplain Augustin Kleinschrodt had sent the soldier Švejk to Korneuburg for wine from Vöslau.

After the soldier Švejk had been cross-examined and had frankly and with a happy smile told how everything happened, there was a long consultation, and the Reverend Chaplain Augustin Kleinschrodt went to visit the good soldier Švejk in gaol.

"The best thing you can do Švejk, you idiot, would be to have yourself 'superarbitrated' so that we have no more trouble with you."

And then the good soldier Švejk looked with great sincerity at the chaplain and said, "Humbly report, sir, I shall serve His Imperial Majesty the Emperor to my last breath."

The good soldier Švejk and the "superarbitration" procedure

IN EVERY ARMY THERE ARE SCOUNDRELS, WHO DO NOT WANT TO serve. They are only too happy if they can become common or garden civilian oafs. Cunning fellows like them complain, for instance, of having weak hearts, although as is revealed afterwards by the autopsy, they probably have nothing more than appendicitis. In this and similar ways they try to get out of their military duty. But woe betide them! There still exists the "superarbitration" procedure, which will damned well put a stop to their tricks. Some bastard complains he has flat feet. The army doctor prescribes him Glauber's salt and an enema and, flat feet or no flat feet, he runs as though he were on fire, and the next morning they lock him up in gaol.

Another rogue complains that he has cancer of the stomach. They lay him on the operating table and say to him, "We'll open up your stomach without an anaesthetic." Hardly have they said that, when his cancer is all done with and he marches off to clink miraculously cured.

The "superarbitration" procedure is a real blessing for the army. Without it every recruit would feel ill and incapable of carrying his pack. "Superarbitration" is a word of Latin origin. "*Super*" means "over" or "beyond", "*arbitrare*" means "investigate, observe". So "superarbitration" means "overinvestigation".

A staff doctor put it very neatly. "Whenever I examine a man, who has reported sick," he said, "I do so in the conviction that it is not a question of *superarbitrare* ('overinvestigation') but rather of *superdubitare* ('beyond doubt'): it's beyond all doubt that he's as hale and hearty as an ox. It is on this principle that I work. I prescribe quinine and a strict diet. After three days he begs me in God's name to discharge him from the hospital. And if a malingerer like that dies in the meantime, then you can be sure he does it on purpose just to annoy us and avoid going to gaol for his fraud. All right, then, *superdubitare* and not *superarbitrare*."

Doubt everyone until his very last breath.

And so, when they wanted to "superarbitrate" the good soldier Švejk, all the companies envied him.

When the prison warder brought him his lunch in his cell, he said to him, "You're in luck, you bastard. You'll go home and be 'superarbitrated' like greased lightning."

But the good soldier Švejk said to him exactly what he had told the Reverend Chaplain Augustin Kleinschrodt: "Humbly report, if you please, sir, that won't do. I'm as fit as a fiddle and

want to serve His Majesty the Emperor to my last breath." With a blissful smile he lay down on the bunk. The warder reported this remark of Švejk's to the officer on duty, Müller.

Müller ground his teeth and shouted, "We'll teach that bastard not to think he can stay in the army. He'll have to get spotted typhus at the very least, even if it drives him round the bend."

Meanwhile the good soldier Švejk explained to his fellow-prisoner from the company: "I'm going to serve His Imperial Majesty to my very last breath. Here I am and here I stay. When I'm a soldier, I must serve His Imperial Majesty and no one can chuck me out of the army, not even if the general himself came, kicked me in the backside and threw me out of the barracks. I should only come back to him and say: 'Humbly report, sir, I want to serve His Imperial Majesty to my very last breath and I am returning to the company.' And if they don't want to have me here, I'll go to the navy so that I can at least serve His Imperial Majesty at sea. And if they don't want me there either and His Lordship, the Admiral, gives me a kick in the backside there too, then I'll serve His Imperial Majesty in the air."

However, the candid opinion prevailing throughout the whole barracks was that the good soldier Švejk would be thrown out of the army. On June 3rd they came for him in the prison with a stretcher, bound him to it with straps in spite of his furious resistance, and bore him off to the garrison hospital. Wherever they carried him, there rang out from the stretcher his patriotic battle-cry: "Soldiers, don't let them take me! I want to go on serving His Imperial Majesty."

They put him in the section for gravely ill patients and Staff Doctor Jansa gave him a cursory examination: "You have a swollen liver and fatty degeneration of the heart, Švejk. You're finished. We'll have to discharge you from the army."

"Humbly report, sir," Švejk put in, "I'm as fit as a fiddle. What would the army do without me, humbly report, sir? I want to go back to my company, humbly report, sir, and go on serving His Imperial Majesty loyally and honourably, as befits a proper soldier."

They prescribed him an enema, and when the Ukrainian

medical orderly, Bochkovsky, was administering it to him, the good soldier Švejk said with dignity in this delicate situation, "Brother, don't spare me. If I was not afraid of the Italians, I shan't be afraid of your enema either. A soldier must not fear anything and must serve. Remember that!"

Then they took him outside and in the latrine he was guarded by a soldier with a loaded rifle.

Then they put him back on to the bed, and the medical orderly Bochkovsky walked round him and sighed. "You stinking hound, you, have you any parents?"

"Yes, I have."

"Don't imagine you'll ever get out of here, you malingerer."

The good soldier Švejk gave him one across the jaw.

"Me a malingerer! I'm completely fit and want to serve His Imperial Majesty to my very last breath."

They put him on ice. For three days he was wrapped up in ice compresses, and when the staff doctor came round and said to him, "Very well then, Švejk, you can go home from the army all the same," Švejk declared, "Humbly report, sir, I have been fit all the time and I want to go on serving."

They put him back on ice and the "superarbitration" commission, which would discharge him from his military duties for ever, was due to meet in two days' time.

However, the day before the meeting, when his discharge papers were already made out, the good soldier Švejk deserted from the barracks.

To be able to go on serving His Imperial Majesty he had had to run away and for a fortnight there was no trace of him.

But imagine everyone's amazement when, after a fortnight, the good soldier Švejk appeared at the gates of the barracks in the middle of the night and, with his honest smile on his round, contented face, reported to the sentry: "Humbly report, I've come to be locked up in gaol, because I dissented so as to be able to go on serving His Imperial Majesty until my very last breath."

His wish was granted. He was gaoled for half a year, and when he still wanted to go on serving, they transferred him to the arsenal, to load torpedoes with gun cotton.

The good soldier Švejk learns how to handle gun cotton

AND IT WAS JUST AS THE REVEREND CHAPLAIN TOLD HIM: "Švejk, you bastard, if you really want to serve, then you're going to serve right in the middle of the gun cotton. Perhaps that will do you good there."

And so the good soldier Švejk began to learn how to handle gun cotton at the arsenal. He charged torpedoes with it. Service of this kind is no joke because when you're doing it you've always got one foot in the air and the other in the grave.

But the good soldier Švejk was not afraid. Like the honest soldier he was, he lived quite happily in the midst of the dynamite, ecrasite, and gun cotton. And from the hut, where he was charging the torpedoes with the dreadful explosive material, his song could be heard:

Piedmont, Piedmont, rataplan!
Behind you have fallen the gates of Milan,
The gates of Milan and bridges four.
Stronger defences you'll need and more.
Build more advance posts. Yours are too few.
A regiment of lancers I raised against you.
But you drove it beyond the gates of Milan.
Rataplan, rataplan, rataplan.

After this beautiful song, which made a lion of the good soldier Švejk, there followed other moving songs about dumplings as big as cartwheels, which the good soldier Švejk used to swallow with indescribable delight.

And so he lived happily in the midst of the gun cotton, all by himself in one of the huts in the arsenal.

And then one day there was an inspection. The inspectors went from hut to hut to check that everything was in order.

When they came to the hut where the good soldier Švejk was learning how to handle gun cotton, they saw — from the cloud of tobacco smoke which rose up from his pipe — that he was a very intrepid warrior.

Švejk, seeing the military gentlemen, stood up and, in accordance with regulations, took the pipe out of his mouth. But to keep it handy, he set it down in the nearest possible place, which happened to be an open steel barrel containing gun cotton. As he did so he declared, saluting, "Humbly report, sirs, there's nothing new and everything is in order."

There are moments in human life when presence of mind plays a crucial role.

The cleverest man in the whole group was the colonel. Rings of tobacco smoke rose from the gun cotton, so he said, "Švejk, carry on smoking!"

Those were wise words; a lighted pipe is definitely better in someone's mouth than in gun cotton. Švejk saluted and said, "Humbly report, sir, I shall carry on smoking."

He was an obedient soldier.

"And now, Švejk, come to the guardroom!"

"Humbly report, sir, I cannot, because according to regulations I have to remain here until six o'clock, when they will come to relieve me. There must always be someone by the gun cotton to prevent an accident."

The inspectors vanished. They trotted off to the guardhouse, where they gave orders for a patrol to go and fetch Švejk.

The patrol went off reluctantly, but they went none the less.

When they arrived in front of the hut where the good soldier Švejk with his lighted pipe was serving His Imperial Majesty in the midst of the gun cotton, the lance-corporal called out, "Švejk, you bastard, throw your pipe out of the window and come out yourself."

"Not a chance! The colonel gave orders that I should carry on smoking, so I must carry on smoking until there isn't a bone left in my body."

"Come out, you bloody fool!"

"But, humbly report, I can't, please. It's only four o'clock and I can't be relieved until six. Until six o'clock I've got to be by the gun cotton, so that there shouldn't be an accident. I'm being very care. . . ."

He never succeeded in saying "ful". Perhaps you've read of that terrible catastrophe in the arsenal. Hut after hut went up into the air as the whole of it exploded in three-quarters of a second.

It began in the hut where the good soldier Švejk was learning how to handle gun cotton, and planks, battens, and iron constructions, flying in from all sides, formed a tomb over it, to pay the last honours to the brave Švejk, who was not afraid of gun cotton.

For three days the sappers worked on the ruins and fitted together heads, trunks, arms, and legs, so that the good Lord on the day of the Last Judgement would have less trouble in distinguishing between the various ranks and in rewarding them accordingly. It was really like trying to solve a jig-saw puzzle. They were three days clearing away the planks and iron constructions from Švejk's tomb as well and on the night of the third day when they penetrated to the centre of that heap of rubble they heard a pleasant voice singing:

> The gates of Milan and bridges four.
> Stronger defences you'll need and more.
> Build more advance posts. Yours are too few.

By the light of torches they dug in the direction of the voice:

> A regiment of lancers I raised against you.
> But you drove it beyond the gates of Milan.
> Rataplan, rataplan, rataplan.

In the glare of the torches they saw a kind of cave, made out of iron constructions and piled-up planks, and there in a corner they saw the good soldier Švejk. He took his pipe out of his mouth, saluted and said, "Humbly report, sirs, there's nothing to report and everything is in order."

They pulled him out of that ruined inferno, and the good soldier Švejk, when he was in the presence of the officer, repeated once more, "Humbly report, sir, everything is in order and may I please be relieved, because it's long past six o'clock and could I also have my mess allowance for the time when it all fell on me?"

The valiant soldier was the only one in the entire arsenal who survived the catastrophe.

That evening a little ceremony was arranged in his honour by the military, in the officers' club in the town. Surrounded by officers, the good soldier Švejk drank like a fish, and his round good-natured face beamed with joy.

The next day he got his mess allowance for three days, just as though he had been in the war, and three weeks later he was promoted to corporal in his company and awarded the Great War Medal. Decorated with this and his corporal's stars, he marched into his barracks in Trient, where he met the officer Knobloch, who started to tremble when he saw the much-feared, good-humoured face of the good soldier Švejk.

"You've certainly done it this time, you bastard," he said to him.

Švejk answered with a smile, "Humbly report, sir, I've learned how to handle gun cotton." And in an exalted frame of mind he went into the yard to look for his company.

That same day the orderly officer of the day read to the men an announcement from the Ministry of Defence about the setting up of an aeroplane section in the army and inviting anyone who liked to volunteer.

The good soldier Švejk stepped forward and reporting to the officer said, "Humbly report, sir, I've already been in the air and I know it, and now I want to serve His Imperial Majesty up there."

And so a week later the good soldier Švejk made a pilgrimage to the aeronautical section where he behaved just as circumspectly as he had done in the arsenal, as you will see later.

The good soldier Švejk operates in aeroplanes

AUSTRIA HAS THREE DIRIGIBLE AIRSHIPS, EIGHTEEN NON-dirigible (because they cannot be driven at all), and five aeroplanes. This is the sum total of the might of Austria in the air. They seconded the good soldier Švejk to the Aeroplane Division so that he could serve to the honour and adornment of this new detachment of the army. At first he towed the planes out to the hangars on the military aerodrome and cleaned their metal parts with turpentine and French chalk.

This shows that he started serving with the aeroplanes from the very bottom. And just as he had carefully cleaned the Reverend Chaplain's horse in Trient, so he worked here too on the planes with the same relish, brushing their surfaces exactly as if he were grooming the horse, and, as a ranking corporal, he led the patrols which guarded the hangars, and instructed them as follows: "We've got to fly and so, if anyone tries to steal a plane, just shoot him."

After about a fortnight he was carrying out the duties of a passenger, which was perhaps a very dangerous promotion. He used to provide weight for the plane and fly with the officers. But the good soldier Švejk was not afraid. With a smile he flew into the air, looking meekly and deferentially at the officer who was piloting the plane, and saluting when he saw below him anyone of higher rank moving slowly over the aerodrome.

And when they sometimes crashed and smashed the plane, the first to crawl out of the wreckage was always the good soldier Švejk himself. Helping the officer to get on his legs, he would say, "Humbly report, sir, we've crashed but we're alive and well."

He was a pleasant companion. One day he flew up with an officer called Herzig, and when they found themselves at a height of 826 metres, the engines suddenly stopped.

"Humbly report, sir, we're out of petrol." It was Švejk's pleasant voice coming from the back seat. "Humbly report, sir, I forgot to fill the tank." And a moment later, "Humbly report, sir, we're falling into the Danube."

And when after a while their heads bobbed up out of the rippled, greenish waters of the Danube, the good soldier Švejk, swimming behind the officer towards the bank, said, "Humbly report, sir, today we've set an altitude record."

It was just before the grand military air flights at the aerodrome at Wiener Neustadt.

They examined the planes, tested their engines, and completed the last preparatory work for the flights.

Lieutenant Herzig had decided to fly up with Švejk in a Wright biplane, to which a Morrison instrument had been fitted. With the help of this device it was possible to fly up without a take-off.

Military representatives of foreign powers were present.

Herzig's plane was of great interest to the Romanian major, Gregorescu, who took a seat inside it and had a look at its controls.

At the lieutenant's order the good soldier Švejk started the engine. The propeller began to revolve and Švejk, sitting by the side of the inquisitive Romanian major, found it very interesting to operate the wire cable connecting the rear elevator. He conducted himself with such circumspection that he knocked the major's cap off his head.

Lieutenant Herzig lost his temper: "Švejk, you donkey, you fly off to hell!"

"Order obeyed, sir," Švejk called out and seized the gear elevator and the lever of the Morrison instrument. As the plane rose from the ground, the regular firings of its excellent engine were audible a long way off.

They flew 20, 100, 300, 450 metres up in a south-westerly direction towards the white Alps at a speed of 150 kilometres per hour.

The unfortunate Romanian major came to himself above a glacier, over which they were flying at a height which made it possible for him to distinguish clearly the beauties of nature beneath, snow-covered fields and chasms gaping sternly and menacingly up at him.

"What's happening?" he asked, stammering with fright.

"We're flying according to orders, please, sir," the good soldier Švejk answered deferentially. "The Lieutenant gave the order 'Fly off to hell' and so we're flying there, please, sir."

"And where are we going to come down?" the inquisitive Major Gregorescu asked, his teeth chattering.

"Please, sir, I don't know where we shall fall. I fly according to orders and I only know how to fly up. I don't know how to come down. We never needed that with the Lieutenant. When we were high up, we just fell down of our own accord."

The altitude meter registered 1,860 metres. The Major gripped the joy-stick convulsively and screamed in Romanian, "Deu! Deu! God! God!" and the good soldier Švejk, deftly operating the elevator, sang above the Alps, which they happened to be flying over:

I'll never wear that ring you gave me.
Lor' lummy, why ever not?
When I get back to my regiment
I'll load it in my gun.

The Major was praying out loud in Romanian and swearing horribly, while through the clear frosty air there rang out once more the clear voice of the good soldier Švejk:

I'll never wear that kerchief you gave me,
Lor' lummy, why ever not?
When I get back to my regiment,
I'll clean my rifle with it.
Lor' lummy, why ever not?

Beneath them there was lightning flash after lightning flash
and a storm raged.

The Major, his eyes wild with horror, stared blankly in front
of him and asked in a hoarse voice, "For God's sake, when is this
going to end?"

"It will end without any shadow of doubt," the good soldier
Švejk smilingly replied. "The Lieutenant and I always fell down
somewhere."

They were somewhere above Switzerland and were flying
south. "Only have patience, please, sir," said the good soldier
Švejk. "When our petrol runs out, we must fall down."

"Where are we?"

"Over water, please, sir. There's a lot of it. Probably we shall
fall into the sea."

Major Gregorescu fainted, wedging his fat belly into the
joy-stick, so that he was firmly ensconced in the metal construc-
tion.

And above the Mediterranean the good soldier Švejk sang:

Who wants to be something,
Must eat some dumpling.
Ein, zwei.
In the army they won't kill him,
Ein, zwei,
Because he ate dumpling,
Army dumpling,
Big as a soldier's head.
Ein, zwei.

And the good soldier Švejk went on singing above those vast expanses of sea at the height of a thousand metres.

Greneville is marching
Strolling through the Powder Tower. . . .

The sea air roused the major from his faint. He looked down at those frightful depths and seeing the sea, shouted, "Deu, Deu," and fainted again.

They flew into the night and flew on and on. Suddenly the good soldier Švejk shook the Major and said good-naturedly, "Humbly report, sir, we are flying down and somehow we're free-wheeling."

In a gliding flight the plane, which had run out of petrol, alighted in a palm grove in Tripoli in Africa.

And the good soldier Švejk, helping the Major out of the plane, saluted and said, "Humbly report, sir, everything is in order."

The good soldier Švejk had registered a world record when he flew over the Alps, Southern Europe, and the Mediterranean Sea and alighted in Africa.

The Major, seeing palms around him, gave Švejk two clouts over the head, which he accepted with a smile, for he had only done his duty when Lieutenant Herzig said to him, "Fly to hell!"

It is difficult to relate what happened afterwards, because it would be very disagreeable for the Ministry of War. They would certainly deny that an Austrian plane had fallen down in Tripoli, for it would confront us with a major international complication.

THE PARTY OF MODERATE
PROGRESS WITHIN THE
BOUNDS OF THE LAW

INTRODUCTION

One of the most curious episodes in the bizarre life of Jaroslav Hašek was his decision to found a political party of his own called "The Party of Moderate Progress within the Bounds of the Law", and to stand as its candidate for the Prague Royal Vineyards (Vinohrady) constituency at the Austro-Hungarian elections in 1911. His object was to find further ways of debunking the Monarchy, its institutions, and its social and political system. He was particularly disgusted by the "immoral" pacts which the parties had concluded with each other regardless of their principles and purely to advance their electoral interests. Not only did Hašek need to satisfy his innate love of exhibitionism, but he had another motive. A friend of his was in love with the daughter of the proprietor of the inn where the election meetings of the new party were to be held. By increasing the inn-keeper's custom they both hoped to persuade him to look more favourably on his prospective son-in-law's suit.

Hašek's cynical and derisory attitude to politics had also been expressed earlier in a poem he had written and dedicated to "The Tortoise", the café-bar, which he happened to be patronizing at the time, and to Karel, its head waiter:

> *Education, gentlemen? The main thing's BEER!*
> *I like to go where there's plenty of cheer.*
> *Our nation's a church, where a candle flames.*
> *Velké Popovice * is one of its names.*
> *Long life to "The Tortoise". Let's get used to Karel.*
> *My politics, gentlemen, are — the barrel.*

* A famous brand of Prague beer.

One of the supporters of the new "Party" was the leading Czech playwright František Langer, who has left us an unrivalled description of one of its electoral meetings in his book They Were and It Used to Be.

Hašek as parliamentary candidate*
František Langer

ZVĚŘINA'S RESTAURANT HAS A BETTER CLAIM TO A COMMEMORA-
tive tablet than The Chalice and other taverns which were only of
incidental significance in Hašek's life. It lay in the very centre of the
Royal Vineyards (Vinohrady), behind the House of the Nation
(Národní dům), in the gardens of which band concerts were held in
the summer. Zvěřina's had the advantage that you could sit there
very comfortably and listen to the music without paying an
admission fee, and always find a seat there if the gardens were full.

Apart from that it had great attractions of its own. It was
bright and clean, and its cuisine was widely praised for the quality,
variety, and moderate price of its food. It was patronized by young
officials, old bachelors, families with relatives from the country,
sometimes wedding parties from the nearby Church of St. Lud-
mila, Yugoslav and sometimes even Czech students, when they
could afford a better meal than they got in their college refec-
tories. . . .

Zvěřina's served a very good lunch for 80 hellers to one
crown including sweet, and with portions of a size to satisfy any
glutton. In the evening it was frequented by many lovers of good

* From *Byli a bylo* (1963) with the permission of the Estate of František
Langer.

beer, of which Mr. Zvěřina was both a renowned connoisseur and consumer. His family boasted five daughters, three of whom were already grown-up, and with their help Mrs. Zvěřina managed the whole kitchen department. It was thanks to this that the cooking was always so dependable and the costs so low. The results of their worthy labours were reflected in the appetizing taste of the dishes and the very moderate prices.

The daughters were not allowed to go into the dining room, where a waiter looked after the service. The mother saw to it that they did not become an integral part of the traffic of the inn. They were very well-educated and pretty girls, lovers of literature and the theatre, and later good friends and, in some cases, patrons of the artists who were customers. Already at that time the dark-eyed Miss Boženka was being continually courted by the most orderly member of our group, Eda Drobílek, whom she later married. He was treated as a member of the family and formed a link between its fortunes and Hašek's circle.

After a time Zvěřina's moved, allegedly because of the rise of the rent, to The Cowshed Inn (Kravín) in what was formerly Coronation Avenue (now Avenue Wilhelm Pieck), also in the Royal Vineyards. This was a less favourable site, because there was rival competition at every corner. . . .

At first after the move Mr. Zvěřina did not do too well. He had to fight for custom against the superior forces of the inns in the immediate neighbourhood, his only weapons being his great experience in the business and his wife's culinary skill. At the very moment when he was going through these difficult initial stages, the writs were issued for the Royal Vineyards by-election. Elections were always a gold mine for innkeepers, as all the contesting political parties set up their electoral offices in different inns in almost every street. Various party leaders and sometimes even the candidate himself came there to make speeches, and the voters stayed there drinking beer and debating politics with party heat until the great day came when the votes were finally cast into the ballot box. These electoral bastions were chosen in the first place from among well-tried party members, and preference was given to such inns and restaurants as had a dance hall, a covered-in veranda, or large spaces in general for an expectedly copious crowd of voters.

Because Zvěřina took no interest in politics and his dining-room was only of moderate size, it was ignored at the elections by all parties. He must have looked enviously through the window at the streams of thirsty voters, who went every evening to the rival establishments just across the street, and sorrowfully calculated the takings by the noise they made as they left the political meeting at night.

I have already mentioned Eduard Drobílek as a link between us and the Zvěřina family. He was then almost thirty and, as an official in the office of the Rector of the Czech Technological College, had an assured existence. He had lively dark eyes, spare features, an angular nose, and fine thin hands. A voracious but discriminating reader, he was playful, witty, and full of ideas which he passed on to others without writing anything himself. Nor did he claim authorship of them, when he found them in his friends' humorous sketches. Further, he was probably the only one of us who was absolutely orderly, punctual, and systematic, so that he was able to organize and keep going whatever he initiated. Above all he had for every one of our group a friendly word, sympathy, and advice. He was wise and experienced and smoothed out quarrels and squabbles. Nothing disturbed his equanimity and good humour. In short he was the good genius of the whole crowd and often its invisible *spiritus rector*. One should add that his partici-pation in Hašek's undertakings was limited to what went on within the walls of Zvěřina's restaurant and ceased on his leaving its doors, whereas Hašek and his other boon companions made pilgrimages to other establishments which stayed open later. But just because of that restriction and because of his loyalty to Zvěřina's, one of his ideas laid the foundations for the most glorious epoch of the life of Hašek and all his boon companions as well as of Mr. Zvěřina's inn.

And so that is how it came about that in these difficult electoral times Drobílek was anxious to help Zvěřina's new restau-rant increase its takings and came forward with the suggestion that, if none of the established political parties would make Zvěřina's their base, we should reverse the process and organize a special political party to help his business.

I was invited to attend what they called an "embryonic" meeting to discuss the plan, but unfortunately arrived too late. I ran into the poet, Josef Mach, at the door, but only when we were both coming to attend the second meeting, and so I do not know whether the Party of Moderate Progress within the Bounds of the Law had existed for years and was only now roused to new life and new aims (as someone maintained) or whether it had come into existence only at this moment and for these elections. This was probably discussed and debated already at the first meeting. Mach always asserted, and even wrote, that it had been only just set up, but he could hardly have had any definite information since he only entered its life at the same time as I did and through the same door. But the preparatory committee commissioned him at once to write a hymn for the Party and he did so on the spot with only slight interventions from the other members. It started as follows:

> A million candidates rose up
> To hoodwink honest people.
> The electorate would give them votes
> And they would gladly take them.
> Let others call for violent progress,
> By force world order overturn.
> Moderate progress is our aim
> And Jaroslav Hašek is our man.

Armed with this hymn, which quickly spread over the Czech lands, the Party of Moderate Progress within the Bounds of the Law (for brevity I shall now call it only "The Party of Moderate Progress") began to acquire a more distinct shape. Further consultative evenings helped the process. Hašek's candidature was accepted as a matter of course, and it was organizational and ideological matters of all kinds which were always gone through late into the night.

It was for example resolved that anyone who liked could sit on the Central Committee, and that the number of its members was limited only by the capacity of two tables knocked together in the middle of the dining-room. . . . *

The preparatory committee had already determined the Party's electoral strategy, which was that at every meeting Hašek would make his electoral address with interruptions, questions, discussion, and free proposals. Before the meeting terminated, a collection would be held for the secret electoral fund, and at the end there would follow a free entertainment for the voters. Drobílek and Khun were detailed to design posters with Party slogans and stick them on the windows.

You can say what you like against the Austro-Hungarian Monarchy, but this electoral campaign was organized and passed off magnificently smoothly. There was no limit on the number of parties participating in the election, except that each party must register the name of its candidate with the authorities. . . so that the votes cast for him should be duly noted and officially counted. Electioneering meetings required no permission and did not have to be reported, even to the police, and no police were sent to them and there was no ostensible surveillance, except for a detective in plain clothes. Moreover, faithful to our anarchist principles, we had completely ignored the authorities, even in the most important matter of all, that of the official registration of Hašek's candidature, but even so the police did not interfere with our meetings. And so we calmly stuck up posters on the windows, announcing that here were the electioneering offices of the Party of Moderate Progress and that on Sunday evening at eight p.m. our candidate, Jaroslav Hašek, would present himself to the politically conscious voters of the Royal Vineyards and its surroundings and expound to them the program of our party.

On Sunday evening the inn was full. A lot of our friends came — artists, journalists, and bohemians — but respectable citizens

---

* Drobílek was their *rapporteur* and among the other members of the Central Committee were Langer, Mach, and Lada (later to be the illustrator of *Švejk*).

from the neighbouring streets as well. They were attracted by Hašek's fame or the name of the unknown political party. An hour before the start, Hašek arrived, clean and sober, together with the whole Central Committee. On the stroke of eight the Committee solemnly struck up the hymn "A Million Candidates Rose Up", and afterwards Dr. Grünberger declared the meeting open according to all the formalities, as he was the only one of us who knew them, and with considerable panache presented the candidate to the electors.

Then Hašek went into action. He portrayed himself in the most favourable light as the most suitable candidate for the seat and for the subsistence allowance which went with it. He outlined his program, which contained a whole heap of promises and reforms, abused the other parties, and expressed his suspicions of the rival candidates — in fact said everything that would be expected of a normal contestant for such office. Dr. Grünberger, who conducted the meeting, occasionally suspended it for five to ten minutes, so that the speaker could go and relieve himself and the waiter bring another round of beer. With these intervals and the time taken up in answering questions and objections, Hašek spoke for a good three hours.

Then, according to the program, a hat was passed round for a collection for the Party funds, and it was chiefly coppers which were thrown into it, I suppose because the voters had not yet begun to take us seriously. Finally came the time for "free entertainment". The Committee shared out the electoral funds and gambled with the proceeds. The guests at the tables stayed until far into the night. Zvěřina was satisfied and Drobílek likewise, since the inn's sale of liquor was greatly helped.

The news of Hašek's candidature spread all over Prague and we had a full house every evening. We even had to borrow from neighbours in the house more chairs for the visitors. One by one the whole of the artistic and café life of Prague came along: Bass, Lada, Brunner, old Anarchist comrades, as well as accepted politicians like Dyk and the Šmeral brothers. They had there and then to listen to many of Hašek's innuendos and accusations of graft and thieving, and to defend and clear themselves before our public. Posters stuck on the windows before each meeting announced how our Party was growing by thousands and what Hašek would speak about that evening.

He, of course, never stuck to the program but said just what came into his head. Sometimes he kept tolerably well to a certain theme. At other times he skipped from one subject to another. Sometimes it was brand new, at other times he repeated what he had had success with before or had already alluded to in one of his stories. In general we listened to speeches about various saints, the fight against alcoholism, the genuineness of the Old Czech Manuscripts,* the usefulness of missionaries and other features of contemporary society. He pillaried abuses, supported or tolerated by the State, like the obligatory fee of twenty hellers charged by concierges for opening the house doors at night, as well as the charge for admission to public lavatories and the fining of poor citizens for using an even more public place, when they had no money to pay such charges and only did what they did because they were obliged to do so in the interest of their health. He thought up grandiose promises, with which he tempted voters of the most diverse occupations and conflicting interests. He hinted darkly that the next evening there would be frightful revelations about the rival candidates, whom he would accuse of various crimes such as having murdered their grandmothers.

With the help of Drobílek and ourselves, who played up to him, his address was sometimes enlivened with a dramatic interlude as, for example, when he elaborated that part of the program of the Party in which it promised to relieve rate-payers by doing its utmost to abolish the twenty hellers paid to concierges. This was received with enthusiastic applause. But so as not to lose the votes

---

* A cause célèbre at the time. Early in the nineteenth century the archivist of the Czech National Museum in Prague claimed to have found two manuscripts which threw a new and flattering light on early Czech history. Most Czechs finally accepted them as genuine but with time T. G. Masaryk successfully exposed them as forgeries.

of the concierges he hastily added that this part of the program was not directed against them; on the contrary, their interests were neglected by all parties and he would take them in hand and ensure that they became State employees with rights of promotion and pension. He asked those voters in his audience, who were themselves concierges, to speak up and give their views on the matter. But no one spoke up, because there were in fact no concierges present. Hašek then proposed the appointment of a commission which should go from house to house, ring at the doors and, when the concierges came to answer the bell, bring some of them to the meeting. This was agreed to and the meeting was suspended until the Commission finally brought in two concierges, just as they were, in shirt sleeves and slippers. They had been tempted by the promise of a few free glasses of beer, to be paid out of the electoral funds. To the delight of the audience Hašek got the concierges to talk about the trials they had to undergo at the hands of the tenants, and let them go with the promise that, when he had been elected, he would see that they would be able to attain inspector's rank.

Sometimes such interludes were fairly short; at other times they were longer. Thus, Hašek once recounted how the government tried to "buy" deputies, but they would not succeed in doing so in his case, he said, because thanks to the generosity of the editorial offices, he always had enough money. Then a voice was heard "from the back row" asking Hašek in that case to return the crown he owed him. Hašek immediately let fly at the interrupter, saying that the Crown must not be drawn into our debates. (To help younger readers understand I should explain that in political jargon the "Crown" meant the crowned Head of State and his family, and their non-involvement in parliamentary debates was always observed by the deputies.) "On the one hand," continued Hašek, "we are supposed to be a party within the bounds of the law and on the other hand there by the door" — and he pointed with his finger — "sits a questionable individual who is known throughout the whole of Prague to be a member of the secret police." The unfortunate man at the door, an entirely harmless neighbour, began to protest and to call witnesses. Hašek, however, started to enumerate the various acts of provocation which he had been caught committing. In the end, however, he took a closer look at him, asking him to stand up, and then begged his pardon, saying that the real police agent he was thinking of was in fact taller than him by two heads. He even invited him to come to the president's table and drink a toast of friendship with him in order to restore calm among the public, who a moment before had been prepared to tear the alleged police informer to pieces.

Hašek's electoral speeches were the most voluminous and the most consistent humorous works of his that I had known before the publication of Švejk, nor did they in other respects fall short of the chief work of his life. They caricatured the hackneyed style, generated by the then political profession of party canvassers, speakers, journalists, and self-styled representatives and spokesmen of the Czech people. Hašek knew how to make literal use of it, guy it, and imitate it to perfection. He had at his finger-tips the complete jargon and slang of posters, the banalities of leaflets and leading articles, together with the bombast and sentimentality of slogans and proclamations. He spouted out whole cascades of this stuff, interpolating them into his address, whether they suited it or not. In addition he thought up false quotations and sayings, which he attributed to various authorities. In the fashion of speakers he was impassioned, enthusiastic, or emotional, but in the wrong places of course. . . .

In the stream of his oratory Hašek produced strings of long sentences, heaps of empty and muddled clauses, which with their rhythm and change of intonation resembled the complex sentences with which speakers lead up to some very important and emphatic conclusion, which should sound like a program or a manifestation and of course be extremely radical. With Hašek all this headed for something which, in its comic and grotesque way, was a piece of unexpectedly colossal nonsense. Often he either knew about it already in advance or invented it in the course of his speech. Even more often he just prayed that something would occur to him at the last moment for this climax and save him from a complete mess-up. When we saw that he had got so mixed up that he was already losing hope of disentangling himself, we helped him by shouting out an interruption or a protest. One only needed to shout "Oh!" or "Shame!" and Hašek at once turned on the interrupter, tore him to pieces, and when, after a digression like this, his audience had forgotten about his unfinished sentence, he immediately set about starting a new one, ten minutes in length.

Many times regrets were expressed that no one ever took down in shorthand these glorious speeches of Hašek's and so preserved them. But even if that had been done, they could not have had a fraction of the effect they made in the heat of their improvisation. For the reader there would have been long and barren passages, which to the listeners did not seem at all long and barren, because they listened to them in the benevolent anticipation that their diaphragms would very soon be titillated by some juicy mouthful. Moreover the reader would not have shared in that collective feeling, which was produced by a combination of listening and seeing and which filled the whole smoke-laden hall; nor would they have been influenced by the receptiveness of listeners well-disposed to the speaker. The core of them were his friends and admirers from the whole of Prague, who voluntarily, gladly, and enthusiastically took part with him in the absurd play at elections, and for whom elections in general meant a ridiculous game. Both afforded Hašek's speeches a sounding-board, which would not have had the same resonance in any written account.

And similarly readers would not have had before them the visible figure of the chief actor in this play, because in Hašek, as we knew him, there was a substantial element of the actor. In these speeches, at every communal session, during the telling of his adventures, wherever he had listeners beside him, even in his every action and very often even in his life-style, Hašek played as a soloist on the stage, who seeks and needs approval and applause.

At The Cowshed Inn the voters saw before them someone who was almost a cabaret candidate. He acted his address with winks at the audience and a foxy smile on his rubicund face. He parried every successful reaction from the audience and supported it with a still broader smile, and he was visibly happy if he could set off a regular salvo of uninhibited laughter. Generally he let it subside and used the moment to refresh himself with a sizeable draught. At other times he assumed the deadly earnestness of a political orator and in a heightened tone made pronouncements about utterly unimportant things, accompanying his words with a fanatical beating on the table, exaggerated gestures, and a challenging and stern stare at the audience. He seemed to be asking whether anyone would dare to express an objection, as though he had just pronounced the most radical truth or announced the greatest discovery. He exploited fully all the advantages of an attested humorist and so had no inhibitions, but allowed himself sufficient time and build-up, which instead of causing boredom, transformed itself into a tense anticipation on the part of the public of what the speaker intended with it and what would eventually come out of it. He liked to act and liked to play tricks and it was obvious that performing this role gave him the fullest enjoyment. When he began to speak, he went on for an hour or two and it was difficult to stop him, so as to pass on to the next part of the program of the meeting. A reader of the account of the proceedings, who would not have the live Hašek before him in his role of popular tribune, would have been deprived beforehand of the main spearhead of the wit of his "Cowshed" speeches.

The Royal Vineyards campaign culminated on the last day, the Sunday, when the voters dispersed all over the streets in the direction of the ballot box. Drobílek rewrote the posters in the window hour by hour, on which the number of votes cast for Hašek up to that moment rose to dizzy heights, and promises were made of a free electoral snack and beer for any new voters. In the afternoon, while the official counting of votes had only just started, we announced on the windows of the inn that our candidate and the Party of Moderate Progress were definitely the victors. Then impassioned voters from other parties began to crowd in front of our electoral offices and stormily urge us to take down the posters. The announcement of such an imposing number of votes for Hašek was regarded by them as a provocation. Finally a policeman came to ask us in quite a friendly way to remove the posters "in the interest of public order". Hašek promised this friendly policeman that for his conciliatory conduct during the elections he would at once at the first session of the Diet see to it that he was promoted police sergeant, which utterly confused the poor man.

That day our Party's committee sat in plenary session from lunch onwards. Towards the evening it transpired that the coalition had won — I think it was the National Socialists and Young Czechs. The Social Democrats with their candidate, Škatula, obtained quite a decent number of votes for that bourgeois quarter of the city, whereas the poet Viktor Dyk, a radical, got altogether only about a hundred votes. Twenty valid voting papers with Hašek's name were cast into the box, but to them we added another ninety of one sort or another, the so-called split votes, which for some formal reason were not assigned to any candidate. And so in this way we presented the improved success of our Party as something stupendous, and our friends, the press reporters, announced it in such terms in the newspapers.

After the announcement of the results of the voting, which the victors celebrated on the streets with speeches, the singing of patriotic hymns and processions to their electioneering inns, the Party of Moderate Progress enjoyed the honour of having all the defeated candidates gathered together in their Party premises in the evening. Each one spoke a few words of farewell. Škatula had a reconciliation with Hašek and they sealed it with a kiss. Dyk made a speech full of aphorisms about the army, the muses, and an electoral Thermopylae. He was proud, he said, to fall and lie beside such glorious dead as, for example, our candidate. Hašek took up the idea of the fallen at Thermopylae and, after his speech, solemnly lay down on the dirty floor. Dyk, although his rotundity made this difficult, self-sacrificingly enacted his metaphor and joined Hašek in that position.

And this was how we bid farewell to the electoral campaign, the climax to the activity of the Party of Moderate Progress within the Bounds of the Law, and as magnificent a practical joke as the heart could desire! With the end of the elections the freedom of assembly, granted under the Imperial and Royal electoral laws, came to an end too, and we were only allowed to meet again as ordinary beer-drinking private persons. This could of course again threaten the turnover of Zvěřina's restaurant.

Then Drobílek intervened once more and refused to allow the enormously increased popularity of Hašek's party to be wasted. He came forward with the idea that as a continuation of its hitherto so beneficial activity the Party should form a cabaret. . . .

THE HISTORY OF THE PARTY

Langer tells us that, after the elections were over, the Party treasurer, Drobílek, refused to allow the "enormously increased popularity of the Party to be wasted". No doubt with his encouragement, Hašek started to write what he called "The Political and Social History of the Party of Moderate Progress within the Bounds of the Law" and completed it in 1911. It has never been traced in its entirety, but seems to have consisted of (1) the Party records, (2) the "apostolic activity" of three of its members, as recorded in the letters of two of them to the "executive committee", (3) the Party's attempts to investigate so-called "scandals", and (4) its electoral activities.

After many adventurous experiences the greater part of the manuscript was traced, placed in the Czechoslovak National Museum (!) in 1963, and published for the first time in that year.

The work, with its pretentious title, consisted of little more than a string of articles ridiculing the activities of the various political parties of the time, satirizing their leaders and parodying their speeches. The humour of most of these can only be appreciated by those with an intimate knowledge of the political conditions in Bohemia at the time. Into this gallimaufry Hašek threw for good measure some humorous personal sketches of his friends and drinking companions, including even his brothers-in-law. Since some of them were highly libellous, if not scurrilous, they obviously could not be published when they were written, and were lucky to survive at all, in view of Hašek's known carelessness in the handling of his manuscripts.

Some of the profiles of the Party members took the form of mock eulogies, the subjects being treated as outstanding members of society and especially of the Party. The totally unimportant Drobílek, for instance, is portrayed as the noblest of men but unlucky in love.

An electoral speech

LADIES AND GENTLEMEN, FUTURE CONSTITUENTS:
...No sooner had I been accorded the honour of adoption as candidate for the Party of Moderate Progress within the Bounds of the Law for the seat of a Deputy for the Kingdom and Lands represented in the Imperial Council than I became at once the victim of a slander campaign... for the opposing side has said of me that I have already been gaoled twice.

My honourable constituents, I declare before you that this is a vile invention and a dirty lie. It is quite untrue that I have been gaoled twice. I have been gaoled three times! And only as a result of prosecution by the police and each time of course when I was totally innocent, like last year for instance, during the autumn demonstrations, when after arresting me they found on me some fragments of granite from the middle reaches of the Vltava and some pieces of pink and blue marble from Slivenec, which I found by pure chance on the street and carried off for my mineral collection. But of course a police official, who hadn't the foggiest idea about mineralogy, thought they were bits of Prague paving stones for throwing at the police! The fact that a piece of brick happened to have found its way in among these minerals was, as I explained, solely due to an error of mine, because in the press of the crowd around me, when I picked it up to save it from being trampled on, I took it for limestone tuff. Another time, although equally innocent, I was sentenced for interfering in official business when all I had done was to advise a policeman, who had just arrested a citizen on the street for committing a nuisance there, to deal with him extremely severely. In this case the police commissioner acknowledged that I had probably acted in good faith, but said that the policeman in question had no need of my advice, and so I was sentenced to a fine of six crowns and, in case of irrecoverability, to one day's imprisonment — which I accepted as more advantageous for a Czech writer, who gets paid for the number of lines he writes. Finally I was sentenced a third time for an article written in *Youth*, the organ of the movement of Czech-speaking theoretical anarchists, and here again I was completely innocent because the article in question was confiscated by the censor and so my friend, the editor, paid me no fee for it.

My friends, that is all there is to it. And, just because of this, is it fair that I should be written off as a degenerate, incapable of looking after the interests of his constituents? My friends, please give this your most careful thought.

Ladies and gentlemen, future constituents. . . .

If we pass from concierges to sextons, we can frankly state that we are now dealing with representatives of religion, whom — be they Mohammedans, Buddhists, or Fetishists of the tribe of Nyam-Nyam around the river Tul in Portuguese Africa — we hold in proper esteem according to the spirit of the statutes of our Party, paragraph 3, point 7. Statistics teach us — and I always go by official statistics, because they are very carefully compounded and, even if they are false, we have no others — statistics, I say, teach us, ladies and gentlemen, that in Prague and its surroundings there are 58 sextons of which 1.3 come under the electoral district of the Royal Vineyards if we include the husband of the charwoman who cleans the chapel in King George's Square. But, not included among those 58 sextons is the sexton of the Church of St. Alfonso, who has been arrested on suspicion of having stolen the church offertories and has thus spoiled the statistical picture. Well, my dear friends, you will certainly be asking yourselves, what use to us are those 1.3 sextons who come under our district? But, my dear friends, I tell you that if you're having any doubts, you are making a mistake, and I shall endeavour to correct you. You must understand that those 1.3 sextons mean 800 votes for our candidate.

You see, sextons have free access to the funeral offices and consequently to the lists of dead voters. These lists, as has been shown in the past successes of the National Freethinking Party (and I sincerely hope that this will be their last), can acquire exceptional importance on polling day. When the electoral campaign is in full swing and is well organized and, of course, generously financed as well, then a dead voter, like one from the 10th electoral district of the Royal Vineyards, knows very well what his duty will be on June 13th, and if the sextons coming under our electoral district are members of our Party, that dead voter will cast his voting paper into the ballot box with my name on it, even if he is unable to walk and has to have himself brought by cab to the ballot box. Incidentally, all the cabs are already hired in advance for June 13th by the candidate of the immoral Young Czech-National Socialist bloc. Now, not even I can say anything good about this bloc, which is no doubt the most appropriate way for me to characterize it.

Our slogan is: "Sextons of the whole of Prague, close ranks and support us in our electoral contest, and you will most certainly be incorporated into a higher grade, as soon as we implement that most important point in our program — the nationalization of concierges and sextons." And at the same time we shall repel the immoral attack of the bloc, which was directed at us, when its top canvasser, Mr. Novák of Charles Street, was sent yesterday to Mr. Fuchs, the undertaker in Rye Street, to find out which voters from the 10th electoral district of the Royal Vineyards have had coffins delivered to them most recently, and to obtain the precious list of their names.

My dear constituents, as far as I can remember, since the time of the coronation of Ferdinand V the Benign, who was the last monarch to be crowned King of Bohemia, Prague has never witnessed such enthusiasm as at these elections, when once more the principles of moderate progress within the bounds of the law begin to sway the whole Czech people as they did on that memorable day in 1835. "We are against violence, and so we withdraw before it," say I, just like Dr. Kalabis when he fell down the steps of the House of the Nation while the police were dispersing his meeting and pushing his supporters out of the hall into the corridor. All the same, I would not like anyone to have any doubts about our enthusiasm and peaceful disposition just because yesterday I happened to break the jaw of a man who insulted me, and because I said that by moral superiority alone I would not be able to achieve anything.

[At the table of the "old medicos" cries are heard once more of "Hašek, the innkeeper has just announced that he's not going to serve any more rounds!"]

Friends, we are where we did not want to be, as the man said when he wanted to go to Budějovice and got into a train going in the opposite direction. He was caught by the Inspector for occupying a second-class seat, when he only had a third-class ticket, and was thrown off the train at Bakov. Because one of the first precursors of our Party, Mr. Galileo Galilei, said as I do, "But, all the same, it goes round," Miss Boženka, please serve one more round: three more beers for me, two beers and one cognac for Mach, two beers and one allasch for Opočenský, a quarter of a litre of white wine for Langer, a beer and a magador for Diviš, and a soda water for Gottwald. So Galileo's words "it goes round" are proved true, and it is also abundantly clear that the Party of Moderate Progress knows how to defend itself and looks after the interests of its voters.

After this digression, ladies and gentlemen, let us return to our theme and devote a few agreeable moments to abusing the opposing candidates.

Just today, at the beginning of the meeting here, the poet Louis Křikava, who not only has the same name as the police director and government counsellor, Křikava, but is in confidential touch with him, gave the executive committee of our Party a piece of information which we gave our word of honour to keep strictly secret. According to this, which is strictly confidential and known to only about three people in Prague, at two p.m. yesterday the

Young Czech candidate, Dr. Funk, knocked at the gates of the Convent of the Barnabites next door to the Schwarzenberg Palace, allegedly only in order to persuade the Mother Superior of that order to influence the votes of the clergy and the electors of his constituency. He did this in spite of the fact that, as a freethinking Young Czech candidate, he must have been aware of the church regulation forbidding Barnabites to have any contact with a man, especially at two p.m. in the afternoon. But Dr. Funk did more than that: he was guilty of an electoral fraud, when he burst into the cosy sanctuary of these innocent ladies: in other words, he went in person — as we have with certainty established — and asked if the Barnabites would pray two hours every morning and afternoon for the victory of Mr. Choc and himself. My dear friends, that is a dirty form of competition. I can tell you that we have an offer from the nuns of St. Ursula and from the Rabbi of the Maizl synagogue to pray for me and my victory in return for a trifling payment, but, honourable constituents, we do not intend to be so moderately progressive in this electoral contest as to rely on God's help. In this case we could hardly rely on it anyhow. Let our enemies play around with that sort of thing, if they like!

My dear constituents, I know similar and even far worse things about the candidates Viktor Dyk and F.V. Krejčí, not to mention the fact that they regard the job of a deputy as nothing more than a quicker way of making a living than by writing, in which they have conspicuously failed. I could say all I know about the widowed sister-in-law's half-sister of Mr. Dyk's cousin on his mother's side and about a widow in Satalice who is related to Mr. Krejčí. But even in an electoral campaign I have some regard for the proprieties and shall therefore wait to say it until next time. As for the candidate of the immoral bloc, I have a confidential meeting with Mr. Choc today at four o'clock, and if I don't force him to resign then don't let us mince matters but "let the truth come out" to quote the headline of *Time*. Yes, everything has its "time".

Today, my dear friends, if I am to recapitulate the statistical data you have already heard me quote, then we must tell ourselves that figures cannot lie. Our principles are such that every politically conscious voter must be guided by them, whatever party he decides to vote for, even if it should be for the parties of the bloc which have conspired together to dig a grave for us, into which they themselves are going to fall. And these principles, my dear friends and voters — whether we look at them from the point of view of the nation, the minorities, social justice, trade, or religion — these principles, I say, cry out to you in the name of moderate progress within the bounds of the law, so that it must be clear, even to every idiot, that there is only one thing to be said and that is — "Elect me!"

Lecture on the rehabilitation of animals

LADIES AND GENTLEMEN, MY FRIENDS, CZECHS AND FELLOW-countrymen: It is indeed a remarkable phenomenon that there should be a party in Bohemia which has had the courage to come forward with a new program, one paragraph of which runs as follows: "Animals, be rehabilitated at last!" Thanks to the way animals have been regarded up to now, every one of them has undeservedly acquired an exceptionally bad reputation.

Take for example, the pig. From time immemorial pigs have enjoyed the reputation of being swine. When people said, "You're a swine," it meant "You're a pig" and vice versa. Indeed there have even been whole peoples who have boycotted pigs. Take the Jews for instance. Moses tried to prove that by eating pork people could contract venereal disease. And so in the time of Moses many Jews pleaded this in excuse for their treatment of pigs. Only under the influence of Christianity, which abolished all the Jewish laws, did the use of pork spread to such an extent that in the end the Catholic Church even introduced pork feasts, to show that Moses was not speaking the truth.

All the same, the pig is still generally regarded as something unclean, because it wallows in mud, which is after all only what

* In Czech animals' names are used as a common form of abuse. To call anyone an ox, cattle, or cow is even more insulting in Czech than it sounds in English.

balneologists recommend for human beings. Take for instance the spa at Piešťany and its mud. Even the aristocracy wallows in it for the good of their health, yet it probably wouldn't occur to anyone to call any aristocrat a pig. Nor is Dr. Kučera, who recommends this type of cure, a swine. None the less, pigs, who have given such a glowing example to suffering humanity, are still despised and their name serves especially now in election time as a term of abuse, by which an opponent seeks to characterize his enemy as a dishonourable creature. But, ladies and gentlemen, have you ever seen a dishonourable pig? Doesn't a scalded pig in the window of a butcher's shop seem to you to be a creature of noble character, when even after death it smiles at those people who are going to eat it? I should like to know what you would do, if you were in its place.

And, as it is with pigs, so it is with all animals, which serve people for the benefit of all humankind and parliamentary candidates as words of abuse. Those of you who frequently attend election meetings at this time must certainly have heard the exclamation: "Shut up, you stupid ox!" This again discredits a certain species of animals, by which term I do not mean the parliamentary candidates. I would just like to mention the fact that it actually redounds to the credit of that parliamentary candidate to whom it is addressed, because an ox like that has much greater value than a parliamentary candidate. It weighs 700 kilos, while a parliamentary candidate hardly weighs as much as 80, and when you sell an ox you get 400 crowns for it, while for a parliamentary candidate you won't get a single guilder.

I've also heard that at a political meeting a man shouted at a candidate "You hound." If this happened to me, I should thank that man for honouring me with the name of a dog, which is the noblest of creatures and I would promise to follow in the footsteps of that animal and "retrieve" from Vienna the electorate's demands. The only thing the public seems to be able to do is systematically to insult animals, calling the humble and faithful dog by the names of various monarchs. A milkman's dog, which patiently and devotedly draws a cart with provisions, is called

Nero. A little toy dog, like a Yorkshire Terrier, which has never injured anyone, and is never tyrannical to anybody, is called Caesar.

People talk of dogs with the greatest contempt, just because their name is used as a term of abuse for human beings. And yet we see that dogs under the name of police dogs perform today yeoman service for the safety of all humanity. It would therefore be only right for animals to be rehabilitated, at least as far as concerns these wisest representatives of the the whole animal kingdom. It would be a good thing if those who insult police dogs were prosecuted for insulting official personages. Let us all in future do our best to see that animals are looked upon as beings which deserve the respect of every political party, and that their names are not used by them for unwarranted agitation in the electoral campaign.

The Party treasurer, Eduard Drobílek

NONE OF ALL THOSE WRITERS WHO BELONGED TO OUR CIRCLE, I must, alas, say, were worth as much as that one simple man of the people, Eduard Drobílek. He had had a very chequered past. Having lost his parents when he was very young — which is always inseparable from a chequered past, whenever a writer with an illustrious name like mine begins to write the biography of an outstanding man — he was left completely alone in the midst of life's vortex. And so he set out one fine day on foot to visit his uncle somewhere across the Elbe above Mělník. And what happened to him on his journey? Did any adventure befall him in the night darkness, which enveloped the valley of the Elbe, when that river, being in spate, roared and beat its waves against the banks (which it actually did not have, since at that time it had not yet been regulated)?

What befell Drobílek was that he met a gendarme.

"May I ask where you are going?" the gendarme asked Drobílek with that gentle sarcasm of which only gendarmes are capable when they meet a suspicious individual in the night hours. The gendarme took Drobílek for just such an individual and the latter answered with extreme politeness:

"May I ask where *you* are going, sir?"

"I'm going to Neratovice," the gendarme replied in some surprise.

"Now that's a coincidence. I'm just *coming* from Neratovice."

"Please then, could you tell me whether Sezemský's inn there is still open?" said the gendarme.

"So you're thinking of going to an inn?" said Drobílek. "Then you're failing to observe the decree of the Ministry of Defence, which enjoins on the gendarmerie of all people to be on their feet without rest day and night and to abjure all worldly delights, because it is just in such delights that there lurks the danger that they will not be able to carry out their duties properly. You have, for example, just asked me whether Sezemský's is open. You, sir, do not know who I am, and indeed I am beginning to suspect that you are no gendarme at all, but some rogue in disguise. Because, if you had been a real gendarme, you would certainly never have asked anyone on the road at night whether there was an inn open anywhere. Your first sacred duty was to ask to see my documents. And, if I did not have any, to arrest me and take me to the nearest gendarmerie station. And then you should have made a report, and, if it appeared that I was a rascal and good-for-nothing, then according to the decree you should have taken me off to the nearest district court, to be tried for the offence of vagabondage. I am going to lodge a complaint against you."

"But, your Honour. . . ."

"Don't 'Your Honour' me. I am now talking to you like a friend. Do you know the Minister of Defence?"

"No, I don't, your Honour."

"Well, all the worse for you. Are you aware of his last decree of May 12, 1901?"

"Pardon me, sir, no."

"Then you are unaware of that decree which lays down that when you meet a suspicious person in the night in your district and you don't know him, you have not only to ask him for his documents, but also to say: 'How much money have you got on you?' Then I would take out my purse and say, 'I have only two kreuzers', or correctly — according to the decree of the Ministry of May 3, 1900 — 'four hellers'. And don't you know that every one of us who travels in Austria must have at least four crowns fifty hellers on him? And since I have only got four hellers, I am four crowns and forty-six hellers short of the sum fixed by that decree, and you will have to lend me the money, even though I don't know you and only know that you have not carried out your duties properly and can be penalized for it."

"I've only got a five-crown piece on me," said the gendarme feebly.

"Then give it to me," said Drobílek. The gendarme looked in his purse and cried triumphantly, "I've got some change after all. By how much did you say you were short of that sum?"

"By four crowns, forty-six hellers." And by the light of his pocket torch he paid Drobílek the whole sum, and so Drobílek arrived at his uncle's with the gendarme's money. Since then people say that that gendarme, whose name is František Kohout, lends four crowns forty-six hellers to all suspicious looking chaps whom he meets on his round and that he has fallen so deeply in debt since the Party has existed that he is going to leave the gendarmerie as soon as possible and himself act the part of a suspicious individual at night.

By this act Drobílek won the affection of all members of the Party and in the next chapter it will be appropraite to tell how heroically he bore the loss of his fiancée in a restaurant.

Drobílek's amorous adventure

THERE ARE NOBLE NATURES IN THE WORLD WHO PERFORM THE passive role of the deceived — people who are doomed in the end to experience every kind of ingratitude. When it concerns the relations of such noble beings with the other sex, the view is often taken that it is just these noblest of all men whom women are most prone to deceive and who suffer the bitterest of disappointments in love. Thus Drobílek, who was always ready to make out a cheque for his friend, Josef Mach, was sometimes very unhappy in love.

He loved Baruška, a cook in the restaurant The Candle, a country wench, buxom and naive, and when he plucked up courage to tell her that he would like to go with her to the cinema, she replied, "You dirty pig! What do you take me for?" From that time on Drobílek felt great respect for Baruška, and whenever there was talk about women he always used to say that he knew only one decent and respectable girl and that was Baruška. She was the girl who some years later wrenched off the water tap in the flat of her employers when she was making the coffee, and when she could not stop the flow of water, jumped out of the third floor and killed herself. It's only nihilists in Russia who die like that.

After that Drobílek fell in love with a dressmaker. He lavished his favours on her to such an extent that in the goodness of his heart and in all honesty, without any bad motive, he invited her to go with him on an outing to the country and arrived at the appointed meeting place with a large package under his arm. "What are you carrying there?" the young lady asked with a charming smile, when they got on to the steamer to go to Závist. "Wait till we get to the forest, miss. There are too many people here," he answered, looking devotedly into her eyes. And when they at last reached the forest and sat down in a spot hidden from all human gaze, Drobílek snuggled up to his second love and said to her tenderly, "I have brought with me two pairs of pants, my love, and two shirts. I've got some thread as well. These pants are torn in the fork, and these shirts have holes in the elbow. Heart of gold, please mend them for me here." And turning round rapturously, he cried out, "Listen how beautifully the birds sing!" And as he told us about this, he always sighed and added, "And do you know what she called me? A vulgar brute! And before I could hand her those pants and shirts, she had gone. I can't imagine what that female thought, when I suggested we should go into the thicket together."

After that he looked on women with distrust for a long time, until finally he announced to us one day that the owner of a wine-tavern was in love with him, because he always spent a lot of money there. But when he stopped spending money, she stopped loving him and Drobílek then discovered that women were utterly worthless. And so he renounced the whole of womenkind until the time when he met the sweet little daughter of the innkeeper, where he used to go to have his lunch. "Strangely enough," Drobílek used to say, "that innkeeper has several daughters and I only love just that one. That is a very strange coincidence indeed. I must marry her, unless something comes between us." But somebody came between them and it was his friend, Förster. "Miss," said Förster one day to the girl Drobílek loved so much, "you must not marry Drobílek, because I love you myself. But if you don't want to marry even me, you would do best to run away from home."

The next day Drobílek celebrated his engagement with Miss Vilma. An hour after it Mr. Förster came along and had a long talk with her, in the course of which he explained that she would not be doing a good thing if she insisted on marrying Drobílek. For one thing she was still young, and for another he loved her himself, so that she would be acting in her best interests if, as he had told her the previous day, she ran away from home and gave up every-thing. . . . And if she would not give up Drobílek, he himself would force him to let her go and to make love to one of her sisters instead. And then he proposed that she should run away that very evening and spend the night in a hotel somewhere. And he said she should write to Drobílek and ask him to forgive her, and that it would be great fun if she did. And if she also wrote to him that she did not love him, that would be even more fun. "We are all curious to see what will happen then," he said. Then leaving her standing in the corridor, he called Drobílek, and told him that Miss Vilma wanted to speak to him alone about her future plans. And so Drobílek stood with Vilma in the corridor for half an hour, and when he came back he said, "That splendid girl is weeping with joy, because I told her that I already have the furniture on order and have arranged everything so that there will be three banns at one go." After that we celebrated Drobílek's engagement and Förster made a speech in which he said that it was true that an engagement was an important step into a new life, but no one should imagine that it was a final one. Then he embraced Drobílek tenderly and said, "Whatever misfortunes may befall you in your life, never forget that I am your best friend."

That very same night Vilma ran away.

When Drobílek came to lunch next day as usual, eagerly looking forward to the sweet which he enjoyed so much, the following scene met his eyes: in the bar sat Vilma's father with a glass of dark beer in his hand, and when he saw Drobílek he called out, "Mr. Drobílek, I am tearing my hair. There is nothing else I need say to you." In considerable astonishment Drobílek walked into the dining room and saw the innkeeper's wife sitting there in the back with a tear-stained face. And from the door of the kitchen there peered out the tearful faces of all five daughters, and a weeping waitress came up to him and said, "Poor Mr. Drobílek, don't you know what has happened? Vilma has run away."

"But you haven't brought me the sweet," exclaimed Drobílek in a panic. When the innkeeper's wife heard that, she wrung her hands and called out to her daughters, "Lord love us, Mr. Drobílek has gone mad." And then the innkeeper himself came up to Drobílek and gave him this letter, written in Miss Vilma's hand:

"Mr. Drobílek, dear Mr. Drobílek. I asked your pardon a thousand times for not loving you and running away. Your loving Vilma".

And while tears ran down Vilma's father's cheeks, Drobílek thrust the letter into his pocket and said anxiously, "But haven't you kept some sweet for me, sir?"

And at that moment Miss Božena came in, and her tears flowed down onto the huge portion of raspberry soufflé which she put before Drobílek, saying, "Poor Mr. Drobílek, you always used to like this. And, think of it, she ran away in the night." And Drobílek began to tuck into his soufflé with a blissful expression on his face. "Thank God," he said. "I was afraid you had forgotten to keep any sweet for me."

And, when the conversation turns on this episode, he always says, "I shall never again get such a huge portion of soufflé as I did that time my fiancée ran away. I really did enjoy it."

THE "APOSTOLIC" PILGRIMAGES OF
THE PARTY

An important branch of the Party's work was its "apostolic activity". Three of its members, the author Jaroslav Hašek, the painter Jaroslav Kubín, and the ballet dancer František Wágner, were sent out on an "apostolic" or "missionary" pilgrimage, the object of which appeared to be to make propaganda for the Party, but which generally involved them in scrapes and had the reverse effect.

In the following story Hašek explains how he came to meet the other members of the "pilgrimage".

The painter, Jaroslav Kubín

MY FRIEND, KUBÍN, WAS ANOTHER OF THOSE WHO STOOD AT the cradle of the Party of Moderate Progress within the Bounds of the Law. I met him for the first time in the gardens of Charles Square, Prague, just as I was studying a large map of Hungary. A young stranger, obviously in a merry mood, came up to me, seated himself beside me on the bench and said,

"Excuse me, sir, that's France, isn't it?"

"No, young man, it's Hungary."

"But I think you're mistaken," he went on. "They've cheated you at the bookshop. That sometimes happens, you know. They make a map of France, put Hungarian names on it and sell it as a map of Hungary."

From the style of his utterance I immediately perceived that it was a painter or someone in that line who was addressing me. At that very moment another young man went by, skipping in time. The stranger seized the astonished man by his arm, dragged him up to me and said, "My good friend, now you must give us the final judgement. Is this France or Hungary?" The newcomer blinked under his pince-nez and said, "It isn't either of them. It's Britain."

"Don't make fun of us, man," the young man who maintained that it was France exclaimed. "Sit down beside us, so that we can enlighten you."

The newcomer began to stammer out something, but he was already sitting beside us, his eyes blinking and his left and right legs beating out the time.

"Well, now," said the newcomer, "a chap never knows when he will be offered a chance of learning something. You should know that this map is in fact neither France, Britain, nor Hungary, but Turkey." And suddenly his face assumed a meancing appearance and he shouted out, "But this is montrous. You sit down here and you don't even introduce yourselves."

And so we all made each other's acquaintances. The first stranger said with dignity, "I am Jaroslav Kubín, Academic Painter." And then the second, "And I am František Wágner, member of the ballet of the Royal Czech Provincial National Theatre in Prague."

That same day I brought them to The Golden Litre, where they became members of the Party. With us the admission of new members was arranged without any formality, except that each new member had to make a speech on a theme which we had decided for him. It was a kind of preparation for courses in public speaking. In addition it was the duty of each member to submit unconditionally to that task which was imposed on him by a general vote as a punishment for his misconduct. And it happened that evening that when Jaroslav Kubín and František Wágner were admitted, the member of the Prague ballet committed that tactless act of starting to fiddle with his nose just when the president was making his speech. As a result the disciplinary committee met at once for consultation in a neighbouring room.

"Who introduced him?" Mahen asked.

"Kubín and I," I answered.

They sent us off to the unhappy Wágner, who could not understand all this and, after a quarter of an hour's lively debate, the president of the disciplinary committee, Mahen, read out the written verdict.

"In view of the unseemly conduct of František Wágner, he is sentenced as follows: he must leave by train for Jihlava tomorrow or the day after at the latest. Thereafter he is to go on foot across

Moravia, Lower Austria, Hungary, Croatia, Carniola, Styria, Upper Austria, and Bohemia and return in four months' time at eight p.m. on Saturday, October 7th of the same year, to our main organizational premises at The Golden Litre. At the same time Jaroslav Hašek and Jaroslav Kubín are invited to accompany him on his journey and to see that the task imposed on him is properly carried out. In the case of any lapse of his, the Executive Committee of the Party is to be immediately informed by telegram. At the same time the sum of forty crowns will be disbursed from club funds to the three persons concerned for expenses on their journey. They are all three instructed to propagate everywhere the program of the Party of Moderate Progress within the Bounds of the Law and every fifth day to send us a detailed report of their apostolic activity."

And punctually at eight p.m., on October 7th of the same year, all three of us reappeared at The Golden Litre, having walked through half of Central Europe.

That's discipline for you, gentlemen!

The apostolic activity of three members of the Party as reflected in the letters to the executive committee

Jihlava, the...

ACCOMPLISHING THE TASK IMPOSED ON US BY THE DISCIPLINARY committee, we report the following:

We came to fetch Mr. František Wágner at four o'clock in the morning and ordered him to dress at once for the journey to Hungary. I believe I am right in thinking that he regarded the whole affair as nothing more than a joke, and only when, after rubbing his eyes, he caught sight of the rucksacks on our backs, our short stockings, and other touristic equipment, did he become scared, and we can state on oath that he started to sob aloud. Only when we told him that he had no idea of what was in store for him, if he failed to obey the order of the disciplinary committee, would he allow himself to be persuaded to dress, and did so with an expression of unusual horror. Because he had obviously made no preparations for our missionary journey, he had to pack his clothes into a great basket, which weighed eight kilos. When he had weighed that basket, he fell on his knees before us and begged us in the name of the Lord to relieve him of the task imposed on him. We were inexorable however and found in his wardrobe long strips of dark green cloth, which this member of the ballet wraps round his legs when he dances in the roles of Sicilian brigands. We wound these strips round his thighs over his trousers, so that they looked like the tourist leggings of that unfortunate English traveller, Lord Everest, who was the first to climb the Himalayas.

Mr. František Wágner watched all these preparations with the rigid gaze of a wild boar from the jungle when fixed by the glare of a cobra. Then we placed before him a half sheet of paper for him to write the news of his sudden disappearance to his old aunt, with whom he was living. And we dictated the letter to him:

> Dear Aunt. Fate has ordained that I must travel round the world on foot. If I should perish on the journey, I shall immediately inform you. All my love. Your affectionate nephew, František.

We dragged him half dead out of his flat together with his heavy basket and in the nearest bar we pumped into him six glasses of slivovice, so that afterwards he was as meek as a lamb. At 6:20 a.m. we left by train for Jihlava by way of Kolín, Kutná Hora, and Německý Brod. At 5:32 p.m. we were in Jihlava, where we went to look for Mr. Bozděch, an official of the local branch of the Živno Bank.

František Wágner's behaviour was exemplary and in the evening of the same day we organized in the Czech club our first lecture on the Party of Moderate Progress within the Bounds of the Law and its attitude towards the Czech minorities. But hardly had the meeting opened, than the town commissioner and an official from the *hejtman's* office arrived and asked us kindly to come with them to the town hall. And so we went along with them and were subjected to a thorough interrogation there. They asked us about the aims of our party, and when Jaroslav Kubín declared that we intended to organize for the Czech minorities in the German towns lectures on the correct standpoint of the Germans in Bohemia, on Czech intolerance and expansionism and give a cycle of lectures on German literature, we were received very favourably and taken off to the German club. Here we were entertained until three o'clock in the morning and on the initiative of the deputy-mayor a collection was made among those present, the proceeds of which amounted to 112 crowns and were given to us as support for our journey. The deputy-mayor, Šafránek, gave us a bed for the night and next morning we went to see our friend Bozděch, who welcomed us with great joy and declared that, after we had been taken off to the town hall, the assembled members of the Czech minority had sent a telegraphic report to *The National* on the violence committed on three Czech tourists by the Pan-Germans of Jihlava. The second telegram had been sent to the Minister of Justice, asking him to prohibit the violence committed on the Czechs on the soil of the glorious Margraviate of Moravia.

If you read in *The National* of our tragic fate in Jihlava, you need not have any fears, because we are just leaving Mr. Šafránek and are taking with us a warm letter of recommendation to the German town council of Znojmo. It would hurt us deeply as Czechs if we had to touch the Czech minorities for money, and so we prefer instead to touch the German majority there.

Another letter from the missionary
pilgrimage

TO THE GLORIOUS EXECUTIVE COMMITTEE OF THE PARTY OF
Moderate Progress within the Bounds of the Law.

I feel constrained to lay before the Executive Committee this
very unhappy account of the treasonable conduct of František
Wágner. I expect that a telegram with instructions on what we are
to do with him will be sent immediately to our address: 7,
Mariahilferstrasse, Vienna. This is what happened:

We arrived safely at Znojmo with a letter of recommendation from
the German town council of Jihlava to the German municipal
authorities at Znojmo and handed it to the mayor himself. Let me
add that we said all the time, "*Jawohl, jawohl.*" The mayor of
Znojmo was president of the Association of German Tourists for
South-Western Moravia, *Provinz Westsüd-Mähren*. He wrote us out a
cheque for 100 crowns for our subsistence, which was paid to us
immediately by the treasurer of that association, when we kept on
repeating, "*Jawohl, jawohl.*"

As no one was controlling us, we went to the Czech club,
where Wágner sang about four popular hits and we made a
collection among the guests. It brought in enough to cover all our

expenses with twelve crowns to spare. Altogether our assets amounted to 142 crowns. According to our rules a different one of us acted as treasurer every third day. On this particular day, it was František Wágner's turn, and he, as was his custom, said, on taking over the money for safe-keeping, "I shan't spend one kreuzer unnecessarily."

Kubín wanted to go and have some wine, but Wágner said he would not allow it; he would not and indeed could not disburse the money for it, as his sacred duty enjoined him only to pay for what was necessary and never for any nonsense. He said that he looked upon himself as the custodian of that little hoard of ours.

I must point out that it was market-day in the town. The surroundings are very agricultural, as you are undoubtedly aware, for Znojmo cucumbers, onions, asparagus, tomatoes, and similar vegetables are staple items of Znojmo's export.

"Why does that fool write all that?" you will certainly be thinking, when you read these lines, which are more suitable for inclusion in a book of commercial geography.

Well, I write it simply because we were very much concerned with all those products and I still today have nightmares about unending heaps of tomatoes; I lie covered with onions, swim in Znojmo cucumbers, and bunches of asparagus rain down on my head. And beside me František Wágner is lying on his bed and howling like an old woman whose last grandson is just being hanged and she is left alone in the world. And Kubín is walking about the room and from time to time stands at František Wágner's bedside and hurls frightful abuses at his head.

Listen now to what that villain did to us. Already in Znojmo we were shouting that it would drive us crazy and now we are shouting about it here in Vienna.

It was that market-day. We took a room in a Czech hotel and bought tobacco for our short pipes. Wágner looked out of the window on to the square and exclaimed joyfully, "There certainly are pretty girls here."

I should perhaps mention that Wágner had already the day before suffered some unpleasantness as a result of his erotic behaviour. On the way to Znojmo he gave a peasant wench a spank and she kicked him in the stomach, so that he was sick for more than half an hour and then said: "But you must admit that she had a very generous bosom."

"Never mind the girls," I said to him with great wisdom, when he started jumping up and down at the window as soon as he caught sight of girls from the region in their folk costumes, whirling round the square near carts full of all kinds of vegetables — those damned vegetables. But he would not take any notice of what we said, and suddenly called out, "Why, that's a pretty girl," and rushed off.

We took no notice and went on lying on the bed and sofa.

An hour passed and there was no sign of him. Another hour went by and still he did not return. He vanished with our money like the town of Messina when it was swallowed up by the earth.

He had gone. Gone! What a frightful word, so horribly short and terrifyingly long as well.

We went to bed hungry without supper. Had he betrayed us, had he left us, or had some misadventure befallen him?

"I have a hope that he has been killed somewhere," Kubín said in the night. "God grant he has been, because then I won't have to shoot him myself for his treason."

"God grant indeed that he has been killed somewhere," I said, "so that we may preserve a pure memory of him."

Then we fell asleep.

He did not even come back that night.

I know that you are already clenching your fists and calling out, "Where is that villain? Hand him over to us!" As I have already said, he is at the present moment lying and tossing about on his bed in Vienna and howling like an old woman.

He did not condescend to come back until noon the next day. Of course we at once threw ourselves on him, but all he did was to weep and scream "Maryša!" But what he now related to us was worse than the whole tragedy of the Mrštík brothers.

First of all, when he ran away from us, he went down to to the square and got into conversation with a girl near a cart. He took a great fancy to her and learned that she came from Drahoňovice, which is two hours' walk from Znojmo.

And so he passed the time pleasantly with her and at the end of it said firmly and resolutely that he would be waiting for her at nine p.m. in front of her farm or wherever she pleased. So she then explained to him where their farm actually was and how to get to it, saying that it would be best if he waited at the back by the orchard.

He could just climb over the fence and the rest would. . . .

Wágner burst out crying. "And so I set out at once on that road and waited there a long time until her father found me in the garden. I have it here confirmed by him. And he took out of his pocket various scraps of paper on which were written in a terrible hand and rusty ink:

"Received from Mr. František Wágner a deposit of 20 crowns for cucumbers."

"Received from Mr. František Wágner a deposit of 20 crowns for small onions."

"Received from Mr. František Wágner a deposit of 20 crowns for tomatoes."

"Received from Mr. František Wágner a deposit of 20 crowns for asparagus."

And so it went on, one item after another. . . .

And between his sobs he added, "What was I to do, when he had caught me there? I had to say I wanted to buy some vegetables."

"How much have you got left, you scoundrel?"

"Ten crowns."

"What, only ten crowns?" shouted Kubín. "Down on your knees, and at once say The Lord's Prayer."

So Wágner got going on The Lord's Prayer, while Kubín went downstairs to a shop. When he came back, he threw at Wagner's feet a ball of twine and said, "Now, I hope you know what to do with that." To me he said, "Come along."

And so Kubín and I went to have a glass of beer and a full breakfast, and when we came back, tearing off the leaves of an acacia branch on our way and reckoning like a girl in love "he hanged himself, he didn't hang himself", and it always came out that he hanged himself, we found František Wágner sitting on the bed and winding the twine round his pants, which had slipped down. So that was the use to which that coward was putting our twine!

We did not let ten minutes pass without continually reproaching him for it. In the night we woke him up and shouted in his ear, "Villain, what have you done with our money?" Whereupon he growled out in his sleep the stock answer: "Carrots, gherkins, tomatoes, asparagus. . . . "

> I now ask the glorious Executive Committee of the Party of Moderate Progress within the Bounds of the Law what we are finally to do with František Wágner. Please telegraph reply.
>
> Jaroslav Hašek

Next morning a telegram arrived with the following brief message: "Sell him to Turkey as a eunuch."

And so Kubín and I decided that it would be best if we actually did take Wágner off to Turkey, and we should certainly have sold him to some brothel there if certain circumstances had not prevented us.

And who was it who suggested the contents of the telegram? Why, Louis Křikava, the poet.

The persecution of the first Christians in the Royal Vineyards

A MR. KOPEJTKO REGULARLY CAME TO OUR PARTY HEAD-
quarters. He was a very pious man and he showed very plainly his
utter contempt for us. You see, we were not exactly devout in the
way we talked about the dear good Lord and at his tenth glass of
beer Mr. Kopejtko considered it his sacred duty to defend his
Maker. And so we called him "the first Christian in the Royal
Vineyards".

Swathed in his Inverness cape, he arrived in a thoughtful and
resigned mood — just as the first Christians came to the ancient
Roman *osterie* when they were cram-full of Roman mercenaries.
And when, in this atmosphere of unfaith, he raised his beer glass, he
did it with a holy sublimity, as though he was raising the *ciborium* in
the catacombs at the time of St. Peter. The most pronounced sign
of his spiteful contempt for us was when on his way out he called
over to our table, "Well, God speed you!"

We tried several times to take his God away from him, but he
always shook his head in dull resignation and said, "You're wasting
your time. Say whatever you like. In the faith in which I was born I
shall live and die." Sometimes also he said: "In the faith in which I
was suckled. . . . "

By profession he was an undertaker, and maybe that affected
his pious turn of mind, although otherwise he never spoke about

those last rites with the appropriate measure of piety. He would say, for instance, "I had a devil of a job again until I had managed to stuff that old woman into her coffin today." Nor did his piety prevent him from being a passionate card player.

And so it happened that one Saturday when we were playing *vingt-et-un* he asked us if he might join in. At first he was in luck, because when the game started he made the sign of the cross. Then his luck turned and he lost every kreuzer of his week's wages. In a vague anticipation that, if he went on playing, he would win it all back again, he asked us to lend him five crowns, so that he could continue. And so he pitted those five crowns of ours against us.

"With all the pleasure in the world, dear friend," we told him, "but let us have your watch as a security, and make a declaration that you don't believe in the Lord God." There was exactly five crowns in the bank.

One of those great spiritual conflicts raged in Kopejtko's soul. He had the same expression on his face which those Christians must have had in the time of Nero, when they were hauled before that ruler and made to declare that they renounced their God.

"Never," he shouted.

"Then we'll play without you."

It was almost as if in Rome the ruler had shouted, "Toss him to the wild beasts!"

Kopejtko's face clearly showed his suffering. It was a dreadful and horrific struggle. Instead of the wild beasts in the Roman circus, his mind conjured up visions of his wife.

"Gentlemen," he said suddenly, handing his watch to us. "Very well then, I don't believe in God."

He was given his five crowns and when the cards were dealt to him again, he called out: "But all the same I do believe in God. I stake those five crowns."

He lost them all. Then he cried out, "I don't believe in the Lord God!" and borrowed ten crowns from the innkeeper on the security of his wedding ring. He lost them, shouting, "All the same, the Lord God still exists."

Then he handed over his overcoat, and in the end his wife came to fetch him away.

The following Sunday he went to the monastery of Svatá Hora to do penance and brought back a rosary for the innkeeper.

Persecution of the new Party by government circles

WHEN MR. KOPEJTKO RETURNED FROM SVATÁ HORA, HE WENT and denounced us to the police, stating that we played prohibited games and slandered the Lord God as well as the great ones of this world and the other one beyond the grave.

From then on Mr. Markup came to join our company. Who was he? He was a good man and an officer at police headquarters. He had a low salary and six children. At this time, when the clouds were gathering in Prague for the great storms over universal suffrage, people of his kind earned extra money by acting as informers to their superiors who in their turn passed the information on to the State police in Vienna. Moreover it happened just after the visit of His Imperial Majesty to Prague.

Mr. Markup was keen on adding to his income. Chateaubriand once said that the police are always romantic. And when Kopejtko on that occasion declared in the Security Department that he could not stand idly by while such things were being said in our tavern, they sent Mr. Markup to us. They did not worry about his being the father of six children.

When the Commissioner asked the pious Kopejtko, "And what sort of people are they?" he answered, "Your Honour, they're villains." And so the father of six children was sent among those villains. He came like a Roman legionary who had been sent to Britain to stand in the front rank on guard in the fog of that strange island.

And he imagined that no one would know him. But he was at once recognized by the Police Chief's nephew, who was one of our company and who said quite simply, when Mr. Markup left the first evening, "That's Markup."

What he told us about him was rather miserable: the man let himself have his face slapped, had six children, and for every slap got two crowns commission. In addition he got daily, or in fact nightly, subsistence allowances at the rate of five crowns a visit to the villains' den. Altogether they paid him 52 guilders a month.

The next evening Mr. Markup arrived earlier than we did and sat down at our table, looking very genial. When we appeared, he apologized and said he would move to another table. But we invited him to stay and said that his company would be most agreeable to us. We told him that we talked politics, but presumed that that would be no obstacle to him.

"So, it's all agreed?" my friend Mahen said to me in a low voice, but loud enough for Mr. Markup to hear.

"Yes, indeed," I said, "I'm making the final preparations."

"Do they know about it already in Moravia?" said Engineer Kún, leaning over towards us.

"Yes, Moravia already knows about everything," I said loudly.

Markup gave a start. "If you pardon me, I know Moravia," he said. "It's a country which always stands shoulder to shoulder with us Czechs."

"I think you are wrong there," I said.

"Pardon me, gentlemen," said Mr. Markup, "you must surely allow that at the Battle of the White Mountain the Moravians fell at the Star Hunting Lodge."

"That's news to us," declared Opočenský. "But, you know, that's something one must not talk about. You could get yourself badly involved. You might find yourself beginning to talk about the Emperor Ferdinand."

Mr. Markup smiled affably. "Don't you think, gentlemen, that the Emperor Ferdinand was an outstanding man?"

"He certainly was," I said solemnly. "A man who in 1620 could stamp on the neck of the hydra of revolt was definitely a most honourable man, especially when you consider that he belonged to the noble House of Habsburg."

"Well, but look," said Mr. Markup, "after all he did have all those Czech lords executed in the Old Town Square."

"Perhaps you regret that, sir?" I shouted out savagely. "Surely it was a very mild punishment for rebels who threw the King's Commissioners out of the windows of the Royal Castle, deposed their own king, called a foreigner to Bohemia and killed in battles more than 20,000 of their own king's troops. And you would defend such people? Are you a Czech, sir? Are you not ashamed of yourself? I'm sure that in a moment you'll start talking about the Hungarian Revolution of 1848, praising Kossuth and saying what a fine chap he was. And that's the blackguard who forged bank notes and stirred up all the Magyars from the *puszta* against the Habsburg dynasty, and, when he should have been hanged, ran away — the scoundrel! And now you calmly come here and begin to defend him, you praise the Hungarian Revolution and shout, 'Long Live the Revolution!'"

"But, gentlemen, I assure you I never said anything of the kind."

I got up. "These gentlemen here are my witnesses that you did. Didn't he say so, boys?"

"Yes, he certainly did," they all chimed in, "and much worse things too."

Then Mahen stood up. "Sir, you wormed your way into this respectable gathering for the purpose of disseminating treasonable slogans here. You blasphemed against the Lord at this very table, where none but the sons of Catholic parents are seated. In your desire to lead astray orderly citizens like us on the path of heresy and unbelief you shouted out that you do not believe in the Lord and you spoke disgustingly about the Infallibility of the Pope. For this there is only one answer — and that is gaol! Landlord, call the police at once!"

"But, gentlemen —— "

"But me no buts, sir. You will have to be investigated by the police and we shall denounce you for offending against religion, insulting Their Imperial Majesties and things like that. Do you understand? Our watchword is: For God, Fatherland and King. And you want to come here and steal it from us. Are you not ashamed of yourself, you, who are a man of education?"

By this time the police were already here.

"Please, officer, be so kind as to enquire of this gentleman his name. In an effort to corrupt our morals he speaks disrespectfully of Almighty God, the Pope, and the whole dynasty. He wants to turn us into anarchists, terrorists, and blasphemers."

Mr. Markup got up and said calmly and solemnly, "I am a police officer."

The Chief of Police's nephew jumped up. "You must be crazy, my good man. Show us your papers. What would my poor uncle say, if he knew about this?"

Mr. Markup started to rummage in his pockets and then, quite crestfallen, was compelled to admit, "I am sorry, sir. I've left my papers at home."

Then the Police Chief's nephew approached the officer and, showing him his papers with that dreaded name, said with dignity, "The Chief of Police, your superior, is my uncle." And, pointing to the unfortunate Mr. Markup, he called out, "Take this man away!"

And while the policeman was leading off the dejected Mr. Markup there rang out after them the sounds of our sublime chorale, "Moravia shall never lose her faith. Preserve for us, dear Lord, the heritage of our fathers."

Mr. Markup never showed his face in our midst again, as he was transferred to the archives department of police headquarters, to dust the old documents.

The struggle of the Southern Slavs for liberation from Turkish rule caused great excitement among some of the Slav peoples. In the nineteenth century many Russians enlisted as volunteers to fight for Serbs or Bulgarians, and at the beginning of the twentieth there was another wave of enthusiasm which even reached peace-loving Bohemia. Hašek here parodies the enthusiasm and bombast of Jan Klimeš, a Czech "volunteer", who came to Prague and told stories about his military exploits in the Balkans. Hašek's attention was first drawn to him by a series of articles he published in the popular illustrated Horizon, describing the life and organization of the Macedonian insurgents. In the following sketch Hašek takes a leaf out of the pages of Baron Munchausen or Conan Doyle's Brigadier Gerard.

Klimeš, Commander of the Macedonian Revolutionary Troops

... NONE OF US KNEW EXACTLY WHERE THIS CHAMPION OF THE oppressed was born. He was very tall of stature, and his enormous beard on his shaggy face, his menacing expression, and his fiery speeches showed him to be a born leader of revolutionary armies. And it was indeed in that capacity that I got to know him in Sofia, two years before our new Party was founded. It would require a whole chapter, and a voluminous one at that, to describe all his glorious deeds, the most renowned of which was when we fought together in that memorable battle on Mount Garvan. It was there that we laid siege to Monastir and, finding ourselves encircled by *nizam* or Turkish regulars, fled from the battle-field as gloriously as anyone can.

I repeat that we had this man in our Party for a certain time and felt extraordinary respect for him just because of his heroic deeds. But what follows should in no way be regarded as a belittlement of him, but rather as magnificent proof of his sterling character.

Truly, that man was totally without fear, but when the worst happened even he had to acknowledge that it was better to retreat, and he always did so in the most perfect order.

The finest moment was when I met him in Sofia. It was just at that troubled time when bands of Turkish *nizam* had surrounded the regions around Salonika and thrown their strongest force at the Bulgarian frontier beneath lovely Mount Vitoša, that magic spot which is so full of poetry. It was at that season of the year when everything is fragrant in the mighty groves and primeval forests of Vitoša. Below the mountain the Turkish guns thundered and there was an answering rattle of rifles from the Macedonian insurgents. And it was just there too that troops of the Bulgarian revolutionary, Sarafov, were advancing on and on and the guns thundering again further and further in the distance.

At that time Klimeš was sitting in an ottoman factory in Sofia, because he was not born a commander but a master upholsterer. And he sat there in perfect calm, quiet unaware that in the air over his head there hung, as it were, the exalted rank of a commander. And it was at that very same moment that I came to Sofia and got to know as a fellow-countryman of mine that man who up till then had known nothing but peace and quiet, and in whose heart were still slumbering the latent qualities of a legendary hero.

And there, over glasses of wine from the Athenian mountains (which was frightfully bad and excruciatingly expensive) and from Mount Olympus (which likewise was no nectar of the gods, but the most common hogwash), he lied to me for the first time in his life, saying that he knew all the passes, all the revolutionaries, and all the bands of Macedonian insurgents including their leader, the hero Sarafov, who was later killed by the comitadji because he misappropriated money intended for the purchase of machine-guns, hand grenades, and other agreeable objects.

I confess that at that moment I felt a great yearning to go with him to the frontier, and he was ready to set off at once or the next day — in brief, to go and fight for the liberty of his oppressed Macedonian brethren. And to prove it to me, he took his hat and exhorted me to follow him.

We went to a small café, which as he afterwards confided to me, he had imagined was not frequented by comitadji, but unfortunately he had miscalculated. And so, all because of this, that good, heroic and valorous soul became the Macedonian Commander.

It happened that at that very same café they were recruiting volunteers to go to the frontier. When Klimeš heard this, he turned pale, but, having already a presentment that glory was in store for him, with the same spontaneous heroism with which the Russian legendary hero, Ilya Muromets, once took his decision, he announced in a Bulgarian which was more broken than fluent that he had with him a fellow-countryman from Bohemia and was ready, together with me, to risk his life for the liberty of his brethren beyond Vitoša, for the sake of their interests, their women and their children, and for everything that was beautiful, heroic, grand, and glorious.

"Give us some rifles, brothers," he called, when he had drunk some *rakija*. And then we swore an oath — an oath to the banner of liberty. I must confess that up to that time I had only shot hares, and now it would have to be Turks. It was a rather unusual thing to have to do, but the second, third, fourth, and fifth *rakija* gave me courage.

As we took the oath, we trembled and our limbs shook. And this was how we set out for the Turkish frontier in the darkest and gloomiest night which I ever remember.

Next morning we came to an arms depot beneath Vitoša. It was a small hut, where first they gave us some cheese and only later handed us weapons. They were Werndl breech-loaders and you loaded them like Mannlicher repeaters, but neither Klimeš nor I knew exactly how it was done.

"Do you understand how to do it?" the leader of the band asked us.

"Of course we do," said the valiant Commander, trembling all over when they put into our hands a supply of cartridges. "You just stick the cartridge into the rifle, brother, and aim it at a Turk, bang! And then that Turkish swine falls down. You then stamp on his throat and cut off his head. It warms your heart. It's no child's play, brothers. Pass the flask along."

They handed him the flask and, when he had taken a swig at

it, he went on: "That's how it is, brothers. The Turk, that unchristian beast, lives like a dog and like a dog he shall die. I swear it, as my name is Klimeš."

And so they put us in the front line to implant fear in the hearts of the Turks — me, because I was wearing European clothes, and Klimeš, because he looked like Goliath. His gigantic figure rose up in all its grandeur, his blue eyes aflame and his bushy beard bristling. He was no longer Klimeš, the master upholsterer, but the terrible Klimeš, the true Macedonian Commander.

On that expedition, we nearly fainted with horror for the first time, when we thought of how the Turks would make mincemeat of us, when they found us in the front line.

Towards evening we set fire to an abandoned barn, which belonged to a Turkish priest. We were on Turkish soil, and the Mullah was insured in Salonika.

And before us there rose the peak of Mount Garvan, the guardian of the Turkish dominion, which swarmed with scorpions. Throwing away our rifles, we scaled that mountain. Being in the vanguard we were the first to reach the summit and see all around below us the fires of the Turkish regulars.

And we fled to the Turks. I knew a few sentences of Turkish and put them together to say, "Turkish gentlemen, comitadji pursue us. We flee." And it was only too true. The Turks formally took us prisoner and decided to bring us before their officer before hanging us. And when they did so, we found that he was a very charming man. He asked me in French why the comitadji were chasing us, and when I said it was because they took us for Turks, he burst out laughing and was very hospitable to us. The next morning he sent us to the frontier by train with a guard of honour.

That was that great battle on Mount Garvan, of which Klimeš, the Macedonian Commander, told the story in Prague and related how we had killed 2,500 Turks there.

But it was not only at the battle of Mount Garvan that the Macedonian Commander distinguished himself by his immense courage, as we have already related. It was principally during the heroic capture of Monastir that he displayed his finest qualities as leader and his utter disregard for any other influences which might have been injurious to the sacred cause for which we fought so valiantly on the mountain.

Whoever followed the account he gave in Prague of that boyar-like struggle could have seen clearly how much the Macedonian Commander accomplished for the cause of oppressed Macedonia, and realized also how decisively we avenged all those atrocities the Turks were committing on the Christian population beyond Vitoša. I should like to mention, moreover that he was always so modest himself that, knowing my own modesty, he never spoke of the part I too had played in that glorious campaign. I am very grateful to him for not having done so, because in our circumstances one really prefers not to hear people say of oneself that one has cut off and truncated hundreds and hundreds of Turkish heads. Here we're above such trivialities. But if someone kills, say, only a kitten, then people talk of him as though he were a monster.

But Klimeš is not the sort who would try to cover up his actions, not the man to be ashamed of what he has done and to make inept apologies for it. There are witnesses in Prague of his marvellous description of the capture of Monastir:

"I can say, gentlemen, that I did not put too much reliance on my troop, who numbered 200 men, because I suspected that there were traitors among them. Moreover the road, along which we approached the city of Monastir, was not exactly the most attractive one, winding as it did through mountainous country which was, so to speak, utterly desolate. On our march through this territory a fortnight before we had poisoned all the wells to prevent the Turkish regular army advancing any further. And now, just imagine it, we could not even ourselves drink out of them in that frightful heat of 38 degrees. Some comitadji, who disregarded my express instruction not to come near the poisoned wells, paid with their lives for their daring. I had to have two of them hanged as a warning to the others.

"But that was not the worst thing. Traitors were to be found not only in our ranks. Behind every little rock there was one hidden, who rushed away to the nearest *vali* to inform against us so that at once the *aga* appeared with his janissaries. And, when I consider that I counted from 2,000 to 3,000 little rocks on that road, you can imagine what it was like for us. You may sit comfortably here over your beer, but you try and sit equally peacefully when shells are bursting over your heads and machine guns and rifles are rattling beside you! Every moment they score a hit, and the horse beneath you takes fright. You have to jump over ravines, because the Turks have torn down all the bridges, and you have to shoot at the same time. This makes the horse even more nervous and it gallops off with you to the enemy's camp. Oh, it's a glorious picnic, I can tell you!

"And so in the end there were only 80 of us left against 28,000 *nizam* infantry, 4,000 janissaries, and God knows how many thousands of other Turkish troops. And they all wore green uniforms and so wherever we looked, we thought we saw forest land and should have the chance of feasting ourselves on wild raspberries, but when we got there we saw that it was the Turks, and they all of them ran away before us, so that we found ourselves again on bare soil. Oh, it was some picnic, I can tell you! But we were favoured by St. Sava, the Bulgarian patron saint, whom the Turks hanged at that time without much ceremony because they found on him a letter from Sarafov. Oh, that was some picnic, I can tell you! And so in spite of all this one fine morning we advanced on Monastir.

"If I may explain it to you, gentlemen, Monastir is one of the most powerful Turkish fortresses in Macedonia. The actual inner fortress is, you might say, just like this table where I'm sitting now. That piano there on the left, that other table there on the right, the landlord there at the door, and there where they are playing cards in the other corner — those are the bunkers around Monastir. And every good strategist, if he wanted to capture Monastir, would have to proceed in the following way: first, he'd have to capture the piano, after that the landlord, and finally that table over there; because, if the fortunes of war changed and the enemy took the

centre bunker — that is to say the landlord — we should have to
blow him up and shoot from the piano on to the table here, after, of
course, having previously slaughtered all those who are playing
cards over there. And of course I too acted in accordance with this
well-thought-out plan. We blew up the centre bunker, occupied
the others, and aimed our guns at the city. For three days and three
nights we bombarded it without stop and then on the fourth day,
towards evening, an enchantingly beautiful Turkish girl came to
our camp. She desired to speak to the Macedonian Commander,
Klimeš, himself and no one else — that is to say to me. I told them
to let her come into my tent and, when she appeared, she fell on
her knees before me and started to kiss my feet, begging me to
spare the city and saying that she gave herself to me completely. I
could do what I liked with her. That was a glorious picnic, I can tell
you! And do you know what I did, gentlemen? Why, I ravished her,
and next morning we took the city, ransacked it, and set fire to it in
six places. We gave the population no quarter but murdered them
and expelled them from Turkey. Friends, this may perhaps seem to
you an act of atrocity and savagery, but it is really not so and I can
easily convince you of the contrary. In the marketplace they had
already set up gallows for all eighty of us and eighty barrels of
paraffin were standing there. Just consider what our fate would
have been if they had caught us!"

Those were manly words, with which the Macedonian Commander, Klimeš, clearly illuminated his activities in aid of the sub-
jugated Bulgarian brethren beyond Vitoša. However, I am going to
take the liberty, very briefly, not, of course, to rectify some of his
statements — this I would certainly not think of doing — but simply
to show that in his heart he harboured no bestial instincts, but that
on the contrary all that he did at Monastir was done only for our
preservation.

Monastir, for example, is not a city. The word means the
same as "monastery", where the monks serve refreshments to
thirsty and hungry pilgrims for their journey further. When that

Turkish officer, to whom we appealed at Mount Garvan out of fear of the Bulgarian comitadji, arranged for us to be accompanied to the frontier by a military guard, we reached that monastery on the Bulgarian side after two hours' marching. And there we besieged its gate and asked for some refreshment. And it is true that the Macedonian Commander, Klimeš, plundered the monastery, because we stayed there a week and ate up all its provisions.

It is also true that a beautiful Turkish girl came to our camp. We crept into the hay stack of that eighty-year-old woman in a meadow and milked her goat. But that was already an hour before we came to Sofia, where afterwards we arrived safely towards evening and Klimeš first showed the wounds he had sustained in the battle beyond green Vitoša. He happened to graze his forehead and elbow when he fell down into the cellar of the monastery, where he had gone to look for the stocks of wine which the monks were carefully concealing from us. And you see, this cannot in any way diminish Klimeš's military glory, for in Prague during his visit here, whenever he was deeply moved by his own stories, he took off his coat and waistcoat, and stripping his shirt off his back invited all his listeners to feel the hard object over his left side, a splinter of a shell which had lodged itself in his body, when it exploded above us — one of those hundreds of shells which the Turkish artillery fired during that glorious battle on Mount Garvan, where we broke through two regiments of the regular Turkish army and completely annihilated a regiment stationed in its rear.

The hard object was actually a floating kidney, which Klimeš had come to Prague to have treated. I can say that his valour and his great commitment to the sacred cause for which he was fighting had a great appeal and won support for the Party of Moderate Progress within the Bounds of the Law. And his accounts of all those numerous battles and glorious victories of his own troops were the first instructive lectures with which the Party appeared before the public. We had taken upon ourselves the task of presenting an enlightening and instructive program, because what do people need to win their independence? Only enlightenment — enlightenment of the kind which permits people to acquire an understanding of the right views on life so that they can learn that they should not be overhasty but go on steadily craving for self-education. And I can say that by the very fact that we included in our program cultural questions, we earned the affection of those classes who until then had had no inkling of the existence of our party.

Our cultural propaganda immediately caused a revolution. In literary and student circles people began to reflect rationally that a party which goes among the people with instructive lectures rather than barren phrases is a party with a future.

And people joined our ranks in flocks, following the theory of Darwin on the social life of higher mammals, according to which as few as six are needed to create a flock.

And so on December 14, 1904, there were altogether eight of us in the Party.